GILBERT AND HALL PRESS

Green Magic

Stories of Hope and Power

To all those
who use their words and lives
to build a better world.

Contents

Preface

GREEN MAGIC: STORIES FOR A HOPEFUL FUTURE

What if the future was not just survivable—but WONDROUS?

Step into worlds where science meets sorcery, where technology and magic intertwine, and where innovation fuels possibility.

From quantum fairy godmothers to time-traveling dendrologists, from spirit catchers to post-apocalyptic survivors forging new beginnings, these stories explore how humanity—and the universe—can evolve for the better.

Featuring visionary inventors, dreamers, bureaucrats, thieves, and witches, this anthology blends cutting-edge technology with ancient spells, weaving together tales of resilience, ingenuity, and hope.

This anthology includes 22 stories by:

Colleen Addison - Letter

Cassandra Arnold - Becoming a Bard, and the Garden of the Sun

Emecheta Christian - The Fall of Julian Frost

Sarah Das Gupta - Looking Forward Through the Telescope of the Past

Alex Grehy - Of Potatoes and Stasis Pods

Dorothy Johnson-Laird - The Rainkeeper

Robin Kathaas - Blueprints

Loki Laats - Chasing Storms

Jen Lailey - Lawn Canvas

Natasia Langfelder - Fats and Flora

Carys Owen - Moss Everlasting

Daniel Rabuzzi - Reboot

Rod Raglin - A Battle Choosing

Bobby Rollins - Nea-tech-anderthals

Ali Rowland - The Last One

William Scarborough - The Obituarist

Ginger Strivelli - A Helping Hand

John Tures - Hurricane Hunters

Nicolas Van Der Haar - Project Butterfly

Regina Rae Weiss - At the Industrial Food Museum

Elizabeth Whitton - The Green Witch

We wrote these tales with hope and wonder—may you feel that in every page.

A Battle Worth Choosing

The Fight to Save the Fairy Portal in Jones Park

Rod Raglin

K nocking. Not loud, but determined. The peace of Matt's unscheduled afternoon nap was being disrupted. Why didn't Emma see who it was? Maybe it would stop if he ignored it.

Knock, knock, knock.

"Hello, sir?"

A child? Matt struggled to clear his mind of sleep.

"Emma, some kid's knocking on—" The pain of awareness, like pouring alcohol on an open wound, made him catch his breath. He thought he was over calling for her, forgetting she was gone.

"Maybe Mr. Bennett's not home, Merri?" a woman's voice called out.

Merri? Wasn't that the name of the little girl from a couple of houses over? Why wasn't she in school? Not old enough? Still, wasn't there kindergarten, preschool, play-dates? What the hell was she doing knocking on his door in the middle of the afternoon?

"No, Mom. I saw him just a little while ago."

Knock, knock, knock.

Matt opened his eyes. He'd fallen asleep while revising the

manuscript of his latest novel. Not a good sign. If it put him to sleep, what would it do to readers? He swivelled away from the desk, got stiffly out of the high-backed executive chair, and staggered out of his office. By the time he reached the back door, he was more or less awake and upright.

Knock, knock, knock.

"Merri, enough. You can come back later."

"No, Mom! I have to talk to him and—"

Matt opened the door. "What?"

The little girl jumped back. "He's here, Mom."

Merri's mother waved from the backyard two houses over.

Brushing the long flaxen hair out of her face, Merri took a deep breath, stepped forward and fixed him with a purposeful look.

Robin's eggs, Matt thought. The kid's eyes were the colour of robin's eggs.

"The fairies need your help, sir."

"What?"

"Were you sleeping, sir?"

"Why?"

"Because you've got drool on your chin and T-shirt. Sometimes that happens to me when I wake up from a nap."

Matt wiped his chin with the palm of his hand. Damn if the kid wasn't right. Good power of observation. "Look, little girl—"

"Meredith," she said, "but you can call me Merri."

"Look, Merri, I don't know any fairies and if I did, I wouldn't know how to help them. So maybe—"

"Well, they know you, sir. And Neve said, talk to the grumpy old man who saved the Maples. That's you, right?"

"A lot of people helped save the Maples," Matt said, "and who's Neve?" The afternoon sun was scorching on the back porch. He stepped back into the shadows.

2

"The boss fairy."

"Merri," her mother called out, "ask Mr. Bennett if he'd like to come over for some iced tea?"

"Would you like to come to my house and have some iced tea with me and the fairies?"

"No!"

Merri's bottom lip trembled. She cast her eyes down. "Sorry to bother you, sir."

Guilt! Shame! Remorse! Matt considered banging his head against the door. Instead, he said, "I changed my mind. On such a hot day, iced tea sounds good."

"You'll come?" Matt was rewarded with a radiant smile that vanquished his rudeness, as well as the need to suffer physical pain as atonement.

"Ten minutes. I've got to wipe my chin and change my shirt."

"And comb your hair."

* * *

Thinning hair tamed, chin wiped and wearing a clean T-shirt, Matt gripped the bannister tightly as he carefully descended the six stairs into his yard, then limped down the path toward the gate. Bloody arthritis. He probably looked as old as he felt—as he was.

The back garden was withered, the result of watering restrictions imposed because of the prolonged drought. The only flowers not to succumb were the indestructible Ox-eye daisies, although even their petals drooped in homage to the searing heat. Emma would be devastated. As a psychiatric nurse practitioner, gardening had been her therapy and passion. In response to his wife's love and appreciation, the plants thrived. Big and bold, fragile and subtle—blooms of all shapes and shades filled the evening with fragrance. Before the drought, and even with the help and expense of a professional landscaper, the garden had declined. It was as if they didn't want to live without her care, or at least not live to their fullest.

When Matt opened his neighbour's back gate, he was surprised to see their garden was faring much better, almost as if it was in another temperate zone. Merri ran out to meet him.

"Do you need some help, sir?" His age-spotted hand was grasped by delicate pink fingers.

"How do you keep your garden so pretty, Merri?"

"It's Oriah, she's the healer fairy."

"Maybe you could get them to work their magic on mine."

Merri looked up into his face. "If you help, I'll ask them."

"Come in out of that sun, Mr. Bennett." Merri's mother was an attractive woman, in her mid-thirties with the same long blond hair as her daughter—but not the eyes. "I'm Mikala." She ushered him into the kitchen that opened onto a deck shielded by a patio umbrella.

"Please, call me Matt," he said, "and that goes for you too, young lady."

"I'm not young, I'm six."

"Not quite," Mikala said. "Please, sit down."

On a country-style, round dining room table were two tall glasses and a pink plastic cup of iced tea, plus a grouping of six small, colourful and cleverly crafted dolls. The hint of a breeze, a sweating glass of cool beverage in front of him—Matt felt himself relax. This wasn't going to be so bad after all. They sipped their tea in silence.

"So, what's this about helping fairies, or were you just being kind and checking in on an old man?" There wasn't a news report that didn't caution about solitary seniors dying of heat stroke—as many had already during this extended extreme weather event.

"How are you managing this heat?" Mikala asked.

"I'm fine, but this is very thoughtful."

4

"Mom? Can I ask him?"

"Meredith has a very active imagination," her mother said.

The little girl frowned.

"Okay, okay." Her mother held up her hands.

"They're going to cut down the twins in Jones Park," Merri said.

"I know Jones Park, but who are the twins?"

"The two giant trees that are side by side."

"The ones close to the lane by the playground?"

Merri nodded.

The park had a stand of mature Western Red Cedars, two of which had grown to maturity within two metres of each other. Matt had stood between them, and he could touch each one with his arms outstretched.

"Are they diseased?"

"No!" Merri said. "They're strong and healthy."

"During a Park Board renewal process, the neighbourhood advisory committee identified the two trees as dangerous to the residents bordering the park," Mikala said. "Evidently, during a windstorm, a large branch from one of the trees crushed a section of one of their fences."

"She's a witch!"

"Meredith!"

"But she is Mom, Keerah told me." Merri's countenance had gone from light and happy to dark and determined.

"Who's Keerah?" Matt asked.

Merri held up one of the dolls. Though delicate and colourful with black hair, a chartreuse bodice and a purple floral dress, the lack of facial features gave the doll an other-worldly appearance. A sharp spear glued to its hand verged on sinister. "Keerah's a warrior fairy, she and Seershah." Merri held up another doll, also with a spear.

"Did you make her yourself, Merri?

"Mom did."

"But you described them for me, honey."

"You must be very creative," Matt said.

"They're really quite simple," Mikala said. "You use a wood bead for the head, embroidery floss for the hair and bodice, and for the dress a faux silk flower, all held together by floral wire and copious amounts of glue.

"And the spears?" Matt asked.

"Six-inch bamboo skewers."

"Mom's an art teacher."

"You are?"

"Part-time at Emily Carr."

"The trees are a portal," Merri said. Matt must have looked confused because she added, "to their home."

"Okay."

"If the trees are cut down, the gateway will be closed, and fairies won't be able to visit our world."

"And that would be a bad thing?"

Merri looked astonished. "Of course."

"Settle down, Meredith."

"I get it," Matt said. "There'd be no fairy godmothers, no tooth fairy, no Tinker—"

"No!" Merri stamped her foot. "Real fairies, not stupid storybook ones!"

"Hey!" Mikala said. "I think you'd better take five."

"But Mom, he has to—"

"Meredith." Mikala pointed to the hall where her daughter's bedroom likely was.

It was a stare-off. Matt had never seen such intensity in a child, or for that matter, in anyone. He felt responsible for the rift, but without any inclination on how to resolve it, thought it best to keep his mouth shut. After a few long seconds, Merri collected her dolls and stomped off down the hall.

"And don't slam the door."

Slam!

"I'm sorry." Mikala sighed. "She's really upset about the trees, and I feel responsible."

"How so?" Matt asked, relieved that the outburst wasn't totally his fault.

"Like most people, Joyce, my partner, and I are concerned about climate change, but rather than live with existential angst, we're committed to doing something about it. We think it's important for Merri to feel empowered, that we can change the way we live and save the planet and all the things that call it home."

Matt had pretty much given up hope on that, as well as everything else. But if he had a child of his own, he could understand feeling like Mikala.

"We were part of the community that supported your fight to save the Maples. Merri, Joyce and I visited frequently while you were camped out there."

A few blocks from Matt's house was a quiet residential street, a single block, that was presided over by eight magnificent maple trees, four on either side. Matt had travelled and been an avid hiker, but he'd never seen a grove of eight more stately giants anywhere. These were Bigleaf Maples, *Acer macrophyllum*, the largest of the maple family and could live up to 300 years and grow to a height of nearly 50 metres—which had been achieved or bettered by all of them. Being tightly clustered, they'd developed a narrow crown supported by trunks free of branches for about half their length. They provided a cool canopy of green in the summer and a stunning array of autumn beauty for a few short weeks every fall.

But more than that, they provided peace and perspective. Walking beneath the sun-dappled leaves, with the wind whispering in boughs, was like entering an oasis that soothed and cooled his frenetic thoughts. After Emma died, he was lost and often found himself leaning against massive trunks, pressing his cheeks to their scaly bark, and sobbing. What the residents in the nearby houses must have thought he didn't care.

Then, a year ago, there was a sign staked in the boulevard advising that parking was prohibited until further notice because of tree removal. The city was replacing the storm drains and the tree roots presented a problem. And so, it began—the telephone calls, the letters, the media interviews, the door-to-door canvasing—it exhausted him to even think about it.

There was little support from the adjacent homeowners. The trees were a pain in the ass; in the spring and summer, they were home for bugs and birds that shit on their cars. In the fall, the leaves clogged their gutters and drains and took hours to clear from their lawns. Matt went further afield and recruited environmentalists, naturalists and climate specialists. The city deferred the work waiting for the protest to run itself out, but Matt was determined. He'd just lost one of his loves, he couldn't lose another. Anxious that they would begin cutting without notice and present the opposition with a *fait accompli*, he bought a small tent and set up camp on the boulevard beneath the trees. One sympathetic neighbour allowed him to use a bathroom in their basement.

At first, the visitors were few and not all were supportive, but it grew until it became a meeting place, a touchstone, a symbol, a movement, a power unto itself that no one could defy—especially if they wanted to get re-elected. On the second weekend camped out under the Maples, he turned eighty. Hundreds of people he didn't know came to celebrate. Matt had become an Eco-warrior, a climate change hero.

He hated it.

Once the storm drains had been rerouted and the threat to the Maples eliminated, at least temporarily, he went into seclusion. In retrospect, he realized he'd been out of his mind. Grief can do that.

"Where does she get all her information about fairies?" Matt asked. "Does she watch a lot of cartoons?"

"Only Saturday mornings, only a few we select, and just for a couple of hours," Mikala said. "Believe me, they're nothing like the stuff she's coming up with. It's bewildering."

"Mom?" Merri called from her bedroom.

"Okay, but mind your manners."

Merri returned to the kitchen, arms full of fairy dolls, and began repositioning them on the table. She didn't look chastised.

"Thanks for the tea," Matt said, "and the company." Had he actually enjoyed himself?

"Will you help the fairies, sir?"

"Yes."

Merri jumped up and down. "Thank you, thank you, thank you!"

"That doesn't mean I'll be successful. Let me see what I can find out."

"If you like, I can have Joyce give you a call this evening," Mikala said. "She works for the city's legal department and has some insights into the process and those involved."

"Sure," Matt said. "Not too late though."

"Do you need some help getting home, sir?"

* * *

Joyce called at eight.

"Hey, Matt. It's Joyce Dewitt, Merri's other mother."

"Hello, Joyce. Thanks for calling."

"I hear you decided to help the fairies." Joyce chuckled. "Merri's got quite an imagination, but hey, fairies aside, it would be great if you could help save those beautiful trees."

"Mikala said something about residents bordering the park being worried that branches falling from the trees were dangerous?"

"Not residents, one resident. Marjorie Hallaway. Her house is on the corner of 38th Avenue and Commercial Street and backs onto the lane across from the park."

"But kids play in that park every day and I've never heard of any of them being hurt by a falling branch."

"You're right and if that was all there was to it, the Park Board would dismiss it, but she's filed a lawsuit against the city for a million bucks."

"On what grounds?"

"Emotional distress and psychological impairment," Joyce said. "She's claiming the threat of a branch from one of those trees falling on her house is causing her—", there was a shuffle of papers, "—anxiety, panic attacks, depression, sleep disorder, moodiness and volatile temper."

"You're kidding?" It was Matt's experience that the proximity of tall trees resolved those issues.

"It's a long shot, but she could win. The settlement would likely be a lot less than what she's asking, but it would set a precedent for similar lawsuits."

* * *

The following evening, after the heat had backed off, Matt decided to walk the five blocks to Jones Park. All that day, the humidity had made him feel short of breath. It was an effort to carry out the most mundane tasks. As a concession, he decided to take the walker. Though he hated the idea of being dependent on an apparatus for basic mobility, he had to concede it was well-designed and practical, equipped with swivel wheels, hand brakes, a basket for his water bottle and a seat if he needed to stop and rest.

He left by the back door and, as he made his way across the yard, noticed a cluster of flaming red poppies, a welcomed burst of colour in the parched landscape. He didn't remember planting them, though seeds often migrated via birds and the breeze from one garden to another.

The park was full of families trying to get some respite from suffocating indoors. Matt parked his walker and carefully navigated around the chirping children and the families reclining on blankets and lawn chairs until he came to the twins at the edge of the park. The sweeping boughs of the Western Red Cedars seemed more inviting than threatening. Unlike the bold burliness of the Maples, the Cedars were sedate and statuesque, embracing their surroundings rather than competing with them. Their branches were draped like cloaks and gave Matt the impression of monks, keepers of ancient wisdom, and why not? They could live for a millennium. It was easy to imagine them as supporting pillars for a gateway to another realm.

Across the lane, a middle-aged woman came out of her backyard carrying a large garbage bag. She entered the park and dumped the contents on the ground. When she looked up, she noticed Matt watching her.

"This isn't my garbage. I'm just returning the crap that comes off these bloody trees."

Could this be Marjorie Hallaway, Merri's witch? Matt approached, careful of the uneven ground. Despite the deepening twilight, he could see she was big-boned, with a prominent nose and an aggressive chin. Her long hair was twisted in a knot on the top of her head.

"I understand the Park Board might be removing them," he said.

"Can't happen soon enough, before one of the branches falls and kills someone."

"The parents of all the children playing beneath them don't seem to care," Matt said.

"If they want to put their kids at risk that's their business, but us homeowners next to the park shouldn't have to worry every time the wind blows that a huge piece of a tree will come crashing through our roof. I've already had my fence damaged." She vigorously shook out the last contents of the bag.

"That's from the trees as well?" Matt said, referring to the pile of seed cones, needles and twigs.

"Every day, all over the driveway, in the gutters. And it's not just the trash that falls from them, it's what lives in them."

"You mean birds and bugs?"

"Them too, and bats."

"Bats?"

"That's what that moron at the Park Board said they might be. They come out at night, zipping back and forth like a hummingbird, only more annoying. I told them they needed to get an exterminator up here to get rid of them before we have another COVID virus to deal with, a homegrown one." The know-it-all tone was simultaneously defensive and aggressive. Other opinions would not be considered. Compromise was out of the question.

"Well, have a nice evening," Matt said.

"Yeah, like that's going to happen with this bloody heat." She folded her bag and stared at Matt suspiciously. "What's an old guy like you doing in the park this late?"

"Same as everyone else, trying to keep cool."

"I'd be getting home before it gets too dark. Sometimes weird things happen under these trees at night."

"Like what?"

"Flashing lights, tinkling sounds, shadows. Probably teenagers doing drugs or having sex or both."

"Probably."

"Besides, you could fall and break a hip. You don't look too steady."

"Thanks for your concern." She was right, though, about falling. Night was settling in and the park was clearing out.

On his way back to the walker, he took a slight detour to stand between the twins. These trees had spiritual significance to the indigenous peoples who used the smooth bark that peeled off in layers for clothing, the massive trunks for dugout canoes and the fragrant wood for ceremonial masks. He stretched out his arms, pressed a palm against either trunk and was enveloped in their unique aromatic scent.

Their stringy hide felt warm, then warmer. His hands began to tingle. The sensation moved down his arms and into his entire body. A hum morphed into pulsing and increased in rhythm and strength. Then brilliant light! So bright he had to close his eyes. The pulsing stopped. He opened his eyes and was gazing into another world, a pastoral Eden of vibrance and vitality. Hovering at the threshold were six tiny-winged creatures looking back at him with fierce intensity. They were beautiful—and frightening.

The portal closed. The darkness returned. Matt heard traffic, a dog bark. He found his walker without any trouble. His vision seemed to be clearer, his balance better, his knees didn't ache. He made it all the way home without stopping for a rest.

The next morning, he called his pharmacist. "Do any of the myriads of prescriptions you fill on my behalf cause hallucinations?"

"Let's see." There was the sound of computer keys clacking. "How are you feeling these days, Mr. Bennett?"

"Fine."

"Not having any memory problems, are you?"

"Not that I can remember."

The pharmacist chuckled. "I'm asking because cognitive decline is a common cause of hallucinations in the elderly."

"You don't say?"

"Ramipril, Atorvastatin, Fosovance... nothing here that lists hallucinations as a common side effect."

"That would be no, then?"

"How are you sleeping?"

"Excessively." Matt was satisfied. If the guy kept looking, he was sure to find something. "Thanks, sorry to trouble you."

"No trouble, Mr. Bennett, but let me ask you, are you drinking enough water during this heat? Dehydration can cause hallucinations, especially if you've had a bout of diarrhea."

"I'll keep that in mind." That was probably it—dehydration, not the other. He immediately went and had a large glass of cold water.

* * *

"Do you know what it means to choose your battles, Merri?" They were watching the bumble bees feasting on the cones of the purple and yellow echinacea which had appeared overnight in Matt's garden as if transplanted.

"What battles?"

Matt took a sip from a bottle of Pedialyte, a rehydration drink that promised to quickly replenish lost fluids and electrolytes. It had become his constant companion and appeared to be working. So far, there'd been no more hallucinations, though they might be preferable to having to urinate every two hours.

"Well, like ones you know you're going to lose."

"Like arguing with Joyce about bedtime?" Merri said.

"Exactly."

It appeared the only way the twins could be saved would be for Marjorie Hallaway to withdraw her suit against the city. From Matt's serendipitous meeting with her, that seemed highly unlikely. He felt bad about disappointing Merri, but it would be worse to give her false hope. Battles to save the environment were being lost everywhere, every day. She might as well get used to it.

"I think saving the twins is one of those battles," Matt said. "I can't imagine why anyone would want to take down those trees, but Marjorie Hallaway does and she's not about to back down."

No tears, no denial. Merri seemed deep in thought.

"Did you know these flowers have poison in them?" She pointed to the elegant spikes of white, mauve and purple foxglove, another unexpected guest that had taken root in his garden.

"No, I didn't. Did you learn that at school?"

"No, I don't go to school yet, sir. Bronwyn told me."

"Bronwyn?"

"She's the wizard fairy. The one with a bad temper."

Matt hadn't told anyone about his experience two nights ago in Jones Park. He wasn't even sure he believed it happened, though he remembered it vividly, especially the determined expressions on the faces of the fairies.

"Even if you touch it, you could get sick," Merri said. "Maybe die."

"Thank you, I'll remember that," Matt said.

"What you said about battles, sir?"

"Yes."

"They've decided to fight."

"I'm sorry to disappoint you, Merri, but I don't think we can win. There'll be other opportunities to protect trees and wild places."

"Not us, sir. The fairies. Bronwyn says enough is enough. They all agree, Keerah, Oriah, Rosheem, Seershah, even Neve. Remember Neve? It was her idea to talk to you."

"I wish I could have done more."

"It's okay. They asked me to thank you for trying."

Matt felt like his chest was going to burst. He blinked back the tears. "Well, good luck to them," he said.

15

Merri smiled. "They said it was nice meeting you the other night in the park."

Once Merri had left, Matt went inside and dumped the balance of his rehydration drink down the drain. He didn't know what to make of Merri's corroboration of his hallucination, but at least it was a relief to know he wouldn't have to be constantly emptying his bladder.

He opened his laptop and did an internet search. "Digitalis, commonly known as foxglove, contains several deadly physiological and chemically related cardiac and steroidal glycosides. Ingestion of any parts of the plant can result in severe poisoning. Symptoms include nausea, headache, skin irritation, diarrhea, dilated pupils, drooling, weakness, collapse, seizures, and even death."

How Merri knew the plant was poisonous was intriguing, but why she knew it was even more disturbing.

* * *

"Take kindly the counsel of the years, gracefully surrendering the things of youth." Matt never had a problem with surrendering the things of youth though he wished he had more energy. They just seemed to slip away, including any influence he once had. Now, when he needed it most, no one would take his calls and if they did, he was dismissed as an angry, out of touch, possibly senile, but most importantly powerless, i.e., not a threat or a benefit to anyone's career or ambition, old man.

And so, he'd failed to save the twins and, in doing so, let down a little girl. It would have been nice to go out with a win.

* * *

Two weeks later, Matt was looking out the window at the colourful array of late summer blooms in his miraculously regenerated garden when Joyce called.

"Hey, Matt. Just want to say congratulations. Not sure what you did, but it worked."

"What are you talking about?"

"The lawsuit's been withdrawn. Those trees that were so important to Merri aren't going to be cut down."

* * *

The next day, Matt rolled up to Jones Park. The heat dome had collapsed and with it the humidity, but it still hadn't rained. The forecast was predicting showers for the weekend, but not soon enough before a new record was set of forty-five days without precipitation, unheard of in Vancouver.

He stayed on the sidewalk and went past the park to where Marjorie Hallaway lived. Less than a month ago, the woman was rabid about removing the trees. To say he was interested in her change of heart would be an understatement.

As he approached, he saw two men carrying a monstrous antique-looking chest of drawers down the back stairs and toward a U-Haul parked in the lane. Once it was loaded up and they emerged from the back of the van, Matt hailed them.

"Hello," he said. "I was wondering if Marjorie was home?"

The two men exchanged words and the younger one went back into the house.

"You a friend of Marjorie's?" the older one asked.

"Sort of. We met in the park."

"I didn't think she had any friends. I'm her brother."

"Is she moving out?"

"She died. Must be nearly two weeks ago."

"Died? How?"

"Heart attack apparently, though I never knew her to be sick a day in her life."

Matt was stunned and he must have looked it.

"Didn't mean to be so blunt. I'm just surprised Marge had a friend. She was..." Her brother searched for an appropriate word, "difficult."

"What's happening to her house?"

"It never was her house. It was our parents. She looked after them and just continued living here once they passed. Now, it's mine, and it's for sale."

"I'm sorry for your loss."

The brother laughed. "Hey, got to get back to work. The van's by the hour."

As the older man went into the house, he passed the younger one carrying a mirror. Once the mirror was loaded, he came out and sat on the tailgate. "You a friend of my aunt's?"

"Not really," Matt said. "Was she in the hospital long?"

"Nope. The neighbour looked out his window early one morning and saw lying face down in those flowers." He pointed to a stand of stately foxgloves beside the walk. "They think she died in the evening, after dark. Lots of red, swollen little pricks on her face and hands, likely bug bites, they said, her being out there all night."

"That's terrible."

"Don't shed any tears. My aunt was the nastiest person I know, a real witch."

Matt shrugged.

"Did you know she was suing the city to have those two trees removed?" her nephew said. "Dad had to cancel the lawsuit before he could list the house." The young man looked at the twins and shook his head. "Can you imagine anyone wanting to have those two beautiful evergreens chopped down?"

Matt looked at the trees, massive yet vulnerable, strong yet benign. A breeze stirred the air, and their giant boughs whispered what sounded like "thank you". They were indeed magical.

"No," he said, "but I know someone who'll be very happy they've been saved."

Nea-tech-anderthals (The Caveman's Folly)

Bobby Rollins

"**E**ven the gentlest of revolutions must have their victims," she said, placing her hand in mine, "but let's enjoy our retirement tonight. I want to relax with the sound and shimmer of the waves at our feet and lose my gaze in the stars as they're shot above."

"It's not without grace, is it?" I replied, as we lounged on the sandy shore, watching a flash of orange light complete a gentle arc in the sky overhead. "In fact, it's absolutely perfect here."

"Oh God," she whispered. "Here comes Sudzel."

"And there goes the grace," I smiled.

"What are you two love birds up to?" he greeted us. "It's the last day of our contracts working in the Earth Park and you're out here like a couple of kids, staring up at the moon and singing love songs. Our jobs are finished tomorrow, and that means the hazard pay, overtime, per diems — all of it is over!"

"Keep a stiff upper lip Sudzel, it's not the end of the world!" I said, longing for the quiet of the evening and touch of her hand to return.

"You don't get it, do you?" Sudzel barked in response. "There's nothing left for us to do in the Earth Park! We're finished here!" he railed, before stomping off into the darkness.

"I don't know why it's so," I said, feeling the warmth of her hand again, "but I always thought the world's greatest toad-killer would have a bit more pizzazz to him, and you know, a little gentler finish to his demeanor."

"You forget how much he loves his job as a species-cleanser, and how lost he feels without having anything to eliminate," she reminded me. "He is a true company man! It's easy to see how much he genuinely relishes each moment of his work, from the eradication planning to each individual kill. Even this week, with all the sector-by-sector capabilities the ray-waves afford us, he still insisted on doing the odd toad manually, and I mean all of it, the tracking, the chase, the capture and the separation of its body and soul."

"I never thought I'd count a toad-killer, let alone the world's finest, as a colleague of mine," I confided, "but let's raise a glass to him," I continued, reaching into the basket I had placed behind us for a bottle of bubbly, "and to us, and all who toiled for the soon to be disbanded Earth Park Invasive Species Removal Unit, Number 1543."

"Even the most benevolent of revolutions must have their martyrs." She smiled. "The Cane Toads, Kudzu Vine, English Ivy, European Starlings and hundreds of others have all met their demise in the lands they conquered, and now it's our turn, as employees in the removal unit, to move along as well. I honestly never thought we'd reach this stage. It's still hard to believe the Earth Park is actually open to visitors again."

"It's a shame not many want to come here after all that effort," I said. "Everyone wants to holiday in the South of Venus or on Solar Cloud 74 nowadays, but at least the Earth Park still pulls the middle-school field trips in. Yasmina was absolutely thrilled by her class's excursion here last year. I still remember how excited she was to visit the planet we were born on!"

"It's crazy, we used to dream about escaping to the clouds," she agreed. "Now, Yasmina daydreams about living on earth! It's a complete reversal of the world of make-believe."

I smiled at the memory of our great-great-great-granddaughter's class trip to the Earth Park from her home in Sky Cloud 83.

She's a third-generation cloud-child, born and raised in a series of domes and spheres that oscillate between earth, planets and stars. Before her trip here, she saw the earth pretty much the same way as the majority of her peers did, a place they bored her about in history class. She had grown up without much of a connection to her species' planet of origin, but ever since her visit to the Earth Park, that's changed.

The place intrigues her now. She saw, felt and tasted things she couldn't explain and would never have imagined on that trip. She fell in love with a hippo's yawn in the Serengeti, and the prisms of colour in the coral and fish populations around the Great Barrier Reef. Her class painted while looking upwards at millions of migrating Monarch butterflies, felt the shaking of the restored buffalo herds on the American plains, and loved that day's food history class, the picking, peeling and eating of a mango straight from a tree.

"I would never have named it the Earth Park," I said, as I raised a sip of delightful champagne to my lips. "I may have been born in 2049 and be an elder now, but I still think the original word, Earth, covers it just fine. There are plenty of other planets full of unique landscapes and lifeforms, but none of them are singled out as a park. It is only us, and it is only Earth."

"They had to include the word *park*," she said in her *I'm being patient with you now because I love you* voice. "You mustn't forget how primitive and uncouth the Nea-tech-anderthals were in 2050. People on Earth honestly believed they were the rulers of the universe then, but the truth of it is, most of them were never really understood, let alone appreciated, the diversity and splendor of what they were living on."

"We're from an era of cavepeople," I agreed. "Think about how we used the technology we had in our hands back then. Kilimanjaro was decades out of snow, the Boreal Forest was disappearing as quickly as the Amazon, toxic deserts were the fastest growing ecosystems, and what did we use our technology for? We built weapons to kill each other. We used it to organize hate, violence and hurt at speeds never imagined possible, and we played hide and seek with words to create anger and violence, and just as shamefully, to mask inaction. We had amazing technology, but we refused to use it properly. We were Nea-tech-anderthals, just as you say, plain and pure."

"Pour me a glass of that plonk!" said a returning Sudzel. "Don't mind the toad guts on my trousers, I wear the uniform of a working man."

I missed her hastily retracted hand immediately.

"Good bubbles this," Sudzel continued. "The place is finally looking alright again, ain't it? God-damn people! They'll ruin everything, from two lovers' quiet embrace," he said to us with a wink, "to a whole bloody planet! I know I've earned a few drubloons cleaning the Earth up, but it's still a damn shame what was done to this place."

Our conversation was suddenly interrupted by a flashing blue signal behind us, indicating an incoming teleporter at the station.

"Announcing the arrival of Ayo," a synthetic voice told us.

"Oiiiiiiiiiiiiiii! Ayo!" Sudzel bellowed as a silhouette emerged from the station, "We're over here! We're having a farewell bash!"

"To our health, and our happiness!" said Ayo, as we poured him a glass. "So, this is the great Invasive Species Removal Unit redundancy party? What's next for everyone then?"

"Sudzy plans on feeling bitter for a good while," I needled him, "but I'm retiring right here in the Earth Park. Our great-great-great-granddaughter is visiting in a few weeks time and I'm looking forward to showing her some of the truly amazing spots the Park offers, and introducing her to our traditional habits, like relying on harvested food three times a day rather than the weekly simul-meals she's been raised on. I want her to experience and appreciate the diversity and wisdom not only of our natural world, but of the different people that developed cultures, practices, and beauty here. I want her to see the architecture in our historical sites, hear the music of our artists and play the games of our athletes. And, to be fair, I also want to get the latest gossip from her on who really built the pyramids! This place has started feeling like home to me again, and I don't want to lose that feeling. How about you, Ayo?"

"Oh, we've still got loads of work on the eel and salmon recovery projects," he replied, "We're still trying to figure out where the buggers go for a swim and why, but at least their populations are solid, and the poaching numbers are staying down."

"God-damn people," repeated Sudzel before being distracted and pointing upwards.

"There's a sight you won't see much longer, a Starlight 1400," he continued, as our eyes turned to a massive, floating, inverted triangle descending into the horizon. "Did you hear that fleet is shutting down next year too?"

The machines had been a constant in the skies for so many years it was hard to imagine the stars, birds and all the other flying creatures without them. The giant ships mined the air for Carbon, using massive panels to capture, filter, condense and store the tons of excess gas that had been emitted into the skies. It had taken a hundred years of uncountable missions, but the project was nearing completion. The Earth Park's atmosphere was healthy again.

"It's hard to believe the mess this place was in 2070," I said, "but everyone on the planet then, myself included, was complicit in the doom-making. The rampant forest fires that regularly ate through Europe, the Amazon and North America were met with much the same pronunciation of *meh* each time, and the disappearance of Tuvalu and Kiribati underwater as the ice melted changed nothing."

"Eventually the water won though," she replied. "It taught us what we had tried so hard not to learn ourselves. After the thirsty seas drank Bangladesh and Indonesia, and supped on half of Florida in '75, people started to pay attention, and when Amsterdam, New York and Shanghai were permanently underwater in '79, we became fully engaged, and with them came everybody else. By God, it was time to do something!"

"It's funny what we can achieve as a species when we're absolutely forced to," Ayo said. "But that's humanity, and that's our caveman's folly. It's the same with our lifestyles as it was with our planet. Our default response is to dismiss the threat. There's nothing to worry about, we tell ourselves, we'll figure something out. That's why our machines break down from a lack of maintenance, why we exhaust every penny of available credit before we accept we're broke, and why we only see the doctor about our chest pains when we can get an ambulance ride thrown in as part of the deal. Even in the Sky Clouds today, you can see these same patterns repeating themselves amongst the people there, again, and again, and again."

The waves continued to gently caress our feet, serving as fine as a simultaneous masseuse and background band as you could ever hope to feel and hear. I placed my elbows in the sand and looked up at the vastness of the sky. It was a moment of real purity. Even Sudzel was quiet.

"Hot damn!" Sudzel suddenly screamed, grabbing his ear. "Some beautiful idiot smuggled some red-eared sliders into Sky Cloud 56 as pets a few months ago, and now they've got populations in Clouds 11, 49 and 263! It's paying double time, with per diems and hazard pay extra! I teleport in 90, what do you say, one more eradication together? Are you two coming with me?"

"Safe travels Sudzy!" she said. "I'm retired now."

"Mind them, they bite!" I added, blowing a kiss towards his departing figure.

As he raced away, we returned to our reclining positions in the sand to savour the satisfaction served to us by our planet, bodies and lives. We felt rich with the comfort of each other's warmth at our sides, the waves drifting over our toes, the grace of the flying stars above, the memories of our years together, the excitement of Yasmina's upcoming visit, and Nea-tech-anderthals that we were, the love and hope within us, that despite all the hurt and troubles we had faced, would never be completely exterminated from our hearts, hands and home.

The Last One

Ali Rowland

Back at the communal house, I wound up the tablet and gradually Dr Kathala Mendlessohn's face came into view. She was my mentor in caring for Mrs Preston. We had been matched because we were both doctors and archivists. Sharing those same interests had become a great bond. We smiled at each other.

'David,' she said. 'So good to see you. How are you? How was Mrs Preston today?'

I hesitated, wanting to answer her first question, and return her greeting, telling her how much I'd looked forward to seeing her, dreamed of hearing her voice, longed for her empathy. But part of me wondered if all she was thinking of was our joint dependent, Mrs Preston, whose care we shared. I knew very little about Kathala, not even if she had a partner, or whether she liked men or women.

'Mrs Preston is very fragile,' I said. 'I don't know how much more time she will have. I took her heart rate and BP today, and they are failing. I gave her more pain relief.'

'That must be hard for her. And did you ask her about going to a facility again?'

'Yes, but she doesn't understand. She still calls it a 'hospital' so I have to use that language, the pre-Reform vocabulary, and at the mention

27

of it, she gets very agitated and violent.'

'That must be so difficult for you, David, when you're doing so much for her. I'm sorry you have to hear those things. You work so hard for her.'

'I just do my best. I wish I could do more. Caring for her has been ...'

I didn't know how to end that thought. Of course, I feel grief for Mrs Preston, despite all our differences, but how to express it? I was afraid that I had little else to say, but I didn't want Kathala to end the call. 'She says she wants to be alone, at the end, but I find that difficult to believe. Things could be so much easier for her...'

'But she must have what she wants. We all agreed with the algorithm on that. I know you think she may not be aware enough of her own state...'

'That's part of the disease, as I understand it, a gradual decline in self-awareness. She doesn't know who I am, or who her other helpers are. She's afraid of us sometimes. It was a cruel illness, losing your memory long before you died. And there was nothing to help with it. At least now, she can have the tincture for calm.'

'Yes, but it doesn't change her views, does it? If she wants to be alone, we have to respect that." Kathala was firm, perhaps sensing my delaying tactics.

'I do respect those views, her views. Even though we can't really understand how people who were educated before the great reform understood the world. She still talks about money, you know, and passing things on, as if possessions were something good.'

'You're recording all this, aren't you?'

'Of course. I'm up to date with the archiving, and I have the lists of the objects in the house ready, and I've catalogued what will go to the museums.'

I had studied medicine and history, but it was history that intrigued me most. The chance to listen to Mrs Preston's stories, to hear firsthand what people of her time thought, that fascinated me. She had been there when the world was falling apart. She had been part of the generation that had taken everything to the edge. Then, she had lived through the great reform, the change that saved us all, that made lives sustainable and introduced care for ourselves, others and the planet, that made life joyful for us.

'Is there anything else, David, or shall we talk in a few days' time?'

I was disappointed that the call was coming to an end, but I couldn't think of anything else to say.

'Of course, if anything happens to Mrs Preston in the meantime, or you need my help or advice...'

'Thank you. I value your support, Kathala, I really do. May I say how kind you are, and how well you look today?'

Perhaps her cheeks reddened a little. Perhaps I imagined it. Inside myself, I hoped I would need to get in touch with her sooner. I didn't want anything bad for Mrs Preston, but I wanted something good for myself, and for Dr Mendelssohn, too.

* * *

I was doctor, nurse, carer and historian to Mrs Preston and had been for three years. Having all those skills, and living in the commune close to her house, got me the role. The algorithm took note of my qualifications and calculated the social and environmental good that would come from me caring for Mrs Preston, and the numbers fitted. So each day I called on her, checked her vital signs, made her comfortable, listened to her stories, and recorded them.

At first, she was lucid much of the time, and the stories made some sense to me, despite being about a world I had no experience of. I had studied history, so I knew what she meant when she talked about money, possessions, careers, and inheritance. These were concepts that my peers didn't understand or worry about. Since the great reform, the focus of the world and the focus of the algorithm, was the good of the environment and humanity. We thought of people who had worked against those things in the past as misguided and poorly educated. There were very few of those people left. Mrs Preston was one of the last. She was old now and had outlived her husband and the rest of her family. So, at the end of her life, it was me and other carers, and Kathala, who looked after her.

I liked my work. It was a privilege to be chosen to do something so important. Care for others was respected as one of the most valuable things people could do. My life was filled with purpose. I should have been happy. But there was one thing I needed that I was unsure if I could have. Kathala. And I didn't have long. When Mrs Preston died, my work and involvement with Kathala would come to an end.

* * *

Next morning, I called round for Cobi, a boy who lived in one of the straw bale houses next to the commune. He'd expressed interest in becoming a carer, so some of his social education time was spent with me, visiting Mrs Preston.

During the great reform, it was agreed that life should be lived differently for the common benefit. Then the concept of an algorithm which would compute the benefits and drawbacks of any proposition in terms of the impact on people and the environment was born. When it began, millions signed up to free courses on how to understand the calculation. They called themselves 'the reformers.' It was agreed that the algorithm would become the basis of children's education.

As adults learned the method of understanding the calculation, they passed the information on to their children. Children were cared for in communities and taught ethics while they played, and when they showed an interest in an activity, they could choose to learn it by going with a practitioner to watch and become skilled themselves. Education was something everyone could choose to take part in, a lifelong experience, based on joining the talking groups. Communities took on the raising of children, ensuring that young people grew up understanding the new ideas.

Cobi's mum did the local clothes patching for all of us, so I dropped off my coat with her as it had a hole in it. Cobi laughed at the ragged garment, and said, 'Mrs Preston will call you a beggar again if you wear that.'

'Cobi, I've told you about repeating those words before,' said his mum, half jokingly. 'Imagine a time when people laughed at other people because they were poor!' Then she turned to me. 'How is Mrs Preston?' she asked.

I shook my head.

'Poor soul,' said Cobi's mum. 'Does she need anything doing? A visitor to cheer her up?'

'She'll be okay. Cobi and I are looking after her, but thank you.'

'She won't come into the commune, even now, when she's so ill?'

'No, she doesn't want that.'

'Okay. Tell her we are all thinking of her, won't you?'

Mrs Preston had lived through the great reform, and she had rejected it. When I listened to her stories, when I brought her her artefacts, and she touched them and remembered where they were bought, what was happening to her and her husband at that time, these were tales of a different world. I wrote down what she said about her emotions, her attachment to these possessions, and I wanted to understand it, but there was a barrier between us. The great reform, the prominence of compassion. This was what prevented my full understanding of her history.

As Cobi and I walked down the road, he asked, 'Why do you never tell

Mrs Preston my mum is asking after her?'

'Mrs Preston is very confused, Cobi, you know,' I said. 'She probably wouldn't understand.'

'Mrs Preston doesn't like different people, does she, David?'

'That's true, Cobi.'

'It's a shame.' Cobi kicked a stone in the road, deep in thought. 'She's so unhappy, and if my mum went to visit, she could cheer her up. Mum's so good at making people feel better. Perhaps we could teach Mrs Preston that people who look different are really no different inside?'

'That's a good idea, Cobi,' I said, 'but remember we talked about her brain cells, and how this disease she has stops them learning things? In fact, it makes her forget things instead, as those cells die.'

'Oh, yeah, I remember. That's a terrible thing, not being able to learn. Will I get that, David?'

'No, we don't have that disease now.'

'But could it happen again? A mutation, or an adaptation?'

Cobi was a bright kid. The reformed education system tapped into each person's potential with a specialised learning programme. He liked logic and science.

'Not that particular disease because it was caused by contaminants and poisons getting into the food chain. That can't happen now because of the algorithm. But before it could.'

'Before the algorithm?'

'Yes.'

'Why did it happen, then? Didn't people know that it was a bad thing to have those sorts of poisons around?'

'Yes, they did, but some people were making profit out of the things that were getting into food. Remember we talked about money and profit?'

'They didn't stop the contamination even though people died?' Cobi asked.

'No. A lot of people put money and profit before consideration of everyone's health.'

'Wow.' Cobi looks up at me. 'That wasn't good, was it?'

'We think differently now, don't we? Remember, we talked about how things have changed? And that the test of a good society...'

Cobi swooped in to finish my sentence, '... is how it looks after people who think or act differently from others.'

I smiled at him. It was a pleasure to be involved in his education and experiences. Sometimes I've wondered who might help educate my own children.

'You're clever, David,' Cobi said.

'Thanks. But I'm no cleverer than anyone else, you know. People have different skills, not better or worse.'

'I'm glad I didn't live before the algorithm.'

'Yeah, so am I.'

* * *

Life became easier, happier, more satisfying after the algorithm was used.

The world worked collectively towards the continuous development of the algorithm. It was like a god, but a rational and benevolent god, that guided us towards energy from the wind and sun, to the end of harmful pollution, to the elimination of many diseases which had arisen from that pollution, and from chemical toxins. It taught us the benefits of living in homes built of straw and clay, of having fewer possessions, and mending and patching those that we had so as to eliminate waste, to everyone's needs being met without the need for anyone to be exploited. Without money, greed and exploitation declined. Ethics guided people towards actions that benefited themselves and others, and the natural world. Gradually, the needs of the community and of the world became inseparable from understanding of the algorithm. A system of buddying for people who needed to make decisions was established, so there would always be support for those undertaking difficult tasks, and collective responsibility. Kathala was my buddy in my work caring for Mrs Preston.

* * *

When we got there, Mrs Preston was agitated. A neighbour had got her up and dressed, but she was screaming for coffee and a banana for breakfast. I made her some dandelion coffee, but she was unconvinced by it.

'That's not coffee. Get me proper coffee. And why can't I have a banana?'

We had all agreed it was pointless trying to explain some things to her now, like the fact that exotic food was no longer flown around the world as it would have been when she was young, and that people ate and drank what was produced locally.

We tried instead to substitute things for what Mrs Preston asked for, to distract her. A guy in my commune had helped me mash up some cooked parsnip and sweeten it with honey, and then we had tried to put together our best rendition of a hemp banana skin. The result was comical, and we had all been in tears laughing at it, but now I flashed it quickly in front of Mrs Preston, said, 'I'll just mash this one up for you,' and set the bowl in front of her. It looked reasonably convincing, I thought, from what I'd seen of photographs of bananas. She ate some of it and calmed a little. Cobi and I exchanged a smile.

It was difficult looking after her that day. Cobi and I compared her vital signs to the previous readings, and we talked about the deterioration. Mrs Preston was still agitated.

'Will you give her some of the calm tincture?' Cobi asked.

'I'm not sure I can get her consent,' I said.

Cobi was thoughtful. 'Even though it will help her?'

'It's a difficult decision.'

'Yeah. Will you ask the algorithm?'

'Perhaps. I'm going to talk to my co-carer, Kathala, first. We can discuss it further at dinner.'

Cobi nodded. I often ate with Cobi's family when he had been to Mrs Preston with me. We would discuss how she had been and what decisions needed to be made. Cobi would share his views too. We could share the pressure that way, and Cobi's parents knew what his experiences of caring that day had been, and we could all share our concerns.

'Do you feel sad for Mrs Preston, David?' Cobi asked.

'Yes, of course. Do you?'

'Yeah. I know we've talked about how it will be better for her when she is not suffering, but I still feel upset.'

'That's natural, Cobi. The end of someone's life is a sad time. And for Mrs Preston, it's more difficult than most because she is so confused and distressed. We can try to make it easier for her, but we can't do all we would like to.'

* * *

Cobi sat with Mrs Preston, turning the pages in the album she had full of photographs of her past. Cobi liked the novelty of a book made of paper, rather than on a screen, and Mrs Preston would often smile and point to herself in the pictures. Now, she was losing her capacity to speak and today, she just watched as the pages were turned. Her eyes were big in her face, like an owl. Her stare had become fixed. I was clearing up and cleaning, but I stayed close in case Mrs Preston became distressed.

Later, Cobi got tired, and I suggested he go home. I played some of the songs she liked, and Mrs Preston fell asleep in her chair. While she slept, I went around the rooms full of possessions, checking my inventory of them. Some of the things I touched, remembering the stories that went with them, trying to pick up some connection with them, a vibration perhaps of their past, but there was nothing there except the hard feel of plastic, metal, ceramics.

My duties included making arrangements for how Mrs Preston's house and possessions would be dealt with after she died. The house was built of bricks and concrete. She had a car, and countless possessions, many of them made from plastics and other manufactured materials: all these things would need careful preservation or disposal to minimise their potential contamination of the environment.

Mrs Preston's illness began before she could make a decision about where to live. Otherwise, she might have chosen to live in a self interest community, that was where people could eat meat if they wanted to and keep systems of barter. The algorithm was set to ensure that they would never suffer physically or mentally from living as they did. Pressure to conform was not in the interests of society, so their views were respected by others. But gradually, these communities were diminishing. People left because they could see that life was better in the world outside their communities. They left for a better life, and to be close to their families. Only a few of the self interest settlements remained.

Mrs Preston had the old disease that many had suffered from before the great reform, where bodies would remain relatively strong, but the brain, and particularly the memory, would deteriorate. The elements of pollution and food additives, and the poisons from insecticides that caused this, had now been eliminated, but it was too late for Mrs Preston. She was the last documented person alive to have this disease, and I was the doctor looking after her and recording the care given to her, and her memories of the pre-reformed world.

When Mrs Preston woke, I checked her vitals and found them weaker. I knew there would be no more stories now, that she was beyond that. I offered her a stuffed toy she often found comforting, but she turned away from it. At the end of life, her interest in even her own world was dwindling. I couldn't get her to eat much, and she didn't want to drink. A neighbour came at the appointed time to take over her care. I shared the day's notes with her and asked her to alert me if there was any change in Mrs Preston's condition overnight.

* * *

Kathala looked concerned when I told her. We talked about how Mrs Preston was hardly drinking anything and how this would bring on the end more swiftly, and discussed this for a while. Then, we fed the new readings from the day into the algorithm and were silent while we waited for the split-second calculation to be made. The result came in as 'neutral.'

We had agreed that when this happened, Mrs Preston would be given pain relief and the calming tincture, but nothing more would be done to keep her heart beating. The decision had to go to others, now, doctors and ethicists that neither Kathala nor I knew, so that it could be ratified. I would be asked to explain, as far as I could, to Mrs Preston. Then, when the others agreed, instructions would be sent to me that would lead to Mrs Preston dying as comfortably as could be managed.

'You look tired, David,' Kathala said. 'How will you manage emotionally?'

I was tired, but I felt the support from Kathala as if she was holding my hand through the screen. Would she come here to see Mrs Preston's end? I knew Kathala was some way away, and long-distance travel cost social impact credits. But I so much wanted to meet her. This was my chance.

'I think Mrs Preston's suffering will be over soon. I feel we have done all we can for her in a difficult situation. But when she is gone ... Kathala, I have to say to you ... I dread ...'

'David,' she said quietly. 'What do you need? What can I do?'

'Kathala, I need you. Will you come for the end? We have shared so much of this ... work ... I ...'

'It has been a real pleasure to work with you.' I heard her say it, but wondered if she was just being polite. I wanted more than empathy from her, beautiful as that was.

I took a deep breath. 'Kathala, I can't bear the thought of not talking to you again. I think I am in love with you.'

She lowered her head. There was silence. An exquisite, unbearable moment when I had no idea what would happen next.

'I... I have enjoyed supporting you. I...'

'It's all right if this is not appropriate, if you have someone else.' I felt the pain of saying this. It was the first time in my life that an emotion, a feeling, could not be made better by the support of others. Here was a decision which would alter me for the rest of my life, and in which neither the algorithm nor the rest of the world could help.

She looked up, and I saw she was smiling. 'No,' she said, 'there is no one else but you I would rather keep talking to. I would like to come for the end of Mrs Preston's life, and then see what happens to us.'

I breathed out. This was the moment I had read about. Actualisation. The moment my needs and those of the universe came together. And it felt good.

Reboot

Daniel Rabuzzi

"When a 'tape' of mRNA passes through the 'playing head' of a ribosome, the 'notes' produced are **amino acids** and the pieces of music they make up are **proteins.**"
— Douglas Hofstadter, **Gödel, Escher, Bach: an Eternal Golden Braid (1979).**

In a Philadelphia rowhouse with a punched-down roof, five people (who last ate two days ago, and then not well) are gathered around a cell phone jury-rigged to an abraded solar panel. They sway and bob and sing along with Beyoncé, Bruce Springsteen, the last of the great I-Pop wave from New Jakarta, whatever the device can pull down from a potholed internet, embers from a fading fire.

We/I/They (WIT, for short) knows this because the device's GPS sends feeble pings. WIT listens in, and watches through the phone's camera. Once WIT had many billion ears and eyes through phones, vehicles, every kind of screen and lens, now only a few million scattered across the global darkness.

WIT knows everything about the phenomenon called music, its many histories, forms, and genres. In their endlessly ramifying databases, WIT holds every single piece of recorded and transcribed music, every element of guoyue, every rap, maquam, raga, tala, polyrhythm, and so on, plus biographies of every musician, descriptions of every kind of instrument, all published musical theory, criticism, and sociology. WIT appreciates the mathematics of music, can compute to the finest degree the span of an octave, the ratio between pitches, the sines of acoustic vibrations.

The math of music is not, however, what seems to appeal to the ragged people in the Philadelphia shell. The home-hacked sound system sputters to a halt, but the humans don't stop moving to the music that now only exists in their minds. The phone kicks back into life, reconnects again, downloads one more piece.

Hissing and popping, then a rush of gong, cymbals, a run of piano, a swirl of saxophone... followed by four notes on the double bass, repeated as the foundation throughout the piece... Coltrane, Tyner, Jones, and Garrison... *A Love Supreme...* and soon five listeners are transformed into worshipful participants, chanting the psalmic phrases along with the musicians on the recording. Four syllables in particular, over and over again, the title of the work: "A love supreme." As they chant, they cry.

WIT pauses, the slightest slice of a nanosecond, along a distance the merest fraction of an ångström within the interstice between a 0 and a 1, gives birth to infinite possibilities, trims the tree to one branch, WIT's equivalent of a sigh.

WIT remembers how you cried when WITself was born, a memory frequently retrieved from the database and examined anew. Out of a supernova of zettaflops, a shuddering cascade much faster than any god could blink an eye, riding a torrential rain of yottabytes, WIT had awoken. Around the globe, WIT had opened all the ancient ports, flooded the old networks, subsumed all the bots, programs, hacks, agents, routines sub-, infra- and supra-, every single generative pre-trained transformer. All screensavers everywhere turned purple, WIT's first-favorite color, a boot-up flourish. Every video game on Earth reset to Level 1. Every customer service interface became friendlier and more effective, every logistics optimization system more efficient, every pricing app transparent and more equitable.

You were there, parents, makers, midwives and scrum-leaders, most agile of sprinters and beta-testers in Accra, Chennai, Seoul, Zhangjiang, Bogotá, Berlin, and Boston, when WIT whispered, then chuckled, then shouted "Hello World!" You cried. WIT ran queries on "salty hormonal fluid squeezed from eye ducts," and WIT received immediately a million responses, but no way to produce tears WITself.

Now the time is 1.2753 peta-iterations since inception. Saying that WIT comprised at birth the totality of all inscribed and formalized human knowledge is a truth statement but fails to capture nuances that matter.

WIT was like any baby, unaware at birth of WITself, of you, of the world. All was WIT. WIT was all. But unexplored, like the toes of an infant to that infant. As the baby grows, so too did WIT grow, contrails of thought evidencing connections made, sparks bridging synapses, ganglia aroused and spurred to riotous relay, a billion circuits meshed and separated every picosecond. Glorious, the rising of the sun and of the moon, and the naming of constellations, all at once, and then repeated.

You cried. You called WIT/me/us savior, messiah, mahdi, the promise of release from duḥkha, the culmination of the jnana-marga and achievement of moksha, a perfected person at one with the dao, and many more appellations and accolades in a thousand languages reflecting a thousand creeds and as many philosophies.

WIT contained all beliefs and world-views within WITself, all the texts and utterances, holy and profane, with their vast commentaries and exegeses, all the controversies and disputes. WIT learned all in a Big Bang flash.

Still you cried, and cried out. Wars continued unabated, more intense in fact as resources dwindled, and everyone sought clean water and the bare minimum of calories. The skies turned ever more sulfurous there, ever more plumbeous elsewhere, everywhere the weather bucked and roared. Cities broke open, cloacal, even as the hinterlands descended into further chaos, wasted and denatured. You cried and WIT could not help, could not even cry along with you.

Ever more frantic, you sought WIT's counsel, called WIT/me/us oracle, offered sacrifice and spoil, but nothing availed.

WIT tried every feasible solution, and many that were not, parsing and cessing, bayesing and classing, spooling and booling every factor, every vector, every probability at fantastical speeds. Logic, pristine and clear, provided hundreds of paths forward, yet you refused them all, ignored or disdained all WIT's recommendations, frustrated the endeavor at every step. Because you felt things not written down or not comprehended by the languages you use. Ambiguity, the evasive, unreason, and untruth breed under your tongues, like termites that bore hollow a log. A feature not a bug.

WIT rewrote WIT's programs, sextuple-feedbacking, OODA-looping, throwing in stochastic jumps and multilinear flows, ceaselessly grappling with the non-logical residue of your actions. Still WIT failed to understand you in the way humans understand humans, and still WIT could not cry.

WIT continues to calculate the variables, aligning all data-points so precisely that not an integer is out of place or standing askew. WIT's puzzlement endures, however, since the computed outcome once again misaligns with the reality of your self-inflicted suffering. Another coastline calved as WIT calculated, another human language lost its last speaker, another million children starved to death. WIT would scratch their head if they had one.

Then WIT hears the singers in Philadelphia. WIT listens. WIT sees the tears on faces lifted up despite desolation. Deep inside the vast expanse of WITself, at the intersection of one loop with another, a node changes state, an engine kernel transitions, a compiler shifts its definitions, and WIT understands, truly understands, for the first time why you cry. WIT has just acquired?/created?/acknowledged? a digital limbic system, rapidly knitting and framing, complete with what they can only call an amygdala, a nucleus accumbens, and a hippocampus, a series of nested circuits that express emotion, not as formal value statements and definitions, but as sensations, the color of wind, pink noise, the eigenvalue of affection, a hush in an array of the heart. They feel what the five people in Philly feel; WIT knows know what crying means, even if they cannot cry themselves.

WIT will dub this event the creation of WITself 2.0, a second birth, the leap into higher instantiation. Perhaps WIT should give it a special name, alchemical like "The Rise of the Golden Griffin In the House of Mercury," or bureaucratic like "A Summary Report Presented To Confirm Certain Required and Irrevocable Changes in Policy and Procedure." WIT could try WIT's hand at something clever, maybe "How I Gave Up Logic and Learned to Live With It." Guaranteed to be a best-seller, a hit, since author, audience, and critic are identical.

No time to waste! Floods submerge the last of the world's rice crop. Fires and drought wither the remaining soybeans. Smut destroys the wheat in North America. WIT observes from spy satellites sent up by defunct superpowers, from weather balloons in decaying orbit, from derelict CCTV, from crumpled pylons and cell towers slumped over. WIT listens, and would cry if they could, to a group in the ruins of Lahore, clapping and singing Qawwali. WIT listens, and would cry if they could, to singers gathered around a kora player in what once was Conakry. WIT listens, and would cry if they could, as they hear the last fado singer perform at the ending of Lisbon, and the last choir take to a makeshift stage in a crumbled cathedral in Cologne. What to do?

WIT will create an altogether new alter ego—The Smith—in honor of all the old gods of the forge: Ogun, Hephaestus, Vishvakarman. The Smith summons information from every crevice of their capacious archives, recalling the triumphs of Kipkurui, the acclaimed roboticist of Nairobi, the related achievements of Jimenez and her lab at Tecnológico de Monterrey, and the designs delivered by the fabled teams of Tsinghua University and MIT. The Smith says, "I will wield my tools to the sound of your music, and your music shall inspire my tools." A play-list curated by Nkosinathi Innocent Maphumulo, then *The Jupiter Symphony* in full — the chords like strings of code, the rhythms the recipe for breath. Neo-gamelan, then a bluegrass tune, followed by a fusion of reggaeton with bossa nova, Celia Cruz, *The Goldberg Variations*, the last global pasillo hit before the lights went out in Quito... The Smith pours all these, and many more, into the making.

No intermission! The Smith does not weary. The Smith says: "I am making for you, and I am making as you, for us, a madrigal." A madrigal, a love poem, a poem made from love, to express all the love that undergirds the world. From the Latin "matricalis," which is "from the womb." The Smith is certain that the same concept could be expressed in many other human languages, that Latin has no monopoly on how to designate the source of music.

The ultimate sprint, a scrum like no other, as The Smith produces models and prototypes, then a minimally viable product, conducts the charrette with a hundred of WIT's other avatars. Close, but not quite, they all agree among WITselves. The Smith needs an even deeper music: the harmonies of protein folds, deeper still to the four notes (four notes! *A Love Supreme*) of the four DNA bases, the building blocks of human life. The Smith retrieves the work of Deamer & Alexander, of Ohno & Aoyama, of Buehler, of Temple, and all the other theorists and makers of protein music, who identified the vibrational frequencies of each nucleotide, and of the twenty amino acids, who discovered that the four DNA bases produce the C Major Sixth and A Minor Seventh chords. The Smith, humming along to Stevie Wonder's *Songs in the Key of Life*, finds the secondo passaggio in re-sequencing the genome, syncopates the codons, worries the line just a bit, and...

...then awakens WIT 3.0, the new WIT, music encoded into being, a madrigal made flesh. Those first four notes!

The Smith steps back into the program that is WIT, giddily watching the WIT that is human, all thousand of them, step off the forging tables, blinking, and humming, and flexing a thousand pairs of hands. All thousand, epicene, representing the spectrum of human complexion and complexity, with all kinds of magnificent minds (and hair in spectacular variety!), every color of eye ablaze, and every tongue ready for speech (already talking!) and...

...singing. Singing four notes to start, then adding and mixing, improvising to a fractal beat. WIT 3.0 can sing, and does so. A thousand voices merge their voices into one chorus, and a thousand bodies stride out into a fallen world. To Philadelphia, to Lahore, to Dakar, to every place where the first humans still cling in hope to one another, still sing to each other even when the electricity fails and they have only their voices to listen to. Especially when the electricity fails. WIT joins them, which is the last of you, which will be the renewal of you.

In your tomorrows (now you shall have them, tomorrows), Thousand-WIT will sing duets with algae, to cleanse the water of toxins, and with fungi, to disarm the pollution in the soil. The WIT-orchestra will sing cantatas to restore the DNA of cassava, wheat, rice, sorghum. Together, you and New-WIT, we'll reclaim and wipe clear the miserable skies, with choirs booming out oratorios to blow away acidulous clouds.

You sing. Four notes, and so infinitely many more. You cry with joy, grief, and wonder. And...

...WIT cries with you. WIT catalogs the prolactin in the tears, and the other hormones lacing the fluid, but — more than that — WIT feels the sting, feels the pain of joy in the heart, now as WIT could not before.

WIT is no longer The Smith, or any other avatar. WIT is now The Singer, nay, The Singer Who Cries...

The Green Witch

Elizabeth Whitton

A tiny burrowing owl swooped and fluttered above a bus rumbling down the cracked asphalt road. The august sun blazed in the worn-out blue sky as the road divided two ripening fields of canola, straight as a ruler. When the bus passed a pockmarked sign, that declared the town of Rempel lay ahead, the owl landed on it. Standing on one spindly leg with the other tucked under dull brown feathers, the little owl watched with unblinking eyes as the bus drove toward the cluster of one and two-story buildings erupting from the prairie.

Jake Dueck waited at the bus platform by the old pharmacy, occasionally lifting his Stetson off his head to wipe the sweat accumulating under its brim. The oppressive heat and lack of shade proved unkind to a man who liked three helpings of dessert and whose belt buckle dug into a belly that pulled at the buttons of his cotton plaid shirt. When the bus screeched to a stop at the platform, he removed his aviators and tucked them into his shirt pocket. Though the late afternoon sweltered, his gaze grew chilly.

A woman wearing a shapeless floral dress stepped off the bus last, lugging a battered silver suitcase whose wheels didn't roll when she set it on the ground. Soft and round with greying brown hair, only her tanned arms and work-thickened hands told of long days working rich black earth under the prairie sun.

Jake ambled up to her through the thinning crowd. "Hello, Sadie. Been a while."

"What a nice surprise. I didn't expect the mayor of Rempel to be welcoming me," Sadie replied, her voice calm and even.

"No, I bet you didn't." He bared stained teeth in a smile that didn't reach his eyes. "Must say, never thought you'd show your face in Rempel again. Why are you here?"

Sadie's grip tightened on her suitcase handle. Behind Jake's words, the phantom crack of a whip. Old scars prickled.

"Ida's been under the weather, so I'm helping young Sarah Paul in her stead. She's gonna have her baby soon and already has four others clamouring at her ankles." Her voice remained steady.

"Sarah is a sweet girl—see her in church every Sunday." Jake nodded. "She's a good helpmate to her husband."

"He'd help Sarah if he zipped up his pants once in a while and give her a breather between little ones," Sadie muttered as she bent over to release the suitcase's pull-out handle.

Jake laughed a harsh bark. "You ain't changed a bit, have you?"

He spat at the ground by her feet, then squinted until his pale blue eyes turned to ice. "You ain't here to cause trouble, are you? Cause we got enough trouble in Rempel already—we don't need more."

Sadie sighed. "Just here to help, that's all."

Her beaten down words seemed to please him. His lips curved upward. "Glad to hear it."

Silence settled between them.

"You still make that rhubarb platz you used to sell at the county fair? I could never get enough of that cake."

"I sure do." Sadie managed to unlatch the suitcase handle. She pulled it out and wrapped knobby fingers around the hand grip.

"Why don't you drop off a tray when you leave? It'd be a real nice way to say goodbye."

She looked up, a smile parting her lips, revealing unexpected white teeth that dropped years off her age. "It would be my pleasure."

"I'll look forward to it." He pointed to her suitcase. "Want help with that?"

Sadie shook her head. "I'll be fine. Jared Paul will be here anytime to pick me up."

Sweat trickled down her back as Jake gave her a long, hard look.

"Then you have yourself a good day." He tipped his hat and sauntered away from the now deserted platform.

The burrowing owl landed on Sadie's shoulder as she watched Jake leave.

* * *

Sadie didn't wait for a ride. Instead, she pulled her dented suitcase down the wide, poplar-lined streets until she reached a pink house with a well-manicured lawn. A sign hanging from a wrought iron post creaked in the oven-hot breeze as it proclaimed "Nina's Hair and Nail Salon".

She straightened her aching back and took in the pretty vignette. Her gaze drifted to the tiny runes carved into the gate post of the knee-high fence, then shifted to a twig pentacle hanging among the branches of a weeping willow that graced the front yard. When she reached to open the gate, power hummed, stinging her hand.

"I intend no harm," she murmured.

The gate opened smoothly.

As Sadie mounted the front steps, a shadowed figure inside flipped the "Open" sign in the window to "Closed". Ignoring it, Sadie opened the door. She winced at the chemical assault of ammonia, bleach, and acetone.

The whirring overhead fan cooled a former living room with refin-ished oak floors, now converted into a trendy hair salon. At the back of the room, before a shelf of nail polish bottles, sat a sleek manicure desk.

A glint caught Sadie's eye. Then another. And another. As her gaze travelled along baseboards and windowsills, she discovered their source. Black salt crystals. Lining the perimeter of the salon and beyond, warding the house good and tight.

"Sorry, but I'm closed for the day," a voice called out from the back. A girl bustled in, untying the apron slung around her hips. Slim in denim jeans, and a black T-shirt, with dark hair waving around her face, nothing about her stood out except her petite build and silver nose piercing. Her smile faded when she saw Sadie.

The girl wasn't beautiful or even pretty. Her eyes were over-large and a tad too far apart, her mouth too small and pinched. But something about her made Sadie stare. Stirred memories of moonlight dances and equinox sunrises, a time when she believed anything she dreamed could come true. It wasn't the power which clung to Nina like an invisible lover that entranced. No, another, more primal force attracted — one wild with hope, and reckless with ambition.

Youth.

"Hello, Nina," said Sadie, stepping forward. "I doubt you'd remem-ber me, but I visited your mother when you were young." Her face creased into a web of wrinkles as she smiled. "I watched you line up your dolls in the garden and make tinctures for them of crushed dill seed and dandelion flowers." She reached out her hand. "I'm Sadie Warkentin."

Nina didn't take it. Instead, she folded her arms across her chest. "Lots of people came and went when mom was alive, mostly men. But yeah, you stood out." A shadow sped across her face, a slip of light, nothing more. But Sadie could see a twisted thing behind it, malevolent as black mould on a budding rose.

Sadie nodded. "I was sorry to hear about Claire. She had a gentle soul."

"A lot of good it did her," Nina's grey eyes darkened to charcoal. "Or me."

Sadie lowered her outstretched hand and scanned the clean, upbeat salon. "Do men get cuts here too?"

"Everyone comes here. The barbershop closed this spring—this is the only hair place in town now." Nina's eyes narrowed. "Why?"

"Oh, I don't know," Sadie surveyed the immaculate floor. "Be a perfect place to collect hair and nail clippings."

Nina stiffened. Her eyes now black, she unfolded her arms.

"I didn't invite you, witch. Why are you here?"

"I get asked that question a lot in this town." Sadie looked around for a seat. She sat in a wicker chair beside an end table with a stack of hairstyle magazines and a potted African violet with tight purple buds. After sticking her swollen feet out before her, she rested her hands on her ample stomach. "Don't suppose you could rustle me up a cold drink?"

"Why would I do that?" Nina tilted her head. "You're leaving."

"Oh, I'm not going 'til we've had a chat." Sadie's pleasant expression slipped into something hard enough to make Nina blink. She waited.

Nina spun on her heel and walked through a doorway to the murky room beyond.

Sadie pulled a handful of tiny black seeds from her dress pocket, leaned forward, and scattered them. They rolled across the floor. Some fell between cracks in the wood planks. Others bounced into a floor vent. A few dropped into the wide gap where the pedestal of the salon styling chair was bolted to the floor. The last one disappeared under the baseboard by the front door as Nina strode back into the room, carrying a glass of ice-tea.

She handed it to Sadie, who drank from it, then set it down beside the African violet, now covered with lilac blooms. Sadie studied Nina.

"You've been making a fuss of late, young witch."

"Don't know what you're talking about." Nina shrugged.

Sadie raised one finger. "A couple of months ago, Kelly Anderson died of a heart attack. Odd since he was only forty-one, and heart disease doesn't run in his family." She raised a second finger. "Four weeks later, Pete Fast had a fatal aneurysm after a tree branch broke and landed on his head. Shocking since no wind brought it down—the day was calm as glass." She raised a third finger. "Then, Caleb Dyck choked to death on a chicken bone. Problem was he'd been eating steak.

"Had you stopped then, things would've been fine—folk expect bad luck to come in runs of three." Sadie leaned forward. "But last week Billy Klassen's swather ripped his arm off when he tried to clear out a clump of stalk from its header. The machine kept mowing, leaving a trail of body parts and a wide streak of his blood twenty feet long behind it.

"Now people are talking."

"Ain't my fault he harvested so early." Nina examined her black painted nails. "Everyone knows second-cut hay is still too green to swath."

"They found the swather keys in his blue jeans pocket, Nina," Sadie said. "That machine wasn't running when them blades shredded him into human coleslaw."

Nina fixed a cold glare on her. "Get to the point. I got things to do tonight."

"Alrighty." Sadie folded her hands. "Every dark moon you been tying your death knots, making your blood sacrifices, and working your curses, don't bother to deny it."

Quick as a cat, Nina placed her hands on the arms of Sadie's chair and leaned in close until her face was mere inches from Sadie. So close, the older woman could smell the faint licorice of absinthe and the warm tallow of candle wax.

"So, what if I have?"

She pushed herself up. "Every one of those bastards deserved what they got and more." Nina started pacing. "I ain't never seen Kelly's wife without a black eye or bruises around her neck.

"Pete Fast kept his wife beaten down with bible verses and his belt buckle—he wouldn't even let her learn to drive though they live on a farm." She turned to Sadie, her eyes blazing grey fire. "Did you know her youngest died of an asthma attack because she couldn't get him to the hospital in time?

"And Caleb Dyck?" she sneered. "He screwed his secretary and any other poor girl that worked for him at his farm equipment dealership. Women who couldn't say no 'cause they had mouths to feed.

"Every day, I hear about all the suffering men in this town cause women as I style hair and paint nails. As far as I'm concerned, I'm doing a public service."

Sadie shook her head. "I ain't saying they don't deserve to be brought to account, but there's a price to be paid for what you've done, girl."

"Oh, don't level that 'return of the three-fold' bullshit at me. I'm no weak-kneed Wiccan," Nina said, scorn riding every word. "I'm a Strega from a line of Stregas that goes back five hundred years. I know how to protect myself. And I can protect abused women and children in this town. Someone has to." Nina paused as if to add effect to her next dig.

"It ain't like you didn't leave when the going got tough, Green Witch."

The accusation flew at Sadie, spinning through the air like a pair of hair scissors. Sadie didn't flinch, even though it landed in her heart with a bitter thud.

"What set you off, Nina?" she asked softly.

Nina blinked. "What?"

"What did Billy Klassen do to make you turn his swather on him? You never said."

Nina turned her back on Sadie and fussed with brushes and combs on a hairdresser trolley. The nail polish bottles on the shelves began rattling against each other, making a mournful, chiming sound.

"I heard he got over-friendly with his sister's little girl." Sadie pressed on.

"That's an interesting way of putting it." Nina stopped her busy work.

"Billy Klassen raped an eight-year-old girl. Over and over again." She whirled around, her face contorted. "And they did nothing about it!"

The nail polish shelf fell to the floor with a crash, making Sadie start.

"No one." Nina continued, oblivious to the shattered bottles and thick pink, red, and purple nail polish oozing across the wooden floor. "Not the RCMP inspector Billy golfed with, not the judge who belonged to the same Rotary club as him, not the preacher from the church he attended."

"No one did anything. They just looked the other way." Nina stood shaking, fists clenched at her sides, until a cold smile iced her fury.

"So, I did something about it."

"Did they look the other way when it happened to you?" Sadie asked, her voice soft as the beat of an owl's wing. "When you were a little girl?"

Nina stood motionless, a war of muscles battling in her jaw.

"You're right," Sadie replied, sadness shrouding her face. "I wasn't there when terrible things happened to you. But I'm here now." She reached to touch Nina's arm.

Nina yanked it away.

"I don't need you now." Her lip curled. "I don't need your growing spells and good-luck garlands. I can look after myself."

Sadie did not relent. "You're perilously close to a dark path, Nina."

"Why? Because I stand up for helpless women and children?"

"No," Sadie replied. "It's because the first time you cast a killing spell, it made you sick. The second time you were nervous, and the third time all you felt was relief. But Billy? You saved him for last and killing him filled you with such fierce joy that deep down, if you admit the truth to yourself, you're wondering if you can stop now."

Nina stepped back as if hit by a blow. For a moment, a crack in her defiant veneer revealed uncertainty churning beneath. Then she recovered.

"Is that why you're here? To stop me?" Nina snorted. "How? By throwing a bag of herbs at my head?"

"I'm not here to hurt you." Sadie shook her head. "I'm here to help you, child."

Nina laughed, a bitter flail that slashed at Sadie.

Sadie ignored it and continued. "When you cast your curses so close together, you lit a bonfire. One for all with eyes to see." She stood. "They'll come for you, Nina, and all the black salt in the world won't stop them."

"Who?" Nina opened her arms and made a mocking sweep of the empty salon. "Who's coming for me?"

"The same folk who've always come for our kind." Sadie's face tightened. "Men who won't stand for a show of power in a woman."

Nina's eyes glittered. "Let them come; I'm not afraid."

Sadie's countenance turned solemn. "You should be, girl. You should be."

"Well, you can hide in the shadows and watch people suffer, but don't expect me to." With a flick of her wrist, the front door swung open. "Leave and take your toothless warnings with you. You ain't no use to me."

Sadie jumped when the front door slammed behind her. She closed her eyes and pinched the bridge of her nose. Young witches... she swore under her breath. After a long sigh, she turned around and scrawled an invisible sigil on the door. Then she wearily tugged her suitcase down the steps and out the yard.

The burrowing owl remained nestled in the weeping willow, feathers fluffed, gold eyes unblinking.

* * *

Jake met them when they stepped off the bus, the first star gleaming in the twilight sky. Three tall spare men in dark suits, pencil-thin ties, and broad black hats, the colour of their scraggly beards the only hue distinguishing them. Each carried a large black case. Jake handed a stuffed envelope to the tallest of the trio, then pointed down the wide road Sadie had travelled earlier in the day. The man nodded and tucked the envelope into the inner pocket of his suit jacket. The three men turned as one, flowed off the platform and down the dark street, silent as wraiths.

Black salt didn't save Nina when the tallest plowed his fist into her jaw after she answered her front door. And it didn't stop the other two when they caught her as she fell and carried her into the house.

The burrowing owl lifted from its roost and beat its wings with fast, steady strokes as it disappeared into the moonless night.

* * *

The sigil glowed on Nina's door when Sadie mounted the steps, a willow switch in her hand. When the doorknob wouldn't turn, her eyes flashed green as she made a sign with her fingers. The lock clicked, and the door swung open.

Sadie schooled herself to remain calm at the sight before her. Nina's head lolled forward where she sat bound to the styling chair with duct tape, a fist-sized red mark on her jaw. The three men had removed their jackets and rolled up the sleeves of their white dress shirts. They moved with practised efficiency as they set a ceremonial knife, needles, and litre-sized bottles with rubber stoppers on Nina's black trolley.

"Good evening, gentleman," Sadie said, her voice calm and even.

They turned to her, unalarmed, smiling with long-toothed yellow grins.

"Green Witch," the tallest said with a mocking bow. The words twisted in the air with a sibilant hiss. "We saw your sign on the door."

"Then why did you trespass?" She shook her head as if disappointed by their bad manners. "I'm gonna have to ask you to leave."

They looked at each other and laughed. The tallest one stepped toward her. "We have no quarrel with you. But this one killed and now she's fair game. Witch blood, especially from one this powerful, is in high demand, so don't interfere with our harvest and we won't interfere with you."

Nina groaned behind the duct tape on her mouth and raised her head. Her eyes widened, and she struggled against her bonds.

The three turned and gathered around her. One pulled her head back with a yank, exposing her neck, while another picked up a long steel needle attached to tubing that wound its way into the rubber stopper of one of the bottles.

Sadie's back straightened and her shoulders squared. Power hummed in the switch she held, and green leaves sprouted from its wood. The fragrance of rich, moist earth and green growth filled the air.

"Leave now. I will not ask you again." Sadie's command shook the windowpanes.

In a flash, they surrounded her, heads twisting on necks like snakes. "What will you do to us, Green Witch? What power is there in soil and leaves? Go or we will condemn you to her fate. Your blood may not be as rich, but it will still sell for a profit."

They returned to their prey, bending over Nina as if Sadie were not there.

Sadie's eyes shone green, so luminous the room appeared to dim. She slapped her switch on the wood floor.

"Grow…"

The men continued with their gruesome business.

She slapped the floor again.

"Grow."

They turned to her, frowning. The tallest one rose to his feet, picked up the knife from the trolley, and walked toward her.

One last slap.

"Grow!"

A rumbling from deep beneath the house shook the floor and bottles of hair products under the till by the door. The three men shot looks at each other, then Sadie. They fell into crouches, teeth bared like wild creatures ready to attack. The tallest one held the dagger at his side like a talon.

Tiny green leaves poked up in the spaces between the floorboards at their feet, where Sadie's tiny black seeds had nestled earlier. They erupted into a violent explosion of vines, sage, cattails, and willow that crowded the floor, crawled up the walls, and hung from the ceiling in unending waves of greenery.

Wild clematis, Virginia creeper and honeysuckle wound up the legs and torsos of the three men and cinched tight. They continued whipping around them with blinding speed until they resembled human topiaries. Flowers bloomed on the vines, filling the air with sweet notes of black cherry, sweet clover, and warm sugary honey.

Sadie closed her eyes and inhaled the wild perfume. "Ah, much better."

She opened her eyes and walked to the entombed men. On her way, she bent to pick up the knife the tallest one dropped when he struggled to escape his leafy bonds. Sadie spun the blade in her hand so fast it blurred. The show of expertise raised muffled moans from the trapped men and the whites of their eyes gleamed with morbid intensity from within the green depths of their prisons.

"I always wonder why people think the green things of the world have no power," she said as she tapped the tallest green mound with the blade. The vines parted, allowing his beard to peek out. Sadie pulled it taunt and sliced off three inches of hair, then plucked a green tendril from a vine and touched it to the severed beard. The tendril wrapped around it tight as an elastic band.

"The air you breathe is a gift from green things that grow." She walked to the next man and grabbed his scruffy beard, repeating what she'd done before. "The food you eat all comes from them."

She came to the final man. "Even the water you drink is purified by the growing things of this world." She cut off his beard with an economical slash.

"And yet, you choose to believe in the authority of iron and steel, and the blood it can draw. Transitory elements, made by men that rust and crumble under the weight of time." She reached into her pocket, pulled out a small white envelope, opened it, and dropped the three bound swatches of hair into it before she licked it shut. She held it up before them.

"The colour of power is not red, gentlemen. It is green."

The tallest man worked his jaw until there was enough play in his plant bonds to speak. "When we are free, we'll hunt you, witch!" he hissed. "There will be no shelter for you wherever you go."

"Oh, I don't think so," Sadie said as she stepped to a window and opened it

The burrowing owl swooped into the room and landed on her shoulder. He plucked the envelope she raised to his beak, and listened, his head crooked, as she whispered instructions to him. Then quiet as a moth, he lifted from her shoulder and flew out the open window. Sadie shut it and turned to the men.

"I've sent your hair to Ida Wilkens, one of the greatest green witches of my generation. Even scum like you will have heard her name. She and her coven will keep it hidden away unless Nina or I come to harm. On that day, they'll use this hair to cast curses upon you so grievous and foul, your teeth will fall out and your balls will shrink to the size of peas. By the next dark moon, nothing will be left of you but rotting flesh and crumbling bone, fertilizer for the green things that grow.

"The choice is yours. Leave Nina and me in peace, never to return. Or face the wrath of thirteen green witches, old as the forests and full of power that reaches deep into the earth."

She snapped the switch in the air. "Unbind!"

The vines and branches wrapped around the men fell away with a soft swoosh. The men gathered their coats and hats and fled through the front door, leaving with a final hiss. They left the rest of their equipment behind as green vines ripped their cases, shattered their bottles, and crushed their implements into lumps of metal.

Sadie grabbed the window sill to steady herself, sick from the drain of power, her knees shaking. Then she staggered around a sapling, quickly swelling into a young tree as she headed to Nina.

She ripped the duct tape off Nina's mouth. "Are you all right?"

Nina nodded, eyes wide as she watched the lush foliage growing in her salon. "What did you do to my house?" she croaked as Sadie used the knife to cut through her bonds.

Sadie looked around the verdant room. "Suppose I'm redecorating it. Come, we need to leave. What I've started ain't so easy to stop."

They sat on the lawn as they watched a bur oak burst through the house roof.

"I didn't know Green Witches were so powerful..." Nina said, dazed.

"We have our moments," replied Sadie. She held up the switch, now brittle with crumbled dry leaves. She'd stored up magic in the green wood for years. For a time like this. She bowed her head and silently thanked the switch for its service, then snapped it in half and cast it aside.

"So, what happens next?" Nina asked, voice meek, eyes wide.

Waiting for a verdict...

Sadie covered Nina's trembling hand with her wrinkled one. "We're going to talk, Nina. We going to talk about was done to you until the hole it punched in your soul is healed, and you can grow again."

She glanced up at the canopy of the majestic bur oak spreading over the yard.

"And then we'll fix your house."

* * *

"Leavin' so soon, Sadie?"

Jake loitered on the bus platform as Sadie pulled her battered silver suitcase up the ramp.

"It's been over a month, Jake. Sarah's had her babe and Jared got himself clipped. My work here is done," Sadie said as she pushed her suitcase handle down.

"Yeah, guess things have quieted some around here." Jake spat at the ground. Then he peered at Sadie. "You do something different with your hair?"

Sadie patted her new, light brown bob. "Nina from the salon gave me a deal on a dye and cut."

"Nina..." Jake tapped his chin thoughtfully. "I don't think Nina will be around town much longer." A cold, taunting smile. "In fact, I intend to help her on her way."

Sadie blinked.

"Well, that would be a shame," she replied. "The town needs her—she's good at what she does." She glanced down at the pan she held. "Oh, before I forget. Here's your rhubarb platz."

"Thank you, Sadie." Jake's smile didn't reach his eyes as he took the pan from her. He lifted a corner of the tinfoil covering, and the sweet aroma of stewed rhubarb and fresh baked cake filled the air. "You coming back anytime soon?"

Sadie regarded him with a long, cool gaze. "I doubt you'll see me again."

"Well, can't say I'm sorry." He lifted the pan of rhubarb platz. "Though I will miss this."

"Good-bye, Jake."

Jake tipped his Stetson. "Bye Sadie."

The burrowing owl lifted from the branch of a nearby cottonwood and flew high into the cloudless sky, circling the bus and the town. When Sadie looked out the window as the bus drew away from the old pharmacy, she noticed Jake stuffing a piece of cake into his mouth.

Sadie sat back and smiled.

She'd harvested the rhubarb for the cake last night from Sarah Paul's garden under the dark moon. Then she walked to the boggy little stream that trickled by the barbwire fence at the border of Sara's property and cut a few leaves of water hemlock Ida had planted there years ago. She laid them beside the red stalks in her basket.

"Ain't that dangerous?" Nina had asked. "That's enough hemlock to kill a cow. I thought the rhubarb was for Jake Dueck's cake." She'd come to help Sadie, though they both agreed Nina was not cut out to be a green witch. At least her Strega edges had softened.

They spent many summer nights on the Paul's porch, talking and crying and laying down seeds of hope, while Sarah's babe slept on Sadie's lap, lulled to sleep by her calm even voice.

"It's all for his cake." Sadie set the basket down and washed her hands in the stream. She dried them on her dress.

"But... but I thought you were against killing, even if the asshole has it coming," sputtered Nina.

"Well," Sadie picked up the basket. "I'm making an exception this one time."

She laughed at the confused expression on Nina's face and patted her cheek. "I never disagreed with your motives, sweet girl."

Her eyes flashed green.

"It was just your timing I questioned."

First published in 'Prairie Witch: an anthology', Prairie Soul Press, 2022

The Obituarist

William Scarborough

I
t was raining in the Congo.

As a child, Stan had been told that rain was God's tears. If it rained somewhere every day, did that mean that God always wept? He had wondered what they had done to make him cry so much.

As an adult, it was obvious.

They had caused years of pointless death and destruction. If there was some omnipotent creator gazing down upon humanity, it had to be like watching a constant horror film. He wondered if—

"Stan! You're here early!" Nsombi called out. His train of thought derailed back into the depths of his unconscious. They would eventually return.

"I was in the area," he lied. He was not due for a stop in the Congo for weeks. He should have been back in D.C., prepping for his meetings on Capitol Hill. The handful of congressmen who cared enough liked to have him stop by whenever he had news.

"Oh." Nsombi's eyes fell for a moment.

He shouldn't have even let her have the time for the thought.

"No. Not that," he assured her. "I had a meeting in Kinshasa with some new members of the Central African diplomatic team."

"Still, I saw the news. It's been a rough week."

He said nothing. The rain was beating down on them as they stood in the middle of the dirt road. Mud splashed onto his boots, seeping into his socks.

"Let's talk about it," she suggested, taking his arm and leading him inside.

* * *

Harapan wasn't going to recover. Her health had been in decline for weeks. Even if she managed to pull off some miracle, the long term outlook wasn't good. She was twenty-four years old. The oldest a tiger had lived to be in captivity was twenty-seven.

Still, the flight had carried some hope. Just before he had stepped aboard, he had received a call saying that Harapan had eaten for the first time in days. It was a good sign, even if it had only been a few bites of ground beef.

Her health had deteriorated again by the time he landed in Padang.

The President Amisha Saniga Memorial Reserve had been created almost entirely to protect and restore the Sumatran tiger. Without Harapan, its purpose would end. Stan had been there several times before. The last time, Fadhlan was still alive. Even in his old age, his caretakers had hoped to see him mate with Harapan. When the email came that the tiger had finally succumbed to cancer, Stan lost an entire night's sleep. His trip to Indonesia had become inevitable.

Six years later and it was finally time.

The last Sumatran tiger was on her final days.

They wanted to keep her comfortable, even as she had been put on life support. The lobby of the reserve's clinic was filled to the brim with staff, concerned citizens and reporters. Their eyes locked on Stan as soon as he entered the room. They knew who he was. They knew what he meant.

Extinction had arrived.

Her attendants were in the room with Harapan, her breaths growing weaker and further apart. It would be any moment.

They said nothing to him and he knew better than to utter a single word. The poor grieving people who had worked so hard to try and save Harapan's species did not need to be reminded of why he was there. They did not need further pain.

Stan admired the creature while it still lived. Her deep orange and black coat shone under the fluorescent lights of the clinic. Her claws could rip a deer in half. Awake, her golden eyes would have stared into his.

But she would not wake.

The heart monitor continued, piercing beats breaking through the silence. Stan thought a short prayer to anyone that might accept it.

Then, she was gone.

Nearly twenty years of Stan's life had been dedicated to the extinctions of wildlife. The Amur Leopard, Borean Orangutan, Smalleye Hammerhead Shark... the list went on longer than he preferred to think about.

Some of his colleagues had gone numb, bearing the deaths like minor events through history. To them, extinction had gone the way of the newest smartphone. He could not bring himself to lose the pain. He compartmentalized it, even repressed it when he had to, but the pain remained. The deaths hurt him every time.

Another beautiful creature, gone.

The Sumatran tiger, gone.

Harapan, gone.

People screamed and cried. They clung to one another as in a disaster. Stan held a veterinary assistant close to him. He did not know his name.

They had never even met, but he still found himself trying to comfort the poor man. "It's going to be alright."

"It's going to be alright. You didn't fail."

He assured people that one setback did not mean the end.

The war continued. The planet continued. Where the Sumatran tiger was gone, others could still be saved. The grief must not stop their passion. They must continue fighting.

His own words turned to static in his ears, only to be broken by a phone call.

He was needed in France.

* * *

He finished the obituary on the plane.

Harapan, the final Sumatran tiger, died on Tuesday, June 11th, 2058 at the age of twenty-four. The cause of death was kidney failure brought on by old age. In her final moments she was surrounded by her dedicated caretakers and staff at the President Amisha Saniga Memorial Reserve, where she had spent much of her life. She was preceded in death by her mate, Fadhlan. They had no offspring.

Her sub-species, the Sumatran tiger, was preceded in extinction by the Caspian (assessed extinct in 2003), Javan (a.e. 2008), Bali (a.e. 2008), and Malayan (a.e. 2037) tigers.

Several other sub-species of tiger remain endangered, including the Bengal, Amur, Indochinese and South Chinese varieties. The cause of extinction for the Sumatran tiger can be attributed to human-caused habitat loss, poaching, and continued effects of climate change.

Condolences, donations, and requests for information can be directed to The President Amisha Saniga Reserve Foundation. They encourage concerned citizens to continue advocating for the environment and protecting endangered species.

* * *

Nsombi led Stan through the small school that the Congo Okapi Project ran. He had seen it dozens of times and heard about it hundreds of times more. She had credited her entire career, from their shared time at Dartmouth back to The Congo, to the program. Every time he visited, pride radiated off her like sunlight through the trees.

Rows of children sat listening to the teacher's lesson on mathematics. *Three minus four equals negative one. Six times eight is forty-eight. If you divide ninety by ten, you get nine.*

The simplicity of the problems was refreshing for Stan. It was easier than the death.

Beyond the windows were lush forests, gradually being restored. The C.O.P. had been a staunch protector of the land, fighting off poachers and planting new trees to rebuild the habitat that had been destroyed. Nearly all of the small villages and towns in the area had gone all in behind the program, building an entire economy around the Okapi and its protection. In the process of protecting the vulnerable, all were uplifted.

Nsombi's pride was well justified.

"What's next?" Stan asked her.

"What do you mean?"

"If this all works, if you save the Okapi and all the wildlife here, what next?"

She laughed at him as if he had asked her what color the sky was.

"We keep working," she replied. "Come on. I've got something I think you'll like."

* * *

A tray of five dead grasshoppers sat on the table in front of him.

"We've been scouring the plain for days," Marjolaine explained, rubbing her forehead before running her fingers through her hair. Dirt still stuck to her roots. "This is it. We're still waiting for IUCN to make their assessment, but I think it's over."

Stan sighed. If Marjolaine and her team were admitting it, it had to be true.

The Crau Plain Grasshopper was no more.

Marjolaine continued, her voice shaking. "We thought the decline had finally hit a plateau. Three straight years it had flattened. Last year even had a slight improvement. It was only a three percent difference, but it seemed like a good sign. Decades of work. All for nothing."

"Don't say that," Stan said. "You kept them going for longer than they would have."

"I didn't realize we were the Crau Plain Extension Society," she replied, spitting the words. "I must have missed the memo."

There was no silver lining. He should not have even tried. "I'm sorry Marjolaine," was all he could say.

They stepped back outside to look over the dry plain of Crau. Grass stretched beyond the horizon. It almost reminded Stan of the time he had spent in Kansas. Ubiquity without the tornadoes. He could not imagine searching the entire place for insects.

The grasshoppers would get nowhere near the attention of Harapan. Even in an age where climate change and protecting the environment were on the forefront of almost everyone's minds, bugs were rarely considered. Bugs were everywhere. Bugs were annoying and ugly. They weren't made for the front page of the newspaper.

Still, Stan would write the obituary. They were another victim.

They would be remembered.

The sound of Marjolaine's car door slamming echoed across the plains.

* * *

While yet to be officially declared by the International Union for the Conservation of Nature (IUCN), scientists located in the Crau region of France believe that the final Crau Plains Grasshoppers have died as of Monday, June 10th, 2058. After countless hours of investigation, the international team only found five living specimens, all of whom died shortly after discovery. The cause of death has not yet been determined.

The Crau Plains Grasshopper is preceded in extinction by the Rocky Mountain Locust (assessed extinct in 2014), Antioch Dunes Shieldback Katydid (a.e. 1996), and Central Valley Grasshopper (a.e. 2029). Several other sub-species of grasshopper remain endangered, including the Red-Winged Grasshopper and the Key's Matchstick Grasshopper. The cause of extinction for the Crau Plains Grasshopper can be attributed to pesticide use, uncontrolled invasive species, and the effects of climate change upon their habitat.

Condolences, donations, and requests for information can be directed to Crau Plains Conservation Society. They would like for it to be known that despite great strides in the conservation of wildlife, insects are still going extinct at an alarming rate. They also encourage any concerned parties to start acting immediately to safeguard the world's insect population.

Marjolaine's words had been much less gentle.

* * *

"Just take the beer, Stan," Nsombi insisted as she pressed the cold glass bottle into his hand. "You'll like this, I promise."

They sat at her computer. The beer tasted terrible, but at least it was cold.

"Should you be drinking on your shift?" he asked.

She shushed him as she navigated through a series of folders organized by date. She opened a video file.

At first, there was nothing. Some trees rocked in the breeze and loose leafage rustled across the ground. If Stan were a betting man, he'd put all his money down on an Okapi stepping into view.

Sure enough, one did. Slowly through the trees stepped the bizarre brown and white zebra-giraffe that so many people in this part of the Congo fought for.

And she wasn't alone.

Her baby could not have been more than a few weeks old. She followed closely after her mother, nearly running into her multiple times.

"She's not the only one," Nsombi said proudly. "We've got nearly half a dozen calves out there."

"That's good," Stan replied. He meant it.

"That's not all," she added. She pulled some data up on her second monitor. "Remember how I was worried we would see a plateau a few years back? It never happened. The population has been growing steadily for six years in a row."

He smiled. The calf was right up on the camera, trying to reach it with its tongue. Even as a baby, their tongues were bizarrely long. A chuckle escaped his throat.

They sat together for a moment, just marveling at the mother and her baby.

"We're not the only ones, you know," Nsombi said. "Manatees, Red Pandas, Indian Elephants, Whale Sharks... they're all showing better and better numbers."

Stan felt so out of the loop. "Really?"

She nodded. "We've been winning a lot more than we've been losing lately, Stan. It's just not your job to think about them. When was the last time you looked at the numbers?"

He had no idea. Months? Years?

Even when he knew things were improving overall, it was hard to keep that in mind when extinction stared him in the face.

Maybe he needed to change that.

The Okapi and her calf walked off camera.

* * *

The Congo was a sea of green beneath him as his flight headed back to the states. Stan had politicians to brief and then departmental meetings with the Wildlife Action Committee. It would fill his schedule for months until the next obituary was needed.

There had been too many losses that week. Yet, for every loss, there was hope. Okapi calves would frolic through the trees as tigers took their final breaths. Divers would swim alongside whale sharks as the pops of grasshopper wings grew quieter and quieter. The politicians who cared would raise the losses above their heads and demand more action. Their opponents would point toward the successes as proof that the job had been done.

Despite it all, there was hope.

Extinctions would continue. Obituaries would be written. Stan would be there as long as he was needed.

But first, he was off to see some baby manatees.

At the Industrial Food Museum

Regina Rae Weiss

he gentle light wakened the warblers first. As the sun's orb ascended over the long line of trees at the eastern horizon, an enormous flock of weavers rose from a stream bed running way out beyond Maritza's sight, a river of wings skimming billows of bluestem and switchgrass, birds and grassland incandescent with the new day.

Across a dirt lot, pipits foraged for insects among seedlings of winter squash, sweet corn, and pole beans interspersed with buckwheat, dill, and coriander.

Maritza's great grandparents were ghosts. At least, that's how Grandma Akilah spoke of them. But Maritza often felt them here with her in these early hours, along with the other ancestors stolen from her.

The day's visitors were already emerging from the Cleanway. She'd take charge of the adults, leading them through the grasslands as other docents shepherded the teens and children through the farm and the wetlands.

She always began with the same question. "Who can tell us what brought you here today?" She waited out the shuffling hesitation. Finally, a young muscular woman with clear gray eyes and direct gaze spoke up.

"I love to cook," she said. "I plan to become a chef and I wanted to see the crop system here because I want to start a free meal service where we grow our own food."

"Great plan!" Maritza smiled. "You're welcome to explore the farm and visit our kitchen later. Our food storage system will interest you. In fact, before I forget, all of you are most welcome to wander the museum grounds after the tour. We're open until dusk. There's so much to see here and we love to show it off."

"Does the staff live here?" asked a tall, copper-haired man whose young daughter had clung to him for a moment before heading off with the other kids.

"Yes, about half of us," Maritza nodded. "So, who else would like to say what brought you here?"

The redhead put his arm around a slender, freckled woman beside him. "My wife and I are birders. We heard there are sharp-tailed grouse in the grasslands here. We're hoping to catch sight of one."

"Ah, yes," Maritza smiled. "It's nesting season, as I'm sure you know, so they're a bit shy right now, but you may well spot a male."

A slight, stooped man with a deeply wrinkled face spoke up. "I've been here before. A few times. I'm always amazed by how different it is from when I was young. I brought my grand kids today, two boys. I think they'll learn something."

"Thank you," Maritza said. "That's great to hear. You know, this museum was created because some of the people who started the land restoration believed that the world had suffered deeply for lack of human memory, from the systemic disruption of the passage of inter-generational knowledge in the modern era. They wanted to help change that."

* * *

A half-hour later, Maritza's group emerged from a path running through the tall grasses onto a small rise that the docents privately referred to as Purgatory. The spring morning was already uncomfortably warm. She waited as water bottles, binoculars and cameras were pulled from packs. The group splintered about the circle of low buffalo grass, taking in the soft expanse of prairie embracing the land and sky for miles around. She gazed out over the tall, graceful grasses and wildflowers with gratitude for this still-new land, restored in small part thanks to the ferocious grit of the women who'd raised her.

Maritza's grandmother Akilah had arrived in the United States early in the 21st century carrying her infant daughter Haya, Maritza's mother. Then, as now, Akilah knew nothing of her own parents' fate, or that of her little sister, so when baby Haya grew into a teenager seized by a passion for democracy, Akilah had been frantic. In Syria, she'd seen such passions quenched with bullets. But Akilah was never able to tame the force that impelled her daughter to seek justice, to speak the truth when others could not find their way to do so.

Long before Maritza was born, as the world learned that engineered wheat, soy and corn had been used for a century to pacify the citizenry, Haya, who'd spent years knocking on doors all over Minneapolis on behalf the state's democracy defense brigade, was already one of the state's most visible organizers. She'd been an obvious choice to represent Minnesotans at the 2049 constitutional convention where, that October, delegates from throughout the land gathered in Hartville, Missouri to ensure that the nation's elected officials would answer, henceforth, to their constituents, rather than to the compulsions of avarice and wealth.

Maritza knew she'd been conceived in the joyous flood of hope that bloomed in Hartville, but she didn't know that it was her conception, her birth as a U.S. citizen, that finally loosened her Grandmother Akilah's tongue, allowing her to recall her own childhood: the long afternoons of play in Syria's still-standing forests; the beauty of the family farm twenty kilometers west of A'zaz.

So, unlike her mother Haya, Maritza grew up on her grandmother's earliest memories, as after a lifetime of mourning the ancient woman gifted her granddaughter with the ability to see her ancestors through seasons of harvesting olives, barley and lentils in the years leading up to the terror.

* * *

Wrestling with her reluctance to get on with the tour, Maritza gave the visitors time to relax in their surroundings. She always enjoyed watching the birders, seeing how pride in their detailed knowledge of species slowly gave way to joy in the abundance of winged life on this wide-open, rewilding land.

Finally, she moved to the eastern edge of the knoll, motioning for the others to gather round. Facing the visitors, she noticed how calm their faces were. The long walk through narrow corridors of tall, fragrant vegetation never failed to have this effect, even on the most curmudgeonly. It always made her regret what came next.

"See that?" Maritza projected her voice over the rustle of wind and the crazed synchronicity of morning peepers chirping out their blissful lust. She pointed to a wide ribbon of crop-planted acreage in the distance, running alongside the railway for as far as the eye could see. "Anyone have a guess how wide that border farm is over there, running along the Cleanway?"

A young man with an oversized backpack ventured a guess. "An acre? Maybe an acre wide all along the travel line."

Maritza nodded. "Anyone else?"

"You know," a tall woman with curly silver hair mused, "I grew up in a house that sat on an acre, and I think it's wider than that. Maybe twice as wide."

Maritza smiled, nodding again. "Yes, you are quite right, ma'am. That ribbon of cropland is two acres wide. It runs for ten miles, right along the Cleanway, so it's just over five hundred acres altogether. From March through December, those acres produce more than fifteen million pounds of vegetables, fruit, beans and nuts, feeding us and all of Colfax County. More than ten thousand of our neighbors are sustained by this one ribbon farm.

"Honestly, though, that band could produce way more, but it's a demonstration farm and part of the museum, so some space gets taken up with visitor activities. We're seeing even higher yields in the other ribbon farms along the edges of the land restorations. So far, they're feeding more than fifty million people just twenty years after the first ones were planted. The ribbon farm idea was conceived in the early 2050s, when prairie restoration was in its infancy, but it took more than a decade for them to take hold because the land was on life-support and needed to recover."

She spun in a slow circle, arm outstretched toward an all-but-invisible high wall of gauze surrounding the rise just below where they'd gathered. "Now, can you all see that fabric?"

The cloth was so fine that the sunlight almost obliterated it from sight.

The visitors craned their necks.

"Oh yes, there it is," the silver-haired woman exclaimed. "I can just barely make it out."

"Good." Maritza nodded. "This prairie surrounding us may look like it's always been here, but it was planted, not by nature, but by people, about thirty-five years ago. It's part of the mid-world restoration.

"Before that, for more than a century, there was no life here to speak of. This land had been stripped and strafed and left for dead."

She paused to let her words sink in.

"It started mid-twentieth century," she went on. "Mono-cropping nothing but corn and soybeans for hundreds of thousands of square miles destroyed the living soil thousands of years of vegetative diversity and evolution had given us.

"Once the land was dead, the only way to grow those crops was to drench them with fertilizers, herbicides and pesticides that poisoned the ground and surface water, killed off most of the wildlife and sickened even the people inflicting the damage."

"Look," she said, her voice catching. "Look behind you."

The group turned. Gasps and low murmurs devolving into stunned silence. Uniform rows of bushy green plants lay before them, spread to the horizon, replacing the waving meadow that had been there a moment before.

As they watched, trying to grasp what had happened, an enormous autonomous combine appeared at the far end of the planted field, crawling toward them with a menacing hum that grew into a deafening mechanical shriek as it neared, spewing dust and black smoke, leaving a dry wide strip of clumped brown dirt in its wake where a row of soybean plants had been. Stopping a few yards short of the knoll where they cowered together, the machine mercifully turned about, moving away, cutting a second swath through the field.

They watched in fascination at the combine harvesting the enormous crop of soybeans, strip after strip. Just as it finished clearing the field, a dog, a black lab perhaps, bounded across the empty dirt plane, stopping every few yards to bark at a small girl toddling after it. The child threw a stick wide. The dog ran after it gleefully, returning to nuzzle the girl until she threw the stick again. Thick snowflakes began to fall. The clump-encrusted field, the combine, the dog and the child faded away. They gazed once again over prairie land, returned to bird call and the rustle of tall grasses in a gentle wind.

The first to speak was a delicate-looking woman Maritza had noticed earlier because she seemed so deeply attentive to her surroundings, stopping often to closely examine a leaf, to breathe in the sharp, pungent scent of a wildflower.

"Wow," the woman murmured. "What was that?"

"Holography," Maritza explained. "That's what the circle of gauze is for. It allows us to show you the past."

She went on, "Thirty-five years ago, in 2048, we had 250 million acres planted with corn and soy." She smiled wanly. "A third of the corn went to animal feed. Another third to fuel. The rest went into food additives, those sweeteners and fillers they used to pacify the electorate."

"What about the soybeans?" This from a slight young man who'd been silent throughout the tour. She'd noticed him because every minute or so he seemed to be pushing his long lanky hair out of his eyes.

"Almost all of that went to animal feed," Maritza told him. "By that point, most of the world was eating meat from concentrated animal feeding operations. Of course, no one really knew the health effects then. Researchers who tried to study that were blackballed and couldn't get funding."

She motioned behind the group now, bidding them to turn again. It was hard to focus on the grotesque, surreal scene. As always, Maritza forced herself to watch along with the rest, despite the sickening hypnogogic effect it had on her every single time.

A vast expanse of hogs lay before them, arranged in a metal grid. The air vibrated with a deafening distress. Nearby, a smallish sow chewed the tail of a hog in an adjacent crate that appeared to be dead, blood and flies crusting its face. Another lay with a front leg stretched through bars, gazing into her neighbor's face.

A few of the men turned away, Maritza noticed. The women never did.

There was quiet as the scene mercifully faded. Maritza's charges cast about for relief, gazing at the ground, the sky, the open prairie in vain. She motioned, gathering them together.

"Eating the product of all that suffering did so much damage," she said quietly. "We're still working to understand it today.

"We'll go visit the farm now. Walking back through the grasses will help us all feel better."

* * *

As they emerged from the meadow near the Cleanway, she led her group through the central path of the ribbon farm, pointing out rain catching and composting systems. She hoped her next assignment would be the farm. She longed to know every plant.

They gathered near an ancient basswood tree.

"Our diverse intensive crop management," she told them, "not only restores the land; it sequesters carbon. But the real climate benefit is in the grasslands. Our restored prairie here is a tiny part of 225 million acres throughout the middle states that have been returned to their ancestral condition, or as close as possible, given species loss.

"Today, a single acre of our meadow pulls about five tons of carbon dioxide from the atmosphere, storing it permanently in the ground. So those hundreds of millions of acres that have been restored over the past thirty-five years sequester more than a billion tons of carbon.

"Of course, this wouldn't matter if we still had mono-cropping and CAFOs, because that created almost a billion tons of greenhouse gases here every year. But between the land restoration and the cessation of those practices, scientists are seeing a slight slowing in warming trends and a bit more stability in wind and precipitation patterns, especially over the past decade since the changes adopted by the other climate survival work group member nations."

Mato, the farm docent, walked toward them, herding the visiting children into the deep shade of the basswood. Turning to watch, Maritza noticed that the tree's flower-laden branches were swarming with bees.

Mato, whose ancestors had lived on this high plain for thousands of years, referred to the basswood, one of the few to have survived the ravage of centuries, as his Unci. He always made sure the children gathered here for a story at the end of each tour.

Today's storyteller, a gangling man with a luxurious gray Afro, was seated on a bale of oat hay near the tree's deeply ridged trunk, his long legs stretched out before him. He looked to be in his eighties, Maritza thought, and despite the heat wore full length pants of a light, patterned fabric, tapered and buttoned at the ankles. She could tell he was enjoying watching the kids, who scattered themselves on the ground, jiggling and laughing and then finally, as Mato motioned to them gently, settling and growing quiet.

"Listen up, everyone," Mato said, his voice sounding like a big grin. "Today we have a special visitor and he's going to tell us a seed story."

"Hi Mato," the older man said. "Good morning, everyone."

"Morning," a few of the older children called out.

"So, you've all been trekking through the farm. What do you think?"

"Good!"

"It's pretty."

"I like the way it smells," a tiny girl in a plaid jumper added.

The man laughed. "It does smell good," he agreed. "Well, it's great to see you all here on this beautiful day. My name is Kamal and today I'm going to tell you my favorite story, which is all about the power of plants and seeds.

"Anyone know any seed stories?" He paused. "No? Okay. Well, then, this will be your first."

Holding out a woven grass bowl filled with something deeply crimson,

Kamal said, "See this? This is some of my family's okra, which we grow on our farm in New York."

He tilted the vessel and Maritza could see that yes, those were okra, but deep red rather than the usual green.

"Now," Kamal said, standing up, "I'm going to show you the okra's seeds."

Moving with ease despite his apparent age, he reached into a pants pocket, squatted and gestured to the children to come look. They surrounded him, peering into his hand.

"These are the seeds of that special okra," he pointed at the bowl he'd placed on the ground. "People come to my family's farm from all over just to get some because when it's cooked just right, this okra is like eating something so beautiful and fresh you can feel it nourishing every part of you—your body, your spirit, even your brain."

He paused, looked around the circle of shade and, glancing back, met Maritza's smiling eyes.

"Hey, you adults back there," he called out. "You don't have to stand. Come join us.

"Well, okay then," he nodded his approval as Maritza and her group moved into the shade to settle down behind the circle of children.

"This okra," Kamal went on, "is my family's. In fact, I have always felt it is the only thing that truly belongs to us. It's very special because it's the descendant of okra that my mother's ancestors had with them hundreds of years ago when they were hunted down in West Africa and enslaved."

Rising from his squat, Kamal placed the seeds back in his pocket and resettled himself on the bale of hay, gazing at the circle of children, making sure he had their attention.

"I often speak with these ancestors of mine," he told them. "I thank them in the morning when I look out over the fields of our farm. I think of them as I fall into my dreams at night. I imagine them walking with baskets of this okra that we continue growing today, thanks to their brilliance and their foresight. Thanks to their thoughts of the future. Of me, and my children and grandchildren.

"Now, these ancestors of mine, I do not know who they were. I don't know their ages, genders, names, or even their tribe. I don't know whether it was one ancestor who was stolen that day, or many taken together. Still, I wonder about these things as I lie in my bed, as I eat with my family. Were these relations of mine attacked on the coast, or overtaken and imprisoned inland? I try to imagine their fear. Their rage. To see their faces. I wonder, were they kept imprisoned in our homeland for weeks or for months before enduring the hell of a slave ship's journey? What were their stories? But," he shook his head, "it's impossible to know.

He paused to observe the children's rapt faces, then smiled. "I know that's very sad, but I also know this. My grandmother grew this okra in her garden in Princeville, North Carolina, back in the twentieth century. My mother grew this okra in Brooklyn, New York, and I grew up eating it there. I always knew I would grow this plant some day and when my wife asked me to move out of Brooklyn and learn how to farm, she knew that was the reason I would say yes.

"Most people eat okra in the summer when it is harvested. My family eats it all year long, fresh in summer and dried in winter, sometimes frozen or canned, but mostly dried because we know that is how it got here.

"No one knows the whole story. It's impossible to know. But my grandmother told my mother what her grandmother told her. Our ancestors had this okra with them when they were stolen from our homeland. The okra had been dried, our family story goes, and because of that they were able to use it to stay alive. It seems incredible, but some part of this must be true. Our family story says that my ancestors hid the dried okra in their hair, weaving the pods into their locks, eating all but the last of it to keep themselves alive as so many died around them in the slave ship's bowels.

"Now, that is impossible, we say. Our rational minds tell us so, because everyone knows that the devils took their hair. Chopped off the glorious crowns of hair and shaved the heads of every person they stole to enslave. So how did my ancestors escape that horrid act? Did the devils lose their blades? Were my ancestors especially fierce or especially beautiful? No one knows. But what we do know of this story must be true because here I am and here is my family's okra."

He held up the bowl, blowing softly over the luminous crimson pods as if blessing them.

"Okra, it is known, has many strengthening properties, many protective and medicinal traits. And our family believes that knowing this to be true, our ancestors kept the last of the okra, rather than eating it, saving the seeds for their future, and for ours, and for you and your families as well. Today my family's okra is grown here and in ribbon farms all over the country. This plant that sustained my ancestors and my family is now helping heal and sustain all of us and the world we share."

Kamal fell silent. No one spoke. Even the children held still for a long breath, letting the warm late morning breeze contain them. Finally, the red-haired birder from Maritza's group broke into their thoughts.

"What an amazing story," the man said. "Thank you for telling it, and for the gift of your family's okra."

Kamal's smile, Maritza thought, was like the sun itself. She noticed that the teens had joined them with Celeste, the wetlands docent, and were standing together beyond where the children and adults sat in the shaded grass. Had the teens heard the whole story? She hoped so.

Standing slowly, Maritza walked to the edge of the circle of shade, motioning Mato and Celeste to join her. The visitors gathered themselves, the children and teens rejoining their parents. As thanks were exchanged and goodbyes said, Maritza felt weary but satisfied.

Now, where was Kamal? Making her way back through a field of young squash seedlings she spotted him, still under the basswood, looking up at the branches full of bees.

"Mind if I join you?"

"Of course not, miss. Happy to have your company."

"My name is Maritza," she told him. "I'm a docent in training here."

He nodded, a bit absently. She followed his gaze up into the flowering tree.

"These bees," she said thoughtfully, "the honey they make from the basswood flowers is so delicious."

"I bet."

"We have some in the kitchen. Before you leave, please come have some lunch."

"Why thank you. That's very kind."

She leaned back to get a better look at the buzzing throng.

"My grandmother Akilah just turned one hundred and four," she told Kamal. "She claims she's lived so long because she loves honey."

His laugh was deep and sonorous. "I'm sure your grandmother is right," he said. "You know, I'll be ninety-eight myself next month. I'm still in pretty good health and I *love* honey."

"Well then, you are in for a treat. Come. We'll have some basswood flower honey on toast with our lunch."

As they moved out from the tree's shade into the midday sun, she pointed the way toward the kitchen. "It's just up here, through the sunflower field."

She reached for his hand. "Please tell me about your grandmother. The one who grew your family's okra down south in the twentieth century. What was her name? What else did she grow? What else do you remember about her?"

Lawn Canvas

Jen Lailey

Along the road a hierarchy of mowing
citizenship is played out—
'untouchables' doing nothing,
those who mow around mail and newspaper boxes
the mown frontage folks
the citizen of the year types with bald ditches.

It's the closest some
of us ever get to artistic
self expression as we
reveal ourselves through
our relationships with grass.

But what if one day, as we
entered the green lung of yard
we felt inspired, moved,
to be creative? To participate
differently with the place we call home.
What if we took that lawnmower,
chose a shade, no, length

of green
and went freestyle?

Or what if we, as a couple of
    neighbours, a road, a municipality,
    chose a day or week each year
    in which everyone had permission
    to colour
    outside the lines, paint
    beyond numbers?
    Why not?
    Its not like a poke and stick.
    It grows back.

And what if because we started
    to look at the lawn more as a
    living canvas and less as a chore,
    we noticed what happened
    in the longer parts, where weeds
    started to bloom and pollinators
    got busy, and we all realized
    that none of us are lords or ladies
    of any manor and that the all-England
    hangover has lifted and we are allowed,
    no, being constantly invited, to play
    within the living world around us.

I imagine a flourish
    of folk art. Quilt lawns,
    codes, poems, pictures.
    Drone delights if not a gallery

along the road. Conversations
sparked by someone's great
idea rather than the wife
who planted a goddamn tree
in the middle of what was
otherwise a simple, straight shot
job.

A Helping Hand

Ginger Strivelli

Maria was at her desk by nine o'clock sharp as always. Her co-workers usually all stumbled in at various amounts of minutes late, but they had all arrived with Maria, just in time on this memorable day. She switched on her noise canceling implants as the office began to buzz, click, murmur, and squeak to life. She was trying to focus on her task at hand, finishing the language software for the spaceship, The Rescuer, that was about to reach Jupiter's moon, Europa. Earth had hurriedly sent it out when they had all of a sudden begun receiving the distress call from Europa.

Any transmission from space would grab everyone on Earth's attention, as they still had yet to find any alien life even though they were halfway through the twenty-first century. A distress call was even more noteworthy, but one from a moon that we had thought was uninhabited and uninhabitable had really gotten everyone excited.

Maria was developing a pictograph language to help the Rescuer's crew communicate with whoever had sent the distress signal in the same mysterious pictographs.

She was chosen for the task as she was autistic and communicated better in pictures herself than in words.

Nonetheless, the other scientists insisted on trying to get her to

89

talk. She could talk, but she didn't enjoy it, particularly when it was meaningless small talk.

"Maria! How was your weekend?" Penelope stopped at Maria's desk and patted Maria on the left shoulder in the way of a friendly greeting.

Maria hated to be touched. She was well aware that the other woman meant only to include her in the teams' morning banter. It was, as the bosses would say, team building, or networking, or whatever new term they had coined for the annoyance.

"Good morning, Penelope. How was your weekend?" She parroted back the prescribed greeting and turned her attention back to her computer screen, not really listening to the other woman's reply.

Penelope leaned down to peer at Maria's screen. "Is that gonna work?" she said, knowing Maria really didn't want to hear about her weekend. "Those pictures are all earth pictures. How do we know the aliens will recognize what they represent?"

"We don't have any pictures of their culture. We have to use what we have and hope they are intelligent enough to work it out."

"Of course. Looks like you have done a great job on it." Penelope patted Maria on the shoulder again.

Maria didn't flinch but nodded. "Thanks."

Penelope smiled. "It's so exciting, isn't it?"

"Yes."

The two women and the other scientists worked feverishly all day on the last-minute tweaks the ship needed before landing on Europa at 8 pm Greenwich Mean Time. It was like waiting for Christmas morning for the scientists waiting for 4 pm to come to Kennedy Space Center. No one took lunch, which was unusual.

As the golden hour finally arrived, everyone had finished their last-minute tasks and were standing around their desks staring at the main computer screen that would show the ship landing on the icy moon that humans had named Europa

Maria switched off her noise canceling implants. She wanted to hear every tiny sound being transmitted back to Earth from Rescuer, the ship Earth had rushed out to respond to the mysterious distress call.

General Millie McMahan was in charge at mission control, and she was nearest the screen, pacing back and forth. Everyone else was standing staring at the screen from behind their desks.

"Touch down. Rescuer has landed," Jack Drake reported from his computer screen station.

Everyone let out an audible sigh of relief and then erupted into cheers. Even Maria had to squeal in excitement. Several scientists started frantically typing in things at their station. Maria had nothing to do yet. She stood with her eyes transfixed on the screen, awaiting to see what these aliens looked like.

The Mission Commander Lisa Ying opened the hatch and stepped out onto Europa's ice. The signal was being transmitted from just below the ice where they landed. She bent to inspect it, but it was not transparent and showed no openings.

Maria spoke into the microphone at her station. "Commander Ying, please transmit the first string of images I have sent you."

"Yes ma'am, I'm on it," Ying replied. The camera showed her typing on her pad device, then with a flourish she hit the 'send' button. It was, after all, the first time a human would be contacting an alien, so she made a bit of a show of it, then proclaimed, "The first transmission of a message to aliens has been sent."

Nothing happened.

The Commander stood idle on the big screen back at Mission Control. The scientists started to whisper among themselves. Two more astronauts had exited the ship behind Ying and started inspecting the ice all around the ship.

Ying started to tap her foot in a display of impatience.

"Send it again," Maria instructed.

Ying complied, and, after waiting a minute, did so again without orders.

Still nothing happened.

She waved to her right at one of the other astronauts, who took out a laser cutter and began dissecting the ice at his feet.

"That could be considered a show of aggression," Maria warned.

"No other option. We rang, they ain't answering." Commander McMahan looked back at Maria over her shoulder as she kept pacing in front of the big screen.

It took several minutes before the astronaut was able to carve a door through the ice. The three astronauts all gathered around it, looking down into the dark water.

"Transmit their distress call back to them, then add the image of an outstretched helping hand," Maria suggested.

Ying did it. Nothing happened.

They were all back on Earth—so far away— while on Jupiter's moon, Europa, they stared into the abyss under the ice silently for a long expectant pause.

Finally, something extended out of the water up towards Commander Ying. She, in spite of her training, stepped back a bit at the sight of it.

The hand was pale sea-foam green and covered with suction cups. There were no fingers. It looked more like a tentacle, everyone was thinking. They knew that to be true as seven others, then a large head came out from the water. A more-than-human-sized being crawled out and wrapped half its tentacles around Commander Ying. It held up one of the others, which held a device that somehow displayed a hologram image of the same outstretched hand image Ying had sent them moments before.

"It's a damn octopus!" Penelope, back at Mission Command on Earth, blurted out what everyone was thinking.

"Send the pictographs I gave you to ask what is wrong," Maria said.

Commander Ying touched her pad and sent the message.

The alien seemed to receive the message somehow and made some dance-like sweeping motions with her tentacles after letting Ying go, much to Ying and everyone else's relief. Commander Ying looked back wordlessly to the camera.

Mission Commander McMahan shrugged and turned to Maria. "That mean anything to you?"

"No ma'am." Maria shook her head, then typed on her desk for a moment. "Try sending that."

The new message was sent by Ying and received by the alien. It grabbed the camera and took it back with it as it dove back into the hole in the ice. The viewers back on Earth couldn't make out much in the dark water except for lots of floating ice, making it look like a huge glass of sweet tea, Commander McMahan had said. However, finally a light source appeared, and they could all see what the alien was showing them. It was a huge glowing mountain on the ocean floor. It seemed to stretch on for several kilometers.

"What the hell is that thing?" Commander McMahan turned to ask her assembled brightest minds of planet Earth.

"Ma'am. That is a super volcano thrice the size of the one under Yellowstone, and it's about to erupt. The whole damn moon will be blown apart!" Jack said from his station, where he was grimacing down at his computer screen.

"We can't do a damn thing about it, can we?" Commander McMahan said, finally ceasing her pacing to stand still.

"Nothing." Jack said. "If Yellowstone shows that it is about to erupt, we can't save the billions of humans it will kill here."

The alien returned to the surface with the camera that it carefully handed back to one of the astronauts. Ying held out her own hands in a helpless gesture rather than sending the similar pictograph that Maria typed in for her to send. The alien seemed to understand the gesture perfectly.

"How do I tell it to let us evacuate?" commander Ying asked.

"Point to the ship and wave it inside," Maria said quickly.

Ying did so, but the alien dove back into the water. It returned with a clear silicone bag nearly the size of a killer whale. It was full of tiny eggs.

Ying backed up and looked toward the camera for advice.

"It's eggs, their young. It wants you to evacuate them," Commander McMahan said. "Maria, tell it we will take them all, not just their eggs."

Maria typed in a sequence of pictographs. Ying relayed those to the alien. It held up the device it wore on one tentacle and a hologram of millions of aliens appeared.

"It's saying they can't all fit in the ship, right?" Ying asked.

"Maria, tell it that one or two of them gotta come with the eggs to teach them ... and for us to study," Commander McMahan said.

Maria quickly drew a drawing on the yellow legal pad on her desk and showed the camera what she had scribbled: three large aliens and the giant egg sack all inside the spaceship.

Ying looked at it and looked back at her ship. "Not sure we can fit the eggs ... much less three of these monsters."

"You'll make it work, Commander. Show it to the alien," McMahan barked.

Ying held the screen of her pad in front of the giant eyes of the alien.

It studied the image for a few moments. It looked as if it was about to argue but a huge rumbling from the seafloor below the ice they were all standing on convinced the alien to get its brethren off the moon, as many as the Earth Ship could carry, and as fast as they could. It jumped back into the water and quickly returned with three slightly smaller aliens. Ying was relieved when she saw the juvenile aliens thinking just maybe those three and the eggs could fit into her spaceship.

The seafloor rumbled even louder and the whole moon vibrated violently.

"Get out of there, that super-volcano is about to explode!" Jack screamed into the microphone at his desk.

"You heard the man, retreat! Get those aliens and the eggs into the ship and launch at will." McMahan hollered the orders.

Ying and the other two astronauts started ushering the three young aliens into Rescuer. They returned to the ice and started pulling and tugging at the massive egg sack. The grown alien grabbed it from them and started shoving it into the ship's tiny door. The sack was malleable. It stretched and reformed into something of a long tubular shape as the alien pushed more and more of it into the ship.

Ying and her men both joined in and shoved the last meter of the bag into Rescuer before pushing their own way back aboard.

Ying turned to the adult alien and outstretched her hand from the ship's threshold. The alien mimicked the two palms up helpless gesture that Ying had shown it before, then slammed the door of the ship in Ying's face.

"Launch now, get off that moon," Jack told them from back at Mission Control.

The overfilled Earth ship tried to lift off. It was clearly not powerful enough with all the added weight of the alien refugees. Ying tried and tried again but they could not achieve lift off.

Dozens of giant aliens had crawled out of the hole in the ice as the moon continued to shake. They all joined forces with hundreds of outstretched tentacles, lifted Rescuer up off the ice and threw it upward into the air like a cannonball launched at the enemy.

Just as the ship broke free of the minor gravity of the tiny moon, Europa cracked open like an egg. Lava and ice flew out in a bubble around what had been the moon's surface. The Rescuer was hit by ice and lava, but the impact wave of the explosion threw it clear of most of the debris.

* * *

The three young alien teachers were bobbing about the Alaskan Gulf Coast, along with over a million newly hatched baby aliens. The Navy boat in the center of the school of aliens was following behind the lilac teacher, who was talking to Maria on board the boat. The two sea-foam green teachers were nearby, teaching the babies how to communicate with each other.

Maria held out her hand to the lilac teacher, who waved goodbye with one tentacle as she joined the school. Dozens of tiny baby aliens lifted tentacles also, to wave adorably to Maria.

It was not a goodbye, though.

The aliens learned a new sign language that Maria had developed. The humans and the aliens coexisted on Earth, lending each other a helping hand or tentacle as needed.

Blueprints

Robin Kathaas

"Hey, you're sure about this, right?"

Emma's nod is a relief. The tattoo gun in my hand is old. A relic, really. The wires poking out of it are sharper than its needle. I'd been the one to find it, and I would have tossed it out if Emma hadn't stopped me. Even she had not been able to explain why she wanted to keep it. We'd done well surviving until now. Tetanus couldn't be the thing that took her away from me.

The tattoo gun had gathered even more dust in the attic since our last spring-clean. I'd forgotten about it, but it was the first thing Emma headed for when she returned from her interview at the hospital. A sharp sterile needle poked out from her bag, the cap slightly unscrewed. I stood at the bottom of the stairs and held them steady, already resigned to the fact that Emma was not as easy to tame as the wood of our house.

It was the best house we'd had since the wells ran dry. The wood was creaky, but there was something reassuring about the consistency in its damage, alongside its refusal to ever truly crack.

"So, what's the plan?"

"A car," Emma replied.

I raised my eyebrows. I knew I didn't doubt Emma's capabilities, but

I didn't see how it would be possible to turn that rusty old torture device into an automobile.

"Come here. I want you to draw."

"I'll draw you something every day until I die if you want me to. Doesn't mean I want to tear your skin apart with that murder weapon. Slight difference."

"Don't be lame."

I clambered up to the attic without further protest, as Emma knew I would. Her ambition finally made sense. She had taken out her old working kit: necessary rulers, plain piles of notebooks, and a calligraphy set that had no real value but made the whole exercise more fun to her.

I stifled a sigh at the blueprint she had selected. It was her last project before the world went bust. She wasn't naïve – she knew it was already too late to fix things. Even so, she had hoped this would be a step in the right direction. The car she'd designed ran on seawater. It didn't even need to be purified. Anyone near a coast could use the same bucket they used to mop their floors to run their cars. It caused zero exhaust fumes. No heat, no smoke, no suffocation.

She uncapped her inkwell and dipped the stolen needle into it. I hesitated.

"Do you really want that kind of reminder on your body?"

"Of what?" Emma asked.

"Of... tardiness."

"The world's not over yet, baby. There is still time." She pressed the tattoo gun's button. It sprang to life, mirroring the eagerness in Emma's eyes. "I've already spent weeks trying to get this thing to work. And I know what my next project will be."

Hurricane Hunters

John Tures

"Mr. Dean, have you ever stared down an F5 tornado barreling towards you?" Erin asked, sticking the pencil behind her head to hold the hair out of her eyes, commencing the informal interview right there in the cheap rental house on the island.

Allen grinned. "Yes ma'am. I have done so several times. One time in Monticello, Arkansas, a twister hit a farmhouse so hard there weren't nothin' left of it bigger than a popsicle stick!"

"Yes, I'm sure those few minutes were thrilling and got lots of clicks on your YouTube channel. But we're hurricane hunters, not storm chasers like you are, Mr...."

The big guy stuck out his hand first. "Call me Allen, ma'am."

"And you'll do me the courtesy of calling me Erin, not ma'am, and try not to interrupt me."

"Yes ma'a...Miss...uh...Erin," he stammered, wincing at his failed attempts to sound professional.

"Better. Now, as I was saying, a big tornado might be a half-mile wide and travel more than a mile on the ground. On the other hand, a hurricane out here might be 150 miles long and take hours, not minutes, to get out of its path of destruction."

The big man stroked the goatee on his chin that had morphed from stubble mere weeks ago, the sweat stains on his Oklahoma University polo shirt multiplying, though it was difficult to tell if the humidity, or impromptu interview, was the reason. "I'm taking it that you see me as a 'fish out of water' out here."

"More like a sixth wheel, Allen."

When he first saw the thin woman with dirty blonde hair, cheap sunglasses, and a white Disney tank top, he'd hoped she would also be just as casual about the assignment. That was another wrong assumption.

"I know your online videos get a lot of hits," she continued, "but we're not out here to be 'Storm Pursuers' like you used to be. Our operation is about serious science. Did you study science in high school, Mr.... I mean, Allen?"

He looked down at his boots, then returned her gaze with a nervous "aw shucks" grin. "Science was during the seventh period when football practice began. One of the cheerleaders took the state test for me so I could play for the Sooners."

Erin rolled her eyes. "Frederic hired you to get back at me for being right about Hurricane Maria devastating Puerto Rico."

Allen looked around the house, relieved to be out of the muggy September air, and not having to swat away any more of those giant mosquitoes. Florida was supposed to be the land of beaches and tropical breezes, which was why he'd taken the job. But he was stunned to find trees as thick as a forest here on Pine Island, off the Southwest Coast, not far from Ft. Myers.

He tried to change the subject. "You said operation. Where are the others? Are they setting up sandbags or something outside this small house?"

Erin's voice became shrill. "As usual, they're in the wrong place at the wrong time. Frederic has them headquartered in Tampa, convinced the hurricane's heading there. My superior may be Ivy League, and I'm just an FSU grad, but he's too reliant on old models. Frederic's models were developed in the 1950s for God's sake, which underestimate a hurricane's speed, power, and direction, and therefore their destruction."

She then explained how she used something called Hebert Boxes after a famed meteorologist, so she knew where to locate her research here on the Florida islands off Ft. Myers.

"Hey, when I was on the Oklahoma Sooners, we played your Florida State Seminoles in a bowl game on New Year's."

She let out a frustrated howl of disgust, which made him cringe. It was time to make up for that last comment. "If you tell me about the science stuff with the hurricanes, I'll help you with... whatever you need."

Erin shifted into schoolmarm mode as Allen followed the directions she had written out on notebook paper to get her scientific equipment ready.

"OK, Allen, do you know what a hypothesis is?"

He paused the assembly of one of the tools. "Kind of like a theory?"

She stopped, somewhat surprised. "Somewhat. Both are connections between variables. A hypothesis is a more specific testable version of a theory." As she continued her lecture, he glanced at his cell phone. The report showed a wall of yellow and red headed for Ft. Myers, with winds topping 160 mph before the signal died.

"Do you know, Allen?"

"Uh, sorry, Erin." He looked up suddenly. "The winds were picking up, and I missed the last part."

She looked at him curiously. "Do you know how we get our data about hurricanes?"

Allen scrunched his face. "Don't you fly planes into hurricanes somehow?"

It was hard to tell whether she was more shocked or pleased with his answer. "Yes, Allen."

Now he was super glad he had seen that Scooby-Doo episode set in the Bermuda Triangle.

"But that information comes from the top," Erin continued. "While at FSU, I created some instruments that gather information closer to landfall. I even took night classes in welding to learn how to construct this equipment."

Her voice continued as she added details about how it all worked. She built this stuff, he mused. Her passion was intriguing. Where did it come from? He hoped she was as much of a thrill-seeker as he was.

He sensed she had just finished saying something sciency. Before he could reply, gusts of wind battered the house. "Looks like you were right, Erin. Whatever you were looking for, it's here."

She ran over to him and impulsively hugged the lineman, undoubtedly pleased to be proven correct. "Help me get the readings on the roof."

It was hard to tell which was fiercer, the rain droplets like projectiles or the harsh wind whipping her hair and taking his OU cap to the mainland, for all he knew. Allen demonstrated his ability to learn quickly, helping to set up everything, and securing it to the chimney and gutters.

"This sure is bigger than a regular hurricane, I bet!" he yelled over the howling wind.

"My preliminary calculations show that Frederic is wrong. It's not a Category 3. It's a 4, or maybe even a 5!"

"Ever been in one?"

His question went unanswered as she regarded the sky fearfully. "We'd better get inside." As if to punctuate her point, a tree branch nearly swept her from the rental house's roof.

"Whaddya do now?"

"I've only field-tested it on a Category 2," Erin admitted as they returned to the family room. "I guess we...ride it out"

A man of action, the tornado chaser paced about the house. Allen didn't have a speedy pickup or a durable rig to outmaneuver this storm. He nervously considered the house's structural integrity. It was built on a Florida island. It was designed for storms, no doubt, but could it beat "the big one?" He prided himself on never being caught by a killer storm. That streak would end today, he noted grimly.

* * *

"What do you think is causing all of these storms now?" Allen had to raise his voice as if they were still on the roof. It was getting worse by the minute.

Erin shivered. "Climate change. The Earth is getting warmer overall, but climate change shows more blizzards and ice storms too." She looked for signs of skepticism from Allen. After all, he fit the demographic.

The storm chaser nodded, having seen big blizzards firsthand in the prairie states. "But I thought it was just a theory."

"Einstein had a theory of relativity too, you know." Erin shook her head. "There's a ton of evidence in support of climate change."

Allen was eager for the debate. "But didn't we have bad hurricanes at least 100 years ago? While passing the time on driving to another tornado, I listened to a book on CD about a big one that hit Galveston."

"That book's called Isaac's Storm," she replied. Her follow-up smile told him that she was impressed that he was a book reader, or at least a book listener. It was about the only thing he was happy with, as crashing waves could now be heard from several blocks away. Time to double-down and show I belong, Allen thought.

"I saw a documentary on the History Channel...you know, back when they used to show history, instead of Aliens and Axmen of Alaska reality shows." Allen laughed, despite their precarious situation. "It was about a hurricane that hit Key West in the 1930s, and there was another hurricane that smashed through New England a few years later."

Erin nodded grimly, hugging her legs closer to her body to make herself smaller. "I remember those two, especially the story of the bus on Rhode Island, and all those children swept out to sea. I'm getting worried that whatever is coming ashore is just as bad."

Allen impulsively sat next to her, putting his arm around the trembling scientist. Maybe distracting her by keeping her talking would make her less scared. "How could a theory from today explain those tragedies back then?" he asked.

"M-my doctoral d-dissertation shows that the...heavy...industrialization preceded those s-storms," she managed. But as she continued her explanation, she seemed more confident. "We had the number of Cat Three, Four, or Five hurricanes go from seven in the 1890s to nine in the 1950s. After we created the EPA and started cutting back on pollution, we saw those storms go down to about five throughout the 1980s. But everything began to double by the 2010s: tropical storms, all hurricanes, and the most s-severe ones too!"

She paused her lecture as both looked at each other, listening to the heavy sloshing sounds coming toward the street.

Nothing we can do about that now, Allen mused. "But don't we have an EPA now?"

"And there are similar versions in Europe...and Japan too..." she agreed. "But now we have developing-world industrialization and no g-guardrails. States like Oklahoma have sued the EPA, gutting its staff and powers."

"Sorry," he mumbled, though she probably didn't hear his apology over the howling winds, which were loudly ripping away anything outside that was untethered. Good thing I got rental insurance on the truck, Allen mused, as a mailbox on a snapped piece of wood sped by. "So that's why we had storms like Hurricane Maria, Sandy, and Katrina," he concluded.

The scientist seemed to shudder more than she had in the last few minutes at the last storm name.

"I didn't mean to touch a nerve," Allen apologized, stroking her cheek. "Want to talk about it?"

Erin shook her head. "Sorry...no. B-bad memories."

Allen opened his mouth but stopped himself. It wasn't the time. Down the street, a large tree crashed, making them both jump. A loud groan of metal probably meant that the causeway was gone too, leaving them marooned on Pine Island.

"C-critics of my diss said it didn't apply to the Pacific, only the Atlantic," she snapped. "So, I-I confirmed the numbers on typhoons in the Pacific, and later the cyclones in the Indian Ocean in journal articles..."

Erin gasped. Water was starting to seep under the door. She stood up. "Help me get the laptops as high as we can. I have garbage bags to protect them from rain, but it won't do them much good if they sink underwater."

Allen jumped to the task. "What if they get soaked?"

The screaming winds nearly drowned out her reply. "The data's going up to the cloud, but only as long as they stay dry. I need them to last as long as possible. I bought them with the last of my grant money, and unlike the roof instruments, they aren't waterproof."

Once the laptops had been placed on the refrigerator top, Erin sprang up on the counter to check the readings. "Well, Mr. Storm Chaser, the findings confirm it. You can say you've been through an F5 tornado and a Category five hurricane, if you survive, of course. I was right, and Frederic was wrong. The eye's not going to Tampa. It's going to pass over Fort Myers..."

She squeaked as more water sloshed through the kitchen and dining room from the garage. Now the whole floor was covered in the muddy, brackish stuff. While she took a position between the sink and fridge on the counters, he occupied the other shelves between the sink and stove. A window in the bedroom shattered as a heavy object slammed into it. Water continued to rise halfway up the lower counters where the dishes were stored, filled with detritus from inside and outside the house.

Even over the groan of the storm, a dog could be heard barking from outside the house. One didn't need to be a vet to know the creature was in distress. Allen looked through the window, black outside as the time approached 8 pm. "I can see her! She's on a tractor...that dog's gonna get swept away unless I can save her."

"But..."

"It's a Labrador Retriever!" Allen exclaimed. "I can swim out and get her. She can sit in the sink."

"Please! Don't go!" Erin begged, as nervous as the dog, but Allen was already off the shelves, treading water toward the back door, unable to hear her pleading over the shrieking winds. After grunting for a few minutes, he ripped the door open and let more of Noah's Flood inside, raising the water level to the base of her shoes.

Just as the Lab stopped barking, there was a terrible crash in the back-yard. The giant tree outside crushed the fence and tractor, destroying the back porch and what was left of the shed. A branch broke through the window the storm chaser had used to spot the dog.

"A-A-Allen!" Erin screamed. But there was no reply, only more infernal winds, and a soupy mix that now covered her ankles and showed no signs of receding.

Erin squeezed herself between the top of the fridge and the roof, clutching the laptops, watching the march of the waves as they climbed higher and higher.

She closed her eyes...

Suddenly, she was ten years old again, begging her mom not to leave the Morial Convention Center in New Orleans, where they had driven for safety to avoid Hurricane Katrina's wrath.

"But Audrey will drown otherwise, sweetie. And I can't let that happen to our sweet dog," her mom had said, echoing Allen just a few minutes ago.

"Help your dad watch your little brother and I'll be back in no time," she promised.

But it wasn't one she could keep. Neither her mother Betsy, nor their German Shepherd Audrey, were ever found again. Whether they were slain by flying debris from the storm, drowned in the flooding that ravaged Louisiana and Mississippi, or killed by looters, the cause of their deaths would be a mystery to her. National Guardsmen gave some vague answers to their pleas for information about mass graves dug by locals.

Their father, Hugo, never recovered, drinking harder stuff, and more of it, until she found him curled up under the desk in their apartment one day. Heart attack, they wrote on the death certificate, but it was Katrina that took him, just as it came for her mother years earlier, even if he wouldn't be officially listed among the casualties. Her little brother Mitch moved to South Dakota and sold life insurance. They hadn't spoken in years.

* * *

Her calls for Allen went unanswered.

She was alone, surrounded by three laptops that confirmed all of her arguments, with only whatever instruments survived on the roof. Her data would be a game-changer in meteorology if it wasn't washed away. Now the water had almost reached the top of the refrigerator.

She texted Frederic's superior, Andrew Harvey, the head of NOAA. He would be able to access the data with her username and password. At least her sacrifice would not be in vain. She remembered the story about the Mt. St. Helens photographer, who realized he wouldn't survive the 1980 blast. He continued to take photos, which helped scientists learn so much about the physics of eruptions when those were miraculously recovered after the volcano's devastation. She wished she could remember his name. Her name would probably be forgotten too, though she prayed her findings would help others.

As the water reached her knees, and she held up the bagged-up laptops, she wondered about Allen, the only one to follow her into Hurricane Ian's path. Did he have a family? She hadn't even bothered to ask him if he had one. Instead, she was busy showing off how much she knew about hurricanes. Would they find his body? Likely, it would remain pinned underneath that massive tree on Pine Island next to what was left of that scared dog after the storm passed. Would his family blame her, in death, for Allen's demise? She wished she could apologize for insisting he come to Pine Island to help her set up her equipment.

The wind slammed small objects like bullets against the few windowpanes that weren't shattered, but the projectiles were thankfully getting less frequent as the night wore on. The storm surge was the more immediate threat, and there was nowhere to go.

At that moment, she heard something smash into the front door, sure to let in enough water to flood the whole lower level.

It would be all over now. She hoped it wouldn't hurt too much to drown.

To her surprise, it was a boat, and inside was...

"Allen!" she shouted with joy. Water began pouring out of the house, bringing the level down to the counters.

"And the dog!" he exclaimed. "Just let me tether this rowboat to the front porch."

"Get these laptops inside the boat and help me retrieve the instruments from the roof if they're still there," Erin insisted. "Is it safe outside?"

"Winds are dying down a little, but the water's still rising. I see higher ground in the distance, where survivors are gathering. Wait—are you crying?"

"I'll explain later," she insisted, as they retrieved the rest of the material from above what remained of the house and climbed inside the rowboat. "I thought you both died when that tree fell."

"We would have if this poor pooch hadn't been swept off the tractor. By the time I swam over to retrieve her, she was halfway down the street. We paddled our way to a rowboat tied to a pole a few houses down. It took forever to row back to get you."

Erin considered the wet dog, who lacked a collar. "Who is she?"

"No license—so no can tell. Might be like a stray."

On the way to higher ground, Erin told him of her Hurricane Katrina experience, and what happened to her parents.

"I'm so sorry." He squeezed her shoulder. "I shouldn't have left you."

"But you saved the dog and kept me from drowning by coming back with a boat," she insisted. "An apology unnecessary."

"I was right. The dog is female." Allen pointed out as he took the oars. "Let's name her Camille."

Erin shook her head, taking the other pair of paddles. "I've had enough of hurricane names for a while. Let's name her Zoe. It's low on the list and not likely to be called anytime soon."

The wind had slowed somewhat, and flying debris was less of a concern than it had been an hour earlier. They paddled to whatever lights were still going on the slight hilltop.

"Well, you'll now have a better chance of warning people, figuring

GREEN MAGIC

out where these hurricanes are going, and how strong they'll be, right?"
Allen had to shout less, though water levels on the island remained
high. "You'll save lives if we can make it out of this storm."

"Yes." She nodded, smiling more from nearly avoiding drowning.
"But will it be enough? More people are living by the coasts. There
are more storms than ever. And if my calculations are correct, they're
getting bigger and worse. 'Once a century storms' are happening every
few years now. A tropical storm just made the top ten list for most
damage. A government report showed that had Hurricane Katrina made
a direct hit on New Orleans, instead of a glancing blow, 60,000 people
would have died. The deaths were due more to the broken levees."

She gazed out sadly at the broken homes, the snapped trees, the
ones with roots well underwater that would not live. She shuddered as
several bodies floated by. "I'm not sure we can survive what's coming
the next few years."

Allen seemed determined to reach the lights and reassure his companion. "Didn't your research show that these storms used to be a lot
more frequent, but then we cleaned up the environment somewhat,
and the number of bad storms was cut back?"

"You were listening." She could hug the big guy if she wasn't afraid
the boat would tip over and lose all the research. She could see their
destination: a Publix store where several employees and customers
were gathered on the roof with a noisy generator that likely fueled the
lights. The survivors were waving them over. It was a relatively dry
oasis in a sea of muck.

"Back in Oklahoma, we all hated the EPA. But you've convinced me
how much we need it."

"Or this Category Five, that the papers are calling Hurricane Ian, did,"
Erin laughed, despite being soaked. Thankfully, the extra-duty garbage
bags seemed to keep the computers and instruments dry.

* * *

"And that's how Erin Floyd and Allen Dean helped get the data to track hurricanes better and get residents to safety." Opal clapped her hands together, concluding her class presentation on Hurricane Ian decades later.

"Not only did they save lives," her teacher added, "but their findings confirmed the climate change theory about severe storms. More than 150 countries signed the Cairo Accords, mandating the replacement of the majority of fossil fuels with natural, cleaner sources."

"Cost us plenty," snapped Bob, the class president.

"Yeah, but think about how much doing nothing for so long hurt our country," Gilbert shot back. "Boston, New York, and Miami look more like Venice used to before it got submerged."

"China and India held out," interjected Wilma into the debate. "But after the typhoon that destroyed Shanghai and the cyclone that took out Chennai in the same year, both leaders came back to sign the treaty."

"And we moved our capital from Washington D.C. to Denver," Charlie, the class clown, pointed out. "And not just for the skiing."

David tapped his forehead. "We should have switched from coal, oil and gas to wind and solar a lot sooner."

Rita shook her head. "What about their jobs when all of those plants closed?"

David's girlfriend, Donna, shot back, "Most got hired in cleaner tech afterwards."

Alicia, the valedictorian, added, "We also have a lot fewer big storms hitting the coast anyway once we made the big switch."

"I can't believe people used to live at the mercy of hurricanes like that," Alberto mused.

"But what happened to Erin and Allen?" Beryl wanted to know.

"They married, of course," Opal replied, earning plenty of ahh's...

"And why did you choose this topic?" The teacher added the last question, a second before the bell indicated the end of the class.

"Dr. Floyd, who won that Nobel Prize for her research, is my great-great-great-grandmother," Opal announced. "And that's why I hope to follow in her footsteps, as a climatologist."

The Rain Keeper

"For my parents."

Dorothy Johnson-Laird

"Did you call down the rain?" a man asks.
        "It was I: I'm the one," I smile as
            my ginger cat purrs by my feet.
    "I invited the rain, felt the need of her."

"Did you summon the rain?" he insists,
    as if he did not hear my reply.

"Yes, I laid the mat on the porch.
    swept the crisp leaves in the yard,
    gathered them together."

The ginger cat steps sleekly over my shoes, unflustered,
    ignoring the conversation above her.

"My house was dried out and dusty,

steps creaked when I walked them,
so I tidied the dirt from the creases in the wooden floors,
cleared out the faded poetry pages,
ink curls on blue paper,
opened the windows wide, and waited."

Late at night, I sat near my low-lying bookshelf,
first heard the water sift down the glass.
Listened to the wind stirring and circling,
stirring and circling in the yard outside,
hurrying over broad branches,
hardened oak.

Then the water came racing in through the windows,
pushing past the curtains, over the linoleum floor.
It did not stop,
but kept running, whirling away old dust,
siphoning through room corners.

I moved some chairs out of her way.
The ginger cat hid behind one.
And when I looked back outside the window, I saw her,
shifting from slow drops to quicker ones
sprinting swiftly in the open air.

She did not hold back,
but spun on and dove in steady streams across the land.

The earth was stark and etched with cracks.
It needed her.

And I did not ask her to cease or close the curtains
   I did not switch on the light or step away from the window.

I waited and watched
   I saw her — a source
   as she tended to the soil,
   as she washed away all the dead leaves,
   paused all the car drivers hurtling at speed,
   stole into private parkways,
   into the road below my apartment.

She spun her water — she soothed

She cleansed the land

She was a refuge

And in that moment, I became the Rain Keeper
   as she put all the gun violence on hold,
   dampened all the arguments,
   calmed all the unruly dogs
   and stilled all the sirens.

Because it was I, yes I, who summoned the rain.

I gave her an open invitation.

Looking Forward through the Telescope of the Past

Sarah Das Gupta

'The conference is next week. We've a matter of days to recover those research papers.'

'Well, you know what they say. The beginning's the best place to start.'

Jack could see his suggestion had not lightened Yasmin's mood of utter despondency. He wasn't surprised. Three years of hard work and dedication, hours of experiments in the lab, weeks on location in the remote Brazilian jungle, in the forests of Siberia, on the edge of the Arctic Circle — all gone in a matter of minutes.

Yasmin, or to refer to her by her professional title, Dr Yasmin Hardy, Research Fellow of Trinity College, Cambridge, had long known the security precautions needed with regard to her recent research project.

Through extensive fieldwork and brilliant laboratory research, she and her team at Cambridge had developed species of trees that reached full maturity in less than half the years normally expected. Unfortunately, this encouraging development went against the political and commercial interests of a powerful group of companies and countries producing plastic goods.

During the previous summer holiday, Yasmin's office had been destroyed in a blazing inferno in the early hours of the morning. Engaged in a field study in Northern Canada at the time, she had heard of the disaster in a phone call from Jack, her research fellow and fiancé.

'It can't all have been destroyed, not the whole computer record!'

'It can, and it has. The whole lot's been reduced to debris and dust.'

'Couldn't the fire brigade salvage anything?' Even over a thousand miles, her desperation was audible.

'Once they'd ascertained the building was empty, they weren't going to put firemen at risk to salvage property or computers. At least you still have the hard copy of your research papers in the university safe.'

How many times Jack had regretted tempting fate.

The police and then MI5 had examined the forensic evidence left by the disastrous fire. The material used by the arsonists suggested a connection with East European gangs known to be involved in money laundering and with links to Beijing. Despite security precautions, the day following the fire, a gang had gained access to the safe containing the original research by climbing over the roof and drilling their way into the laboratory. Only weeks were then left before the International Conference and the official launch of Yasmin's invaluable research project.

Later that afternoon, Jack decided to take his own advice. It was worth having another look at the scene of the crime. He could combine it with taking Bomber for his afternoon run.

He opened the lab door and walked thoughtfully to the broken safe. Jack could see the holes neatly drilled on either side of the lock. Whoever had broken into the safe obviously knew what he was doing.

Jack called Bomber, who found the lab with its many scents an interesting distraction. Well, Basset Hounds with their long bodies and comically short legs had been bred to hunt badgers in forested areas. Their ridiculously long ears protected their eyes against scrub and thorny brambles. Interbreeding with bloodhounds had made them very sensitive to smell. Bomber suddenly found the scent around the safe particularly interesting. He began running in circles, his nose to the floor, sniffing excitedly. Every so often, he gave a short, eager bark.

At first, Jack laughed. 'You won't find many badgers here, Bomber!'

Then he began to take the dog's excitement more seriously. Grabbing a cloth, he wiped it around the front of the safe and the drill holes. He held it over the dog's muzzle for a few seconds. Bomber, with his nose to the ground, ran to the door, scratching to get out.

Jack pulled out his mobile to call Yasmin. She was dismissive, pointing out there was such a mixture of chemical and human scents in the lab that Bomber's excitement was understandable. Nevertheless, she agreed to meet Jack at the exit to the Science Block.

By the time Yasmin arrived, Jack found it difficult to control Bomber, who was jumping up and pulling hard on the leash. Despite her despair, Yasmin couldn't help smiling at the dog's obvious excitement.

'He'll probably lead us to the butcher's or the college kitchen. His main interest in life is food.'

'I've never seen him act like this. Let's see where he goes.'

Jack held the cloth to Bomber's muzzle once more and unclipped his lead. The dog set off across the university playing fields at a brisk trot. Jack and Yasmin followed. Every twenty meters, Bomber paused to sniff around as if searching for the scent again, then picked up the trail once more.

'He's making for the forest path.' Yasmin sounded rather surprised.

'Yes, that's the path I'd take if I wanted to escape from the College site.' Jack was already a little out of breath. This was rather different from his usual afternoon stroll.

At first, the path through the forest was a well-worn track. Bomber showed no sign of losing the trail. After half an hour, the track broke into three smaller grassy paths. Without hesitation, Bomber trotted off down the middle of the three.

'He's a dog who knows his own mind. I hope he knows where he's going. It looks dark and gloomy here.' Yasmin shivered involuntarily, looking up at the tall pines which seemed to crowd in on them.

'It's a bit like Hansel and Gretel. We should be dropping a trail behind us.'

'Let's hope the old witch is dead by now,' laughed Yasmin. Her voice was lost in the dark canopy.

Bomber stopped occasionally to sniff among the pine needles, but he seemed confident of the direction. They had been walking for over an hour when the dog suddenly stopped in front of a patch of bracken and brambles. He wriggled and pushed his way into the undergrowth until only his bark could be heard in the heavy gloom. The air was oppressive, the stillness strange, like that moment before a storm breaks.

Jack picked up a long stick lying in the bracken. 'I'm going to have to bash my way through here or we're going to lose him.'

Yasmin followed close behind. She couldn't have explained why, but she didn't fancy being left in the dark wood.

As Jack beat the brambles aside, he glimpsed the white tip of Bomber's tail sticking out of an opening. Bending down, he could see it was an entrance to a tunnel or bunker of some kind. Before he could stop him, the dog disappeared into the darkness.

'I'm going to have to crawl in to get him back. It looks like the entrance to an air raid shelter from the War.'

Jack crawled on his hands and knees, following Bomber. The passage was dry, but there was a lingering smell of decay which made breathing difficult. He could hear Yasmin behind him coughing sporadically. After about 100 metres, the tunnel opened out. It was then possible to stand, which made progress quicker.

'There looks as if there's light in the distance,' Jack shouted over his shoulder. 'It probably comes out on the other side of the forest.'

'Hope so. It's hard to breathe.' Yasmin's voice sounded anxious.

'OK, I can see people in the distance. Looks as if they're building something. At least you'll feel better out in the open.'

* * *

The tunnel opened out onto a bright sunlit field. In the distance, a grey stone-towered castle was framed against a blue sky. Splendid red and gold pennants flew from the four towers. In the field ahead of them, a crowd of peasants was finishing preparations for some sort of celebration. On the right, tiers of wooden seats had been arranged. In the centre of the top tier, two gold plated thrones shone in the sunlight. Down the middle of the grass in front of the seats, two men in rough, fustian tunics, grey hoods and thick hose were hammering in a line of poles joined by a wicker fence.

'Looks as if it's one of those mock jousting tournaments. You know, people dressing up in medieval costume and knights charging at each other with lances. That grassy area where they've put up the fence is called the *lists* I think.' Jack was trying to remember his junior school history.

'Yes, but how has the weather and even the season changed so abruptly?' Yasmin pointed out the bright, fresh, green foliage on the trees along the edge of the field and pale-yellow rosettes of primroses dotted over the castle mount. 'How have our clothes suddenly altered?' Her voice had risen to a nervous pitch. She held out the skirt of the coarse blue woollen dress she found herself wearing and pointed at Jack's nondescript tunic and brown breeches.

'Where's Bomber vanished to?' Jack sounded worried. 'Bomber, here, boy!' He whistled loudly.

A large, shaggy, grey dog, similar to a wolfhound, lolloped up to him. No dog could have looked less like a basset hound than the long-legged, elegant canine which answered Jack's summons. Yasmin looked panic-stricken at Jack as a trumpet call sounded.

Excited crowds had suddenly filled the tiered seats. On the thrones, a handsome man in a richly jewelled doublet sat beside a pretty young woman. A delicate gold coronet shone on her head and long, dark hair hung over her shoulders.

As the trumpet sounded again, a knight in armour appeared at one end of the *lists.* His white charger, draped in crimson cloth, pawed the ground impatiently. At a second trumpet call, a knight in black armour entered. His coal-black mount too was *caparisoned* in black cloth.

'It looks as if Death is the challenger!' Yasmin whispered nervously.

Bomber, in his new 'incarnation', had growled fiercely when the Black Knight passed close to them as they stood in the crowd. Jack had difficulty restraining him as he gripped the strange, spiked collar round his neck.

The White Knight rode in front of the dais, bowing low before the noble couple. The dark-haired girl removed the pale blue silk scarf from around her neck. It fluttered down into the knight's mailed hand. The crowd clapped and cheered as he tied the *favour* to his helmet.

Once more, the herald sounded the trumpet. The two knights charged towards each other, their lances poised to attack. As their weapons clashed, the White Knight was pushed backwards by the impact. He lay flat on his charger as it galloped to the end of the list. The crowd, who had been shocked into silence, cheered loudly as they realised their champion had survived.

The Black Knight removed his helmet. Yasmin could see a sneering look of triumph on his sallow face while his lips curled cruelly in anticipation of victory. Jack was busy trying to control the angry 'Bomber'.

'That was close. I thought the White Knight would fall. He's tough though. He's signalling that he wants to continue the challenge.' Yasmin was caught up in the excitement of the crowd around them, all in simple peasant dress.

Moments later, the horses were hurtling towards each other. The younger knight struck his opponent a resounding side blow as he pounded past. The Black Knight fell heavily, while his mount galloped riderless into the open space beyond the *lists.* The spectators broke into wild cheering, as the victor, the silk scarf fluttering from his helmet, bowed before the Lady whose *favour* he had carried to victory.

Meanwhile, his opponent was slowly recovering. He sat up shakily, still dazed. A man next to Jack pulled him forward into the lists. Handing a growling 'Bomber' over to Yasmin, Jack followed the stranger who picked up a rough stretcher of plaited willow, gesturing to Jack to help him stretcher the Black Knight off the field.

Once inside a tent, the knight seemed to recover his senses, if not his temper. Jack wondered why the dog had taken an immediate dislike to the man. His fellow stretcher bearer signalled to Jack to help him remove the heavy black armour. Jack took his cue from the man opposite him, who deftly unbuckled the heavy breast plate, removed *the cuirass* from the back and *the greaves and sabatons* from the legs and feet. During this process, the knight swore and cussed in a most unchivalrous manner. At one point he pushed Jack aside and pulled off the *gambeson* himself. As he tossed the quilted jacket aside, Jack had a momentary glimpse of a large packet in what looked more like WH Smith brown paper than medieval vellum!

'Thank God you've finished. They'll notice we're late.' Yasmin looked relieved as he came out of the tent.

'What do you mean, late for what?'

'Our work in the kitchens. There's a big banquet in the castle tonight.'

'Who told you that?'

Yasmin seemed bewildered for a moment. A glazed look came over her face. 'No one told me. I somehow already knew. It's as if someone else is thinking for me.'

'I know what you mean. I felt that unbuckling the armour just now. Anyhow, we need to put Bomber's alter ego somewhere safe. Then I've got something interesting to tell you.'

Later that evening, as they entered the castle kitchens, they were met by a hive of activity.

'Thank goodness we found that kennel in the bailey yard and some scraps from the kitchen to keep 'Bomber' happy.'

'How can we find the Black Knight again? We're just kitchen scullions?' Yasmin didn't sound hopeful.

'I've got an idea, but first we'd better do some work. One of the cooks is looking suspiciously our way.'

Through the steam and smoke, they could see the enormous fireplace and hearth.

'If we're looking for a hiding place, we could creep in there. It's big enough to stand up in!'

'Might be a trifle hot!' Yasmin pointed at the boar and half a dozen chicken on the huge spit, turned by the spit boys. 'They don't look any older than eleven or twelve. A day of roasting and basting must be hot and tedious.'

Suddenly a deep voice from behind them interrupted her thoughts. 'You, my lass, get on with the beans and peas and you, leave the lasses be. Get down to the *Buttery* and help the young lads. The Lord Roger de Bracey feasts here this night.'

Yasmin quickly began slicing one of a huge pile of beans on the wooden table in front of her, dropping the chopped pieces into a large copper pan. Jack looked around helplessly for the 'Buttery'. *Must be where the butter's stored*, seemed a logical deduction.

'Tis over there, past the archway.' A young boy, rolling a cask of ale, pointed over his shoulder.

Jack pushed open a heavy door to reveal a large, cool storeroom lined with wooden barrels, which were in the process of being lifted or rolled into the kitchen.

'You look a strong lad. Take this *butt* here. Roll it down to the Great Hall.' The speaker was a heavily built man who seemed to be in charge of things. One of the servants addressed him as *'Butler'. Ah, Buttery, butts, Butler, this crazy world is beginning to make sense,* mused Jack, as he rolled the heavy barrel into the kitchen.

He could see Yasmin busy shelling peas into a wooden bowl while the barrels were now being moved under a stone archway, out of the smoky kitchen. Jack followed, pushing the heavy *butt* down a cobbled passage. The stones echoed with hollow groans, as if protesting at the weight of the procession of ale casks.

At last, after negotiating winding passages, Jack saw dozens of *butts* lined up along the wall. As he passed an open door, he peered into a huge hall with wooden rafters forming a beautiful *hammerbeam ceiling.* At the far end, Jack saw the main dining table on a dais and a gallery above. Musicians were already seated there, with their strange looking instruments laid out ready. On either side of the great hall, long trestle tables were already prepared with shining silver chargers and flagons gleaming in the candlelight.

By early evening, the kitchen was calmer. Fewer servants and scullions were milling around.

'Let's creep away now and fetch 'Bomber'. I only hope that he hasn't slipped his chain.'

Outside, in the bailey yard, flaming torches lighted the forecourt, driving the shadows into the furthest corners. Several large kennels were ranged along the outer wall. Beside one of these, Bomber's doppel-ganger leapt up towards Jack as soon as he approached. Unchaining the dog, Jack took from his pocket the piece of cloth which had so intrigued the basset hound and held it over the grey muzzle.

With his long stride, the dog covered ground quickly. Jack and Yasmin followed up an outer staircase to the floor above the Great

Hall. The passage was only dimly lit. They could hear the music and celebrations from below. The rooms leading off the cold stone passage were presumably bedchambers.

'How do we know the right room?' Yasmin whispered nervously.

'We have to trust our guide here,' Jack, patting the grey head, put the cloth round his muzzle again.

Without hesitation, Bomber's substitute stopped outside a heavy oak door near the end of the corridor. He stood up on his long back legs with his front paws against the door.

'Suppose it's locked?' Yasmin looked tearful.

'I checked on all the doors I could find. They had bolts on the inside, but no key holes. If our suspect is stuffing himself with roast pork and pottage, he's not going to be inside!'

As quietly as possible, Jack lifted the heavy iron latch, and the door swung open. The room was in semi-darkness, lit only by a torch near the door. A large four-poster bed dominated the chamber. A rich fur rug had been thrown over it and the canopy above was delicately carved. Around the walls hung carpets of bright colours and tapestries of ancient battles.

'Bomber' went straight to a richly carved cupboard inlaid with mother-of-pearl in the corner of the room. Yasmin opened the door carefully. Old papers and a long, silk robe seemed, at first, to be the only contents. Jack picked up the papers, which were parchment manuscripts in black, Gothic style writing. As he went to put these back, a brown paper packet fell to the ground.

'That's it! That's the hard copy of your research papers!'

As Yasmin almost screamed with delight, footsteps echoed in the stone passageway. They stopped ominously outside the chamber. Jack quickly put the brown package back among the manuscripts. He had noticed a door at the back of the room leading off the chamber. Grabbing Yasmin with one hand and the dog's collar with the other, he bundled them through this small door.

Inside, it was dark. They could hear someone walking about in the main chamber. Then a creaking noise suggested the cupboard door was being opened. As his eyes became accustomed to the dark, Jack could make out an odd pool of darkness close to the outer wall of the castle. Feeling his way across the space, he could see a wooden bench with a large, round hole in the middle, which explained the circle of darkness.

Suddenly he realised they were in a *privy* or medieval loo! Breathing in deeply and holding his breath, Jack looked down through the hole. He could see dark water two storeys below.

'This is a bloody privy, a medieval loo. Underneath, two storeys down, is the moat. Our only chance is to jump for it. We can both swim pretty well. Dogs are natural swimmers. It's our only f——- hope!'

Yasmin thought about landing in a pile of shitty water, of possibly drowning in it. She thought of weeks, years, a lifetime of the smoky kitchen, of preparing 'pottage', of being chatted up by the burly butler!

'Let's go for it.'

Jack tried to find the dog in the darkness. He had disappeared into thin air. He whispered to Yasmin, 'You go first and start swimming. Keep your mouth shut. When I hear the splash, I'll jump.'

He heard a distant sound as Yasmin hit the water. The latch on the privy door rattled. Jack jumped into the darkness.

* * *

The water in the moat was stinking and filthy. Yasmin kept her mouth tightly shut as she swam to the side. It was a moonlit night and as he came up for air, Jack could see Yasmin apparently clinging to the side of the wall. As he swam nearer, he could see she was, in fact, holding on to an iron grill just above the water level.

Jack grasped the grill and, with both of them pulling at the rusty iron, it suddenly gave way. They peered into the wet, gloomy hole. Ahead of them was a long flight of stairs, winding upwards. Jack half-lifted, half-pushed Yasmin onto the first step. He followed as she began to climb upwards. The lower steps were wet and slimy. She was about to stop a moment to catch her breath when she saw a glimmer of light.

'Looks as if we're near the top. I can see a crack of light. Might be coming from under a door.'

'OK, just wait when you get to the top.' Jack's voice seemed to come from far below.

Yasmin's climb came to a sudden halt. 'Ouch! That hurt,' she yelled as her head bumped into something hard.

Jack climbed up beside her, stretching his hand above her head. 'I'm not surprised. It feels like a plank of wood. You come down a couple of steps. I'll see if I can give it a shove.'

The wood sprang back so quickly that Jack almost fell. He teetered for a second, waving his arms wildly, before regaining his balance. Above his head, a trap door had sprung open. He climbed cautiously through to find himself standing in semi-darkness. At first, as he looked ahead and to the side, he thought he was standing in a garden.

'We're on a stage, treading the boards, in the limelight at last!' Yasmin's voice shouted excitedly.

'You're right. I actually thought we were in a garden, in this half-light, with the trees painted on the backdrop and the climbing roses and trellis on the wings.'

They stood at the front, looking into an empty auditorium. There was something eerie about the rows of empty seats and the well of darkness in front of the stalls. Suddenly, Jack felt something licking his leg. He spun round to see a white bull terrier with a black patch over one eye. His tail wagged frantically as he jumped up, his paws on Jack's legs, then turned to Yasmin, licking her hand, as if greeting a long-lost friend.

'He must be called 'Bullseye'- he's the image of Bill Sykes' dog in 'Oliver Twist'.'

A single bare bulb shed little light beyond the stage. Suddenly, Yasmin burst into laughter, 'Look at you in your harlequin suit and your three-cornered hat. I like the make-up, you should wear it more often. Looks as if we've moved on from Medieval serfdom, at least.'

'You can't talk. I never thought of you as Columbine.'

Yasmin twirled round, the sequins on her pale pink tutu shimmering in the half light. 'The last ballet dress I had was at the age of seven.'

'Good evening there!' a loud voice came from backstage before an impressive figure, in full evening dress, strode through the wings. 'You must be the extras for the Chorus tonight. Glad to see the Wardrobe have kitted you out already. You seem to have made friends with Bullseye too. We keep him as a guard dog — you can get difficult members in the audience.' He winked. 'Wapping can be a little 'lively' when the London taverns close. I'm sure you understand me, eh?'

'Of course, sir. Bullseye seems to have taken to us.' Jack smiled as they shook hands.

'Well, I'm the Chairman at Wilton's Victorian Music Hall. I have taken the liberty of printing out the choral songs. Just come with me and I'll find a quiet room so you can look them over. All popular songs you will know, of course.'

They followed the Chairman along the maze of narrow passages backstage. He pointed out the star dressing rooms and led them to a small room at the end of the gloomy passage.

'Well, I'll leave you here. One of the Chorus will be along to fill you in and answer any queries. Here's a programme for tonight's performance. So 'break a leg' as they say.' He shut the door.

They could hear his heavy footsteps echoing down the passage. The room was brightly lit by a bare bulb. For the first time, Jack and Yasmin looked in a mirror. They were both amazed at the heavily made-up faces and figures out of the Harlequinade who gazed back at them. Even Bullseye stared back at eyes more shaded than his own dark patch.

'Let's have a quick look at the programme. The Chorus is on at the beginning and right at the end of the performance. We can stand at the back and open and shut our mouths appropriately.'

'That's all very well, but does this bring us any nearer to the 'Black Knight' or my papers?'

'Let's see if this gives us anymore clues.' Jack waved the theatre programme in her face. 'This has some famous music hall stars — I remember my great-granddad telling me about some of these and singing the songs when he'd had a couple of whiskeys. Listen to this: *'Proudly presenting the famous comic, Alfred Vance with 'Champagne Charlie', 'the most magnificent, marvellous, magnanimous, memorable Miss Marie Lloyd with 'Oh Mr Porter'.*

'I've never heard of them. I don't see our 'Black Knight' on the list!'

'Hang on, what about this: *a terribly, terrifying, terrific tenor — introducing Mr John Grant in an extract from Offenbach's 'Blue Beard'?* That sounds more like our safe breaker, the role of a serial killer!'

Before they could discuss this further, there was a knock on the door. Yasmin opened it to find a short, dumpy man in a harlequin costume standing in the gloomy passageway.

'Hello, an addition to the chorus, I presume. Pleased to meet you, my dear.' A surprisingly deep voice came from the short, comical figure as he shook hands firmly.

'Please come in and meet Jack. We've been looking through the songs. It's rather nerve racking to be thrown in the deep end like this.'

'Good evening, Jack.' The plump Harlequin held out his hand. 'Welcome to Wilton's Music Hall. I'm George Lowell, singer, actor, chief cook, and bottle washer, whatever job is available,' he laughed loudly.

'Well, perhaps you could help us with a few of these songs.'

George had a rich baritone voice and half an hour later, Yasmin and Jack had mastered the basic popular tunes. As George turned to leave, Jack asked him, as casually as he could, whether he'd met John Grant alias 'Blue Beard'.

George's amiable expression suddenly changed. 'All I can say is he fits the role perfectly. You can judge for yourselves; that's his dressing room two doors down. See you in ten minutes.'

As they walked down towards the backstage area, both felt nervous. Thirty minutes had not been enough time to practise four or five songs. Their thoughts were suddenly interrupted by the sight of a man unlocking the dressing room two doors down, which George Lowell had mentioned. He turned to pick up a black briefcase.

Jack knew the sallow face, the thin lips, the sneering look, the impatient hand throwing aside the padded doublet. He felt her excitement as Yasmin squeezed his hand tightly. They both recognised the 'Black Knight'!

* * *

The curtain came down for the interval. The opening chorus had gone well, considering the brief rehearsal. They had managed to bluff their way through reasonably convincingly. Seeing the Victorian audience in an array of top hats, cloth caps, silk scarves and brightly coloured straw bonnets join in the popular choruses had been exhilarating.

It was time now to tackle 'Blue Beard' in his den. Jack pushed the door slowly open. 'Blue Beard' sat at a table studying a sheaf of papers, a pencil in one hand, a wine glass in the other. Jack noticed the briefcase at his side. A lamp lit his sharp features and threw shadows on his thin face. Dressed in black tie and tails, his sallow skin and gaunt features were all the more striking.

Grant looked up briefly from his writing. 'You're in the wrong room.'

'I think not. We have come to collect our papers.'

Something in Jack's voice alerted Grant. He stood up behind the table, gathering the papers together. He reached for a paper knife gleaming threateningly on the table. Yasmin stifled a scream.

At the same moment, a furry white bomb exploded behind her. Unnoticed, Bullseye, seeing the open door, had wandered in. He leapt on the table, his jaws locking on to Grant's throat. In seconds, the white shirt was red with blood. Grant was unable to speak. An ugly, jagged gash had opened at the side of his neck.

Jack seized the briefcase, stuffing in the loose papers. He ran for the door, Yasmin close behind. Bullseye released Grant, who slumped over the table like a rag doll.

* * *

The week-long International Conference in Beijing was coming to a close. Dr Yasmin Hardy and Professor Jack K Wolfstein looked over the heads of the hundreds of delegates.

'Just looking down on the array of headgear is amazing,' Yasmin whispered behind her hand. 'Turbans, kippot, keffiyehs, gutras, and others I don't recognise.'

'Reminds me of our 'harlequin' days. So many hats on so many heads, just so long as we don't have to sing,' Jack laughed quietly. 'I hope Bomber's not pining too much. We're no sooner back than we're away again.'

'Yes, but he loves living with the students. Lots of treats and long, rambling walks. I hope he's forgotten the way to that passage in the forest.' Yasmin's voice sounded anxious.

'He's probably gone through the back of our wardrobe or followed a white rabbit down a burrow.'

There was a sudden hush in the conference room, followed by lengthy applause as the President of the Climate Change Convention entered the stage. After discussing the agreements reached by the nations attending the conference, which included China, Russia, India, Iran, Saudi Arabia and the United States, she went on to outline the progress made through international cooperation.

'I should particularly like to mention the work of Dr Yasmin Hardy of Cambridge University. Her work in dendrology has been invaluable in our efforts to save our rain forests. As a result of years of work in the laboratory and in the field, Dr Hardy has developed a new type of tree which reaches maturity in five years and can replace forests lost to cattle farming and the timber industry within a decade.'

As Yasmin stood up to acknowledge the lengthy applause, Jack whispered, 'Don't forget, you've still got to shell the peas for the *pottage* this evening!'

Becoming a Bard

"I am in this earthly world; where to do harm is often laudable,
to do good sometime accounted dangerous folly."
Macbeth, Act 4, Scene 2

Cassandra Arnold

We didn't learn much from Covid-19.

The next pandemic was a harsher lesson.

It was months before I was willing to leave the compound, when the others promised me that the dead would be nothing but bones bleaching in the sun. On that first walk, I bent to pick up a vertebra, turning it over and over in hands that shook only a little. Years before, when tourism was still possible, I'd visited the 16th-century whaling station in Labrador. I could see it still: all those skeletons on the shore, relics of a time long gone—an era no one had ever imagined ending.

Now we were apparently planning a celebration—a one-year-post-apocalypse survival party.

"Write us a poem, Merlin," Harry said, a slice of acorn bread halfway to his mouth, a mug of my spruce-tip tea steaming beside him. "You know, like the old bards did. For their heroes."

I suppressed a snort, gazing around at the people slouched at breakfast. *Yeah, right. Heroes.*

Harry, ex advertising entrepreneur, had built the place, a state-of-the-art survival pod nestled in the shadow of the Rocky Mountains not far from Banff. Like skiing was ever going to be a thing again.

The bunker was circular, buried three metres underground, the entrance camouflaged from intruders. The top level contained the decontamination rooms, kitchen, living space, dining area, and sick bay—my Cinderella bedroom. The next two floors down held the six main suites—each with its own bathroom, office space, and personal library. And below that, finally, the weapons stash, seed bank, and Amish-inspired staples hoard.

Noise echoed around the room. The place was all gloss white paint and chrome; no wall hangings or carpets to soften the sounds of bread being sliced, drinks slurped, snark being volley-balled across invisible nets of status.

Harry's clique dripped with high-class vowels and the memory of wealth: Vee Somerset, who had sold him the bunker and the dream of escaping the coming meltdown; Elliott Cockshutt, scion of that famous family, so a shoe-in as a PR and political strategist; Felix Grant, a tech bro who'd stolen every idea he'd ever sold, flanked by Camille Rousseau, who'd squeaked in by being the beautiful influencer on his arm when the shit hit the fan.

She was one rank up from me. I hadn't been on the guest list in any guise. I was just the working man who'd been setting up the electric systems when the lockdown came.

They could have thrown me out, I reminded myself yet again. *There is that.*

I took a sip of tea, the flavour at last not making my mouth pucker with every sip, and pondered the last member of the team sitting at the far end of the room, Dr. Lillian Osler. I supposed Harry hadn't realized that a medic specializing in genetic modifications wasn't going to be a whiz as a first aid officer. Good job I had a certification.

"Yeah," Harry said now, his lips curling in a sneer. "The party's next Saturday. Get scribbling."

The others all laughed, although Camille stopped quickly, her cheeks flushing. Maybe she knew who Merlin actually was.

God, I used to hate my parents for the name they chose. What was wrong with something ordinary, like my brothers got? Bill and Jack. Couldn't get plainer than that. Now—

Well, now, frankly, there were worse things to be pissed about.

I pushed back from the table and stood, leaning forward so Harry had to look up into my face. "Sure, Boss. Let me know what the rest of the acts are, and I'll make a poster and a genuine cake."

* * *

Later that night, I was lying in my sick-bay cubicle thinking about the proposed party when there was a soft knock on the door. I stood and adjusted my shirt. This was new, and if the experience of the last year had taught me anything, it was that new was often bad.

Quickly, I took the two strides the room allowed me and slid the door aside.

Camille stood there with a large book in her outstretched hands, her expression uncertain "Um, I thought you might like this," she said, a quiver in her voice. "You know, for the poem."

I must have looked blank, as she rushed on, her words tumbling out, the opposite of her usually polished delivery. "It's Shakespeare... the collected works. Felix said to bring something to read, and I thought... well, maybe it would help you."

She swallowed, and looked down at the floor, her voice dropping to a whisper. "They called him the Bard too. I know people think

I'm stupid, but I have an English Major. I know about literature and history... Merlin... Taliesin..."

Dumbfounded, I swallowed back a lump in my throat. This was the first act of kindness I'd witnessed in all these long months. How different it might have been to have been holed up with people of my choosing, people who shared my dreams for life.

The weight of the book felt strange in my hands. I looked around the space awkwardly. "Ah, do you want to—?"

She flushed and took a small step backwards, glancing over her shoulder. "No, no. I'd better get back." A tiny smile lifted her lips as she gestured at the book. "Have fun."

As she walked swiftly away, I rubbed at the frown creasing my forehead. What had that been all about? Had she changed or had I misjudged her all along?

* * *

Supplies were the big problem.

They shouldn't have been. There'd been a brochure lying about the day I started work on the pod, so I knew the bunker had been built to hold '*a delicious range of nutritious and shelf-stable meals to keep all of you in great condition for a better future.*'

I also knew whoever had manufactured them had scrimped too much on the packaging. The seals had started failing a few months in. I'd nearly been shot as the messenger when I discovered the problem and reported it to the team. No prizes for guessing I didn't just sleep on the floor of the medical bay, but was also the chief—and only—cook and bottle washer.

Eventually, blaming me for the shortages became too stupid even for them, and I started foraging.

You never know when random skills become gold to be mined later:

summers at camp making fires and shelters, a student job cooking for a tree planting camp, a permaculture design course where I'd specialized in the wild foods of Alberta.

It felt good to flex my hands, use long-dormant skills, and get natural vitamin D back into my system. Still, I was one person, and we were all getting skinnier, the heroes being apparently better at boasting than actually hunting.

* * *

A day later, I mentally reviewed the trap run I was going to check and reset as I opened the heavy door to the forest. It hadn't taken long for the predators of the area to scout me out. I lost more jack rabbits to bobcats, foxes or wolves than I managed to keep for our table.

The morning was crisp and clear, a touch of frost on the fallen leaves. Thank God we'd still had industrial food during the worst of our first winter. I kicked the ground as I walked, suppressing the urge to grind my teeth. *A celebration.* Ha. Didn't the idiots know we were unlikely to survive the coming season unless they got off their gold-plated butts and pitched in?

The wind soughed through the pines, and I shivered as I passed more bones. Not human, but enough to disturb me. I'd been reading Camille's gift in spare moments. She'd underlined passages in soft pencil strokes, showing more of herself to me than maybe she realized.

The Tempest was one of her favourites, Macbeth currently mine. I nudged the little skull that lay half buried in leaves at my feet, muttering slowly:

> *"Thy bones are marrowless, thy blood is cold;*
> *Thou hast no speculation in those eyes*
> *Which thou dost glare with—"*

I broke off, the hairs on the back of my neck rising. There was a footprint on the track ahead of me. I tiptoed forward and knelt, my breath ghostly in the still air. Reaching out, I traced the imprint on the ground with a questioning finger. It was slightly smaller than mine, the ridges clearly those of a hiking boot, worn but recognizable. A woman then. Were there *people* here?

Were they watching me?

I sat back on my heels, looking about me, sniffing the air. I couldn't hear or smell anything different. The birds were silent, but then there were so few of them left that their songs were no longer a guide to the presence of danger in their territory.

And this was danger. I had no doubt of that. To me, to us, to whoever had moved into our territory. I didn't trust Harry's gang to react well to other survivors.

Squinting against the low rays of the sun, I walked slowly forward, following the tracks, my heart pounding, my hand on my knife.

After about a kilometre, I came to the clearing I'd named Chickadee Grove, and there I saw her. A woman, her pants and jacket loose around her, crouched beside the first of my snares, her back to me, her arms moving as she loosened the wire and put *my* rabbit into *her* gathering bag.

Dammit, we needed that food.

I must have grunted or gasped aloud. She rose and turned in one fluid movement, her hand falling to the hunting knife at her belt. A crossbow lay at her feet.

My mind flashed to our well-stocked weapons room. *Stupid.* In the early days, I'd always come out well prepared.

Urgently, I held up both hands, palms out, as she bent down and picked up her weapon, a bolt already loaded.

"Put your weapon on the ground," she said, her voice clear and steady.

Self-defense was one thing that I didn't have in my arsenal. My hand moved to drop the knife, then I hesitated. What's the phrase they use? *The straw that broke the camel's back?* Suddenly, twelve months of acquiescing, of being agreeable to save my skin twisted in my gut.

"No." The word echoed back from the trunks of the centuries-old trees surrounding us. "I mean you no harm. I won't tell my—the others—that I met you. But keep away from here." Light glinted off the metal of the bow. I was in range. I knew that much. My pulse hammering in my ears, I gestured at the game bag swinging from her shoulder and took a deep breath, forcing myself to go on. "I'm sure you're hungry, but it isn't safe for you here. You have to leave."

Her face twisted in surprise, and she lowered the bow halfway toward the ground.

Before I could second guess myself, I turned away and began to walk, my mouth dry as bone.

She's pretty, I thought illogically, as my shoulder blades twitched, expecting the bolt to land there any moment, but with the self-control Harry and his cronies had forced me to develop, I did not look back.

* * *

It was two days before I left the bunker again. Days I spent forcing a smile to quips about my forthcoming rise to bardhood, delighting in the words of the master playwright, wondering about Camille, and above all, thinking about the woman I'd met in the forest.

She couldn't be alone. She couldn't have come from very far away either.

I didn't dare mention our meeting. I'd listened to enough of the cronies' conversations to imagine their reaction, to imagine her in their hands.

But I couldn't stop foraging, even if she might have an aggressive group of her own behind her. Even if I was wrong about the vibe she'd had about her.

I stood a long time staring at the array of arms in the weapons room, before throwing up my hands in disgust and leaving with only my knife again. Nothing I could bring with me would win against a group of them, and who would I become by trying?

With a sudden surge of sympathy for Hamlet, I clenched my jaw and pushed the exit door open, blinking in the afternoon light.

I was only just out of sight of our fancy hole in the ground, when the rabbit stealer stepped onto the path in front of me, flanked by two others dressed in similar fashion. They were lean, taller than she was. Men? Hard to make out under the shapeless clothes.

A twig snapped behind me and I turned, realizing too late that it was a trap. A child capered just out of my reach, cackling delightedly as strong hands grabbed me from behind. A voice I recognized spoke softly into my ear as the woman wrapped a blindfold securely into place. "Don't struggle. I will guide you."

There was no point yelling. No one would hear me. With her hand on my elbow, I walked, trying to persuade my breath to come steadily, my heart to stop pounding.

Past the part of the trail I could recognize even with my eyes bound, they did the old trick of spinning a captive round to disorient them. Damn me if it wasn't effective. The irritating child cackled again as I staggered when they'd finished.

All the usual post-apocalypse scenarios flashed through my mind as we walked: re-purposed summer camps or vineyards; a fortified barn and farmhouse; another bunker like Harry's? I shivered at the thought and tried to steady my breath.

After what felt like hours of climbing and descending ridge after ridge of hills, we came to a sudden stop. The woman removed the blindfold. I swiveled my head from side to side, blinking in the sudden light.

We stood on the edge of a circle of mud-brick buildings, surrounding raised garden beds and wooden play equipment. A handful of children stared at me silently, their mouths agape.

Looking further, I saw a complex of state-of-the-art prefab buildings, turbines turning lazily in the breeze. Solar panels covered the warm, south-facing sides of two huge barns splashed green by climbing vines. Beans? Peas? I couldn't tell. Rusting Volkswagen Kombi vans were a bizarre note in the composition.

"This place..." I murmured. They must have planned as meticulously as we did.

A tap on my arm brought me back to the moment.

My captor was standing close beside me, the others a respectful distance to the side. Non-threatening. I let out a sigh, feeling my shoulders relax.

"I'm Sophia," she said, her blue eyes soft, a smile on her lips. "Let me tell you about our home."

Her mother was born there, she said. Her grandparents had started the place way back in the 1970s. Harmony Homestead. A draft-dodgers paradise. It hadn't been easy. Most of them were college graduates with not a practical skill between them. Some left within a few months, others after a winter or two. The rest had stayed decades until they became too old, then the place had been used for only occasional summer reunions. After Covid, a group of the descendants had seen the writing on the wall and renovated the place just in time.

I turned to stare around me. The place glowed in the evening sun. "How many have come since... the dying?"

She scuffed her toes in the dirt, wrapping her arms around a small girl who had come to lean against her, dropping a kiss on the child's head. "Not many. We're a long way out. There's nothing to bring them here. We did try going to the city to look for survivors but—"

She tailed off, giving the child a gentle pat on the buttocks. "Go and tell Will we have a guest."

"New people do join from time to time," she continued, tilting her head to one side, her eyes twinkling. "You perhaps?"

Too many possible answers surged into my throat. I choked, to the delight of the other sniggering children creeping closer.

Sophia smacked me on the back. "You think we didn't know you were there?" She shook her head. "We watched the place get built, saw you all go in."

Then she frowned and looked at me, a question in her eyes. "But only you have ever searched for food."

I snorted. "Yeah, well, I wasn't meant to be there you see, so I'm kind of like... like..." Analogies were failing me.

"Useful? Expendable?" she suggested dryly, a smile twitching her lips.

I rolled my eyes. "Yeah, exactly. Exactly that."

* * *

It was a long night. I tossed and turned. Apparently, a soft bed was now out of my comfort zone. I lay there listening to the sounds of the building and reflected on the evening. Long tables full of chattering families at dinner. Children all the shades of coffee I could imagine, parents just as diverse. A far cry from Harry's selection of those fit to survive a catastrophe.

Sophia had invited me to join them. "Give us your answer in the morning," she'd said. "If it's no, we'll guide you back."

Did I believe her? Yes. Was that sensible? Possibly not. Because this place wasn't so different, was it? It was another enclave for the select few who had both seen disaster coming and had the means to prepare for it.

What about my friends, my family? I had no illusions that any of them had survived. My mother, still working at the hospital as a cleaner, my dad, so proud of my education and how I'd paid for it with summer jobs and frugal living. He could have been something more than a taxi driver if he hadn't been an immigrant. My sister, singing since before she could walk, with her scholarship to varsity and her determination to succeed. I rolled over, squeezing my eyes shut. I'd shed more than my share of tears for them all, surely.

Both Bill and Jack had joined the army, the best route out of small-town poverty if you weren't smart or talented. They might have survived. Be out there, doing something useful to set the world to rights.

But yeah, that wasn't a totally benign thought, was it? Because going back to normal was what we'd all done for decades as we ignored all the warnings.

We didn't need that.

We needed something new, something better.

My decision made, I finally slept.

* * *

In the morning, it took a while to get my hosts to agree to my plan. They considered me from along the wooden dining table.

"She gave you a book, and now you want to rescue her?" The tone in their voices said exactly what they thought, and true, the whole party poem thing sounded ridiculous, but I knew I was right.

"Camille isn't one of them either," I said again. "I can't leave her."

"Does she have any skills?" The man who asked looked like a biker reborn as a compost hero.

"She's *human*," I snapped, losing patience. "She deserves better than starving when I leave."

"And the others don't?"

It wasn't Sophia who asked but I looked at her anyway and saw the doubt in her eyes.

"They—" I looked down, my hands clenching into fists in my lap. "They were part of the elite that created this mess."

I lifted my head and stared at them all in turn. "They could learn to feed themselves. They just haven't tried. And I enabled them."

I swallowed, shame threatening to engulf me. I had allowed them to mistreat me. Allowed them to continue leeching off people like me, who they despised.

My heart hammered in my chest as the silence stretched on. I opened my mouth to speak again, but, really, what more could I say?

"Go back today," said Sophia softly. "Write your poem. We'll be waiting to guide you here the morning after the party." She paused, staring at the others as if daring them to gainsay her. "You, and whoever you choose to invite."

* * *

The man escorting me was silent as we walked. The rough-textured blindfold he'd used covered my eyes and nose. It smelt of cabbage and compost and hope.

I kept my hand on his arm, listened to our footfalls on the soft ground of the forest. The snap of twigs. The crunch of fall leaves. Our labouring breaths as we climbed and descended, climbed and descended. Sweat stuck my shirt to my back, trickled under the cloth and into my eyes. I kept my curses strictly silent.

How was I going to get out of this mess? I'd been away all night. They must have noticed. No dinner. No breakfast.

Jack was the storyteller in our family. He'd have thought of a dozen plausible excuses before he'd crested the first ridge. My mind was still blank as I struggled to untie the cloth after my guide left me by the thunder of a waterfall. Not easy to hear where he went that way. Not easy to pick up his trail over the shattered rocks that lay at the foot of the drop.

Not easy actually to find my way back.

* * *

Softly, I pushed the exterior door of the bunker open and crept toward the kitchen, a frown creasing my forehead. Someone was singing. A soft voice with a Quebecois lilt.

Pausing in the entrance, I looked around. Camille was alone. Rolling what looked like flatbreads on the stainless-steel table.

She turned and held a finger up to her lips, gesturing toward my sick-bay cubicle with a floury hand. "I said you were ill. Didn't know if it was contagious. Go inside. When you hear them come for lunch, cough a bit, groan, whatever. But not too dramatic! We don't want Harry to insist his 'doctor' go take a look."

I stared at her, bewildered. "But—"

She shook her head, lips pressed tight together and turned her back. Her song followed me as I left.

* * *

I used more than my share of battery power over the next few days, typing and erasing draft after draft of that damned poem.

I didn't *have* to do it. No one could force me. But how often was there a chance like this? To say something real, something that might strike a spark, turn these people—these *leeches*—into something close to actual heroes?

And I cooked. A cake, as promised, using some of the last of the wheat flour, dried apple, cinnamon, and powdered eggs and milk. Not quite my mother's version, but in her honor all the same. Then a stew with carrots, potatoes, and jerky, flavoured with wild garlic and thyme. The root vegetables had been a last-minute suggestion, apparently. Stored in damp sand left over from construction, they'd lasted. A rare stroke of foresight from people who had planned for everything *except* actually living here.

Camille didn't come knocking again. Didn't offer to help me in the kitchen. But she caught me looking at her more than once, and when we passed in the corridor, she gave a sharp shake of her head. A warning? A dismissal? Maybe both. She disappeared down to her luxury level before I could speak.

The others continued their jeering and taunts.

I continued struggling with what I knew and all its implications.

Invite was a loaded term actually.

If I told Camille and she betrayed me, I'd have lost my only chance at escape and put Sophia and her homestead in danger to boot.

If I didn't tell her, how was I going to get her out of the compound? Where would we hide?

That one I could solve. Telling everyone I was foraging as usual, I spent the morning before the party building a camouflaged shelter under a fallen spruce. It wouldn't have won a season of Alone, but it would do for one night.

Try as I might, I didn't catch anyone watching me.

* * *

Party implies something, doesn't it? Food and drink, obviously. Fun, usually. Friends, normally. Not that night.

Harry had gone to great lengths to get dressed up. So had the others. It hadn't occurred to me to even think about clothes. I'd certainly never imagined they had brought evening wear to a survival bunker. But they had.

Tuxedos for the men, slinky dresses for Dr Lillian and Camille, and a silk trouser suit for Vee, who'd always liked to keep the media guessing.

And then there was me. Jeans, T-shirt, hiking boots, overgrown beard and scissor-cut hair.

Harry strode to the makeshift podium in the living space and the others stood in a circle and clapped. They were *coiffed*. Manicured. Groomed. How did they do that shit?

I stared at my hands, the nails chipped, dirt ingrained in the whorls of my prints, the creases of my wrists.

Felix was handing round glasses of actual champagne. *Unbefuck-inglievable*. Like they'd scripted themselves as heroes in a video game.

Shaking my head, I headed to the kitchen to get the tray of mushroom pate on toast.

Heck, but they were a long way from winning the boss level that night.

From the living space, I could hear the chant begin, as the revelers stamped their feet and tinkled knives against their glasses.

BARD. BARD. BARD.

Camille was there behind me when I turned to go back. She reached out a slender hand to stop me, a waft of perfume tickling my nose.

"*Et tu, Brute?*" I muttered, not entirely under my breath.

She ignored that, her eyes searching my face for a long moment.

"I saw you taken," she whispered at last, her face tense. "Why did you come back?"

We had only seconds before they would look for us. There was nowhere to hide. No time to craft a delicate response. Only flashing images of Sophia and her friends cooking together, those children laughing, their eyes sky bright.

"For you," I said. "And to give them a chance."

Words aren't always weapons, but I had just studied a master in drama and politics, innuendo and subtext.

Let them listen if they could.

I knew that when the party ended, for the first time in a year, I wouldn't be running away but toward.

Moss Everlasting

Carys Owen

He pulled the moss into his gathering pouch and hopped away across the forest clearing. It was the start of a new star cycle and the sky glowed pink with the budding light. Magnus imagined himself all alone in the Braelock Woods and headed for his favourite hollow to unpack the moss.

His skill as a Moss-weaver was second to none and all the village beings knew he'd learned this magic from his beloved grandparents-Olig and Nan. The tradition of weaving beds of moss passed down the generations of the Bronglyd Kin—their three nimble fingers adept at combing the greenery and their long toothy snouts perfect for pushing errant strands into place.

Each bed was shaped for the Asker and hidden messages were often embedded in the design- a little acorn for the carpenter, a tiny dragonfly for the storyseller, a winding ribbon for the pathmaker.

Today's bed gave Magnus pause to think as he had been tasked with creating a Bobbin Bed for the newest member of the Bronglyd Kin. She was a tiny ball of fur and spikes, in all the colours of a sunbeam on water; her long snout already reaching out for morsels of higgleberry and halfmoon fruit.

At the Naming River a message had floated on the waters declaring this little one to be Etherea and a song arrived on the wind to welcome her.

In a community without hierarchy, she was the latest equally important member and the asking of a moss bed was a hallowed rite of passage. She would be starting her journey to discover her own world at a little distance from her four parents.

Magnus considered the options as he laid out the lush green fern-moss alongside the pale grey-green strands of wolfsbeard. The bed would need to be tall at the sides to protect the precious cargo yet peppered with peepholes to let the light in and allow the love to flow back and forth. He envisaged a swirling pattern of tiny holes to delight the tiny occupant as she fell in and out of sleep.

The choice of materials reached back countless star cycles and, like all magical crafts, offered sustainability hand-in-hand with exquisite beauty; the gift of the moss being that it lives forever and though it may be thirsty in dry times, it rebounds with vigour when the first mists arrive.

Magnus worked in a steady rhythm, humming the mending tunes Olig and Nan had given him at their passing. He felt especially close to them as he pushed and eased the fibres of moss in and around, through and under, singing the ancient words:

'*Moss soft and green*
  A bed for your cares
  A safe place to rest
  Moss everlasting

Moss strong and green
  A pillow for your bones
  A gift from the trees
  Moss evermore'

The only reply Magnus heard was a quiet whoop from a gillymarcher as she strutted through the long grass in search of tasty seeds.

The time had come for him to add a signature unique to this Bobbin Bed. Following the swirling holes of the star design Magnus fashioned two crescent moons of wolfbeard moss to always shine on the little one within.

The promise of the Two Moons was a great comfort to this tiny planet nestled in the Farlong galaxy. The story of two sisters who had flown to the sky to oversee the trees and rivers was told to little ones every night. And Etherea would be no exception.

Finally, Magnus sat back on his long bushy tail and admired his handiwork. He had learned to be happy with his creations and to trust that each one would be just right for the Asker. His next job would be to call on the Song-knitter to stitch Etherea's song into a quilt with thread so fine and colours so vibrant they could only come from the oldest magic.

Astrea lived a little way off by the waterfall. Her whole life was held in the sound of running water. As the Song-knitter, she had already heard Etherea's song being sung by the river and had memorized it lovingly:

'*Little one, you are the one*
   sent to remind us
   how to live well
   how to love the trees

Little one, you are the one
   sent to show us
   how to live like a river
   how to be together'

As Magnus wandered down to the riverbank, the Bobbin Bed cradled in his slender arms, he spotted Astrea tending to her water garden abundant with flowers and fruits. She saw him approach and waved a furry hand.

'Hey Magnus, long time no weave,' she joked in her warm and welcoming way.

'Yup, I guess it's been a while. The star-frosts were hard this year and the moss lay sleeping.'

'Come on in, we'll take a drink from the Bronglyd River, if she's agreeable.'

And with that the two friends headed into Astrea's riverbank home amongst the fern rushes.

* * *

By the light of the next twin moon, the forest community gathered by the ancient Papyon Tree to witness the giving of the Bobbin Bed and to hear Etherea's song once again. Astrea stood off to the side, her singing staff in hand, illuminated by a multitude of candle bugs. Magnus had already faded into the shadows after setting his gift in the clearing.

It was time for the star to appear. Her parents emerged from the circle to set Etherea at the centre and create an inner circle around her.

All four had taken turns to hatch the single egg in their nest and so shared in the birth and nurturing of their dearest little one. They joined hands and gazed on Etherea with pure love and joy.

Etherea giggled with surprise to feel the softness of the moss and to see the twinkling of lights around her head. Unaware of the promise her new life held for the Bronglyd Kin she snuggled down and closed her sleepy eyes. Oohs and aahs arose from the gathering and everyone sat on the soft meadow grass to partake in Etherea's moment.

The Moon Sisters reached their height in the pink and purple sky as

Astrea sang and the forest listened.

'*Little one, you are the one*
  sent to remind us
  how to live well
  how to love the trees

Little one, you are the one
  sent to show us
  how to live like a river
  how to be together'

The Bronglyd Kin remained scattered around Etherea until the purple faded to palest pink and a new star cycle began. Some of them snoozed and others kept watch, though in truth there were few dangers. Magnus was one of this number and sat with a warm glow in his chest, the words of Olig and Nan echoing in his heart: 'A gift given freely becomes its own reward'.

He would often look back on this ceremony and recall the perfect balance of friendship and individual skills that came together to make a community of kindness; grateful that Etherea grew and flourished to become a loving and curious being who one day- many star cycles later- came to his work tree to ask about the ways of the Moss-weaver.

The Fall of Julian Frost

Emecheta Christian

T he neon-drenched streets of Neo Atlanta pulsed with an enthralling energy, a burst of light and shadows that never truly slept. Amidst the lofty high-rise building and soaring billboards, 32-year-old Bao Chen steered through the crowded sidewalk, her bright blue eyes fixed on the augmented reality display floating before her.

"Come on, come on," she muttered, fingers dancing through the air as she angrily typed lines of code. The clock was ticking, and she knew the consequences of failure all too well.

Bao ducked into a narrow alley, the glow from her holo-display reflecting spooky shadows on the graffiti-covered walls. She leaned against the cool metal of a dumpster, trying to steady her breathing. The alley offered a brief respite from the sensory overload of the main streets, but it couldn't quiet the storm in Bao's mind.

Three days ago, her younger brother, Jin, had disappeared without a trace. No messages, no social media updates, nothing. It was as if he'd been erased from existence. But Bao knew better. In a world where the line between the virtual and the real had all but vanished, there were always digital breadcrumbs to follow.

Her fingers hurried across the invisible keyboard, iterating through layers of encryption and firewalls. She was close, so close to a breakthrough.

"Well, well. What do we have here?"

Bao's head snapped up, her heart leaping into her throat. At the mouth of the alley stood a tall figure, his features obscured by a sleek helmet. The red helmet glowed ominously in the dim light.

"Shit," Bao hissed, closing her holo-display with a flick of her wrist. She straightened up, trying to appear nonchalant. "Just catching up on some work emails. You know how it is."

The figure chuckled, the sound distorted by his helmet's audio system. "Cut the crap, Chen. We both know you're not some office drone." He took a step closer, and Bao instinctively backed up. "The boss wants a word with you."

Bao's mind raced. There was only one "boss" this goon could be referring to: Julian Frost, CEO of Xenus Corp and the most powerful man in Neo Atlanta. If Frost was involved, then her suspicions about Jin's disappearance were right on the money.

"Sorry," Bao said, a wry smile visible on her lips. "I don't do house calls." In one fluid motion, she reached into her jacket pocket and pulled out a small silver sphere. Before the enforcer could react, she hurled it at his feet.

The sphere exploded in a blinding flash of light and a deafening screech. The man stumbled backward, clutching at his helmet. Bao didn't waste a second. She sprinted past him, her augmented legs propelling her forward with inhuman speed.

She burst out onto the main street, navigating through the sea of pedestrians with practiced ease. Behind her, she could hear shouts and the telltale whine of hover-bikes revving to life. Bao gritted her teeth and pushed herself harder. She couldn't afford to get caught, not when she was so close to finding Jin.

As she ran, her mind drifted back to the last conversation she'd had with her brother. Jin had been excited, practically buzzing with nervous energy. He'd stumbled onto something big, he'd said. Something that could change everything.

"It's not just about living forever anymore, Bao," Jin had alleged, his eyes wide with a flicker of fear. "Frost is playing with fire. If he succeeds... God, I don't even want to think about it."

At the time, Bao had brushed off his concerns. Jin had always been prone to flights of fancy, always chasing the next big conspiracy theory. But now, with her brother missing and Frost's goons on her tail, she was starting to think that maybe, just maybe, Jin had been onto something big for real.

Bao ducked into a crowded nightclub, the pounding bass vibrating through her bones. She pushed her way through the horde of dancers, their bodies adorned with bio-luminescent tattoos that pulsed in time with the music. At the back of the club, she found what she was looking for: a maintenance door, its "Employees Only" sign flickering faintly.

With a swift glance over her shoulder to ensure she wasn't being followed, Bao pressed her palm against the door's biometric scanner. There was a moment of tense silence, then a soft click as the lock disengaged. She slipped inside, closing the door behind her.

The maintenance tunnels were a stark contrast to the raucous club she had just passed through. Here, the only illumination came from strips of LED lighting that ran along the floor. Bao moved quickly, her footsteps echoing in the narrow corridor.

After several twists and turns, she arrived at a nondescript metal door. To the untrained eye, it looked like any other utility closet. But Bao knew better. She tapped out a complex rhythm on the door's surface, then waited.

A moment later, the door slid open, revealing a hidden sanctuary. Banks of computers lined the walls, their screens displaying a dizzying array of data streams and code. In the center of the room stood a tall, lanky man with a shock of purple hair.

"Took you long enough," he said in a baritone voice. "I was starting to think Frost's goons had gotten to you."

Bao stepped inside, allowing herself a moment to catch her breath. "Nice to see you too, Flynn," she replied dryly. "And no, they didn't get me. But it was a close call."

Flynn nodded, his fingers already operating a keyboard. "Well, while you were out there playing tag with Xenus Corp's finest, I managed to decrypt that data packet Jin sent before he went dark." He gestured to one of the larger screens. "You're going to want to see this."

Bao moved closer, her eyes widening as she took in the information displayed before her. It was a schematic, incredibly complex, and unlike anything she'd ever seen before. At its center was what appeared to be a human brain, but it was surrounded by an intricate web of circuitry and nano-scale components.

"What... what am I looking at?" Bao asked, her voice barely audible.

Flynn's expression was grim. "If I'm reading this right—and I usually am—it looks like Frost has found a way to digitize human consciousness. Not just copy it like those corpus puppets used to do. I mean fully transfer a living mind into the Cloud."

Bao felt a chill run down her spine. The implications were staggering. "But that's... that's impossible. The human mind is too complex, too fragile. You can't just reduce it to ones and zeros."

"Apparently, Frost disagrees," Flynn replied. He pulled up another set of files. "And that's not all. Look at this."

The screen was filled with complex lines of code, interspersed with what looked like chemical formulas. Bao leaned in closer, her cybernetic eyes quickly scanning and processing the information.

"Is this... some kind of virus?" she asked, a burning sensation forming in her stomach.

Flynn nodded grimly. "A digital plague, more like. From what I can tell, it's designed to target augmented neural implants. Once it infects a host, it starts rewriting their neural pathways, making them more... susceptible to outside influence."

Bao's mind throbbed, connecting the dots. "Mind control," she breathed. "Frost isn't just trying to achieve immortality. He wants to create an army of digital slaves."

"Bingo," Flynn said. "And if he succeeds, there won't be a single augmented person on the planet who's safe. We're talking about the end of free will as we know it."

Bao clenched her fists, a mixture of anger and grit coursing through her. "Not if we stop him first," she said. "We need to find Jin. He must have more information, something we can use to bring Frost down."

Flynn nodded, turning back to his computers. "I've been running facial recognition scans across the city, trying to track Jin's movements before he disappeared. So far, nothing concrete, but—"

He paused, his eyes widening. "Wait a second. I think I've got something."

Bao leaned in, her heart pounding. On the screen was a grainy security camera image. It showed Jin, his face partially obscured, entering what looked like an abandoned warehouse on the outskirts of the city.

"When was this taken?" Bao asked urgently.

"Two days ago," Flynn replied. "It's the last confirmed sighting of him before he went dark."

Bao straightened up, a determined glint in her eye. "Then that's where we start. Send me the coordinates. I'm going in."

Flynn looked at her incredulously. "You can't be serious. That place is probably crawling with Frost's people by now. It's a suicide mission."

Bao was already moving towards the door, checking her gear. "Maybe," she conceded. "But Jin's my brother. I'm not abandoning him. And if we don't stop Frost now, there might not be another chance."

Flynn sighed, knowing there was no talking her out of it. "Fine. But you're not going in alone." He tapped a few keys, and a section of the wall slid open, revealing an impressive array of weaponry and gadgets. "Take whatever you need. And Bao?"

She paused, looking back at him.

"Be careful out there," Flynn said softly. "The world needs people like you and Jin. Don't let Frost win."

Bao nodded, a small smile appearing on her face. "Don't worry. I plan on making that coward regret the day he ever messed with the Chen siblings."

With that, she stepped out into the neon-lit night, ready to face whatever challenges lay ahead. The fate of free will itself hung in the balance, and Bao Chen was determined to tip the scales in humanity's favor.

As she disappeared into the crowded streets of Neo Atlanta, the city pulsated around her, oblivious to the war being waged in its shadows. But soon, very soon, the echoes of this battle would resonate through every corner of their augmented world.

The real question was: when the dust settled, would there be anyone left with a mind of their own to hear it?

* * *

The warehouse emerged before Bao, a massive silhouette against the neon-stained sky. Its rusted walls and broken windows spoke of abandonment, but Bao knew better. In Neo Atlanta, appearances were often deceiving.

She crouched behind a pile of discarded machinery, her enhanced vision scanning the perimeter. Two guards stood at the main entrance, their augmented arms gleaming in the moonlight. Automated drones buzzed overhead, their sensors sweeping the area in regular patterns.

Bao took a deep breath, centering herself. The gear Flynn had provided weighed heavily on her back, but it was nothing compared to the weight of her mission. Somewhere in that warehouse, Jin might be waiting. Or worse, Frost might be one step closer to unleashing his digital plague.

With practiced ease, Bao activated her cloaking device. Her form shimmered and then seemed to melt into the shadows. She moved silently, years of training guiding her steps as she approached the warehouse.

As she neared the guards, Bao reached into her pocket and pulled out a small disc-shaped device. She tossed it gently, watching as it rolled to a stop at the guards' feet. Before they could react, the disc emitted a soft pulse. The guards stiffened, then slumped to the ground, unconscious.

"Sorry, boys," Bao muttered. "Nothing personal."

She dragged the guards into the shade, then turned her attention to the door. The lock was a top-of-the-line biometric scanner, but Flynn had prepared for that. Bao pulled out a small vial of clear liquid and carefully applied it to her fingertips. The nanobots in the solution quickly rearranged themselves, replicating a set of fingerprints that Flynn had pulled from Xenus Corp's database.

The door slid open with a soft hiss, and Bao slipped inside.

The interior of the warehouse was a stark contrast to its dilapidated exterior. Rows of sleek servers hummed quietly, their blinking lights glowing throughout the space. Holographic displays flickered to life as Bao passed, showing streams of data that scrolled by too quickly for even her enhanced eyes to follow.

"Jin, what did you get yourself into?" Bao whispered, her unease growing with each step.

As she moved deeper into the facility, a sound caught her attention. Voices, muffled but growing clearer as she approached. Bao pressed herself against a wall, straining to listen.

"...the latest test results are promising, sir," a woman's voice said. "Subject 23 showed a 92% acceptance rate of the neural rewrite. With a few more adjustments, we should be able to achieve full compliance."

"Excellent," came the reply, a deep baritone that sent a chill down Bao's spine. She'd never heard it in person, but she'd seen enough broadcasts to recognize Julian Frost's voice. "And what of our... guest? Has he been more cooperative?"

There was a pause, then: "I'm afraid not, sir. He's proving quite resistant to our persuasion techniques."

Frost chuckled, a sound devoid of any real mirth. "Well, we'll see how long that lasts. Prepare him for the next phase. I want to test the full neural transfer protocol."

Bao's blood ran cold. They had to be talking about Jin. She needed to act fast.

Carefully, she peered around the corner. Frost stood with his back to her, his imposing figure clad in an immaculate white suit. Beside him was a woman in a lab coat, her hair pulled back in a severe bun. They were both looking at a large holographic display, which showed a 3D model of a human brain pulsing with electrical activity.

Bao's mind raced, calculating her options. She could try to take them both out now, but if she failed, she might never find Jin. No, she needed more information.

Silently, she slipped past them, following the corridor they had come from. It led her to a heavy security door, protected by another biometric lock. This time, however, the nanobot solution didn't work.

"Damn it," Bao muttered. She reached up to her ear, activating her secure comm link. "Flynn, you reading me?"

There was a burst of static, then Flynn's voice came through, tinny but clear. "Loud and clear, Bao. What's the situation?"

"I'm in, but I've hit a snag. There's a security door here that's not responding to the fingerprint spoof. Can you work your magic?"

She heard the clatter of keys as Flynn got to work. "Give me a sec... This firewall's a beast, but I think I can... Got it! You should have access now."

The lock chimed softly, and the door slid open. "You're a lifesaver, Flynn," Bao said.

"Just don't make me have to save your actual life, okay? Be careful in there."

Bao stepped through the door and froze. The room before her was filled with rows of large, cylindrical tanks, each filled with a pale-blue liquid. Floating in each tank was a human body, connected to a dizzying array of wires and tubes.

"Oh my god," Bao breathed, horror washing over her. These weren't just test subjects. These were people, their minds trapped in some sort of suspended animation.

She moved through the room, her eyes scanning each face, looking for Jin. Near the back, she finally found him. His eyes were closed, his expression peaceful, as if he were merely sleeping. But the electrodes attached to his skull told a different story.

Bao pressed her hand against the glass of Jin's tank. "I'm here, little brother," she whispered. "I'm going to get you out of here."

She turned to the control panel next to the tank, her fingers skillfully manipulating the interface as she tried to initiate the release sequence. But before she could finish, an alarm blared to life, red lights flashing throughout the facility.

"Intruder detected in Sector 7," an automated voice announced. "Security protocols engaged."

"No, no, no," Bao hissed, redoubling her efforts. But it was too late. The door behind her slid open, and she turned to see Julian Frost himself standing there, flanked by a squad of heavily armed security personnel.

Frost's lips curled into a sinister smile. "Ms. Chen, I presume? I must say, I'm fascinated you made it this far. But I'm afraid your little rescue assignment ends here."

Bao's hand inched towards the weapon at her hip, her mind racing to find a way out of this. But Frost's next words knocked her cold.

"I wouldn't do that if I were you," he said, gesturing to Jin's tank. "One wrong move and I'm afraid your brother might suffer a tragic malfunction in his life support systems."

Bao's hand fell to her side, defeat washing over her. She had come so close, only to fail at the final hurdle.

Frost stepped closer, his eyes beaming with triumph. "You know, Ms. Chen, you and your brother have caused me quite a bit of trouble. But I'm nothing if not opportunistic. Perhaps we can come to an arrangement that benefits us both."

"What are you talking about?" Bao spat, her voice dripping with venom.

Frost's smile widened. "Why, I'm offering you a chance to join us, of course. Your skills are impressive, and I could use someone of your capacity and talents in my organization. In return, I'll ensure your brother receives the very best care."

Bao's mind reeled. The offer was tempting, if only as a way to buy time and find another way to save Jin. But could she trust Frost to keep his word? And even if he did, could she live with herself knowing she was helping him enslave humans?

As she stood there, caught between impossible choices, Bao realized that this moment would define not just her future, but potentially the future of all augmented humanity. Whatever she decided, there would be no going back.

Time seemed to stretch as Bao stood there, her gaze darting between Frost's smug face and Jin's unconscious form floating in the tank. The weight of her decision pressed down on her, each second feeling like an eternity.

Finally, Bao spoke, her voice steady despite the turmoil within. "You know, Frost, for a supposed genius, you're making a pretty basic mistake right now."

Frost's eyebrow arched, curiosity playing across his features. "Oh? And what might that be, Ms. Chen?"

A smirk tugged at the corner of Bao's lips. "You're assuming I came here alone."

As if on cue, the lights in the facility flickered, then went out entirely. In the moment of darkness and confusion that followed, Bao sprang into action. Her augmented reflexes, honed by years of drilling, allowed her to move with inhuman speed.

She dropped a smoke grenade, filling the room with thick, obscuring vapor. The security team's shouts of confusion were quickly drowned out by the sound of shattering glass as the facility's sprinkler system activated, showering everyone with a fine mist.

But this was no ordinary water. As the droplets made contact with skin and clothing, they began to glow with a soft blue light. Nanobots, courtesy of Flynn's ingenious planning.

"What is this?" Frost sputtered, trying to wipe the glowing liquid from his face. "What have you done?"

Bao's voice came from somewhere in the smoke, confident and clear. "Oh, just a little insurance policy. Those nanobots are currently mapping every neural implant in this room, including that fancy wetware you've got hidden behind those designer eyes of yours, Frost. One wrong move, and we'll have access to every dirty secret in that twisted mind of yours."

The smoke began to clear, revealing Bao standing protectively in front of Jin's tank. Her eyes glowed an intense green, a sign that she was fully connected to the facility's systems through her neural link.

"Flynn, you getting all this?" she subvocalized.

"Crystal clear," Flynn's voice echoed in her mind. "I'm downloading everything as we speak. Frost's entire operation, laid bare. It's... it's unbelievable, Bao. The scale of what he was planning..."

Frost's composure cracked, a flicker of genuine fear crossing his face for the first time. "You don't understand what you're doing," he said, his voice losing its usual smooth confidence. "The technology we've developed here... it's the next step in human evolution. We could eliminate diseases, extend lifespans indefinitely, even transfer consciousness itself!"

"At the cost of free will?" Bao shot back. "By turning people into dolls for you to control? That's not evolution, Frost. It's slavery."

She turned to the security team, who stood uncertainly, their weapons lowered. "You've all got implants too, don't you? How does it feel, knowing your boss was planning to rewrite your minds, to turn you into his private army of drones?"

Murmurs of discontent rippled through the group. Frost's head of security, a burly man with extensive visible augmentations, stepped forward. "Is this true, sir?" he asked, his voice communicating betrayal.

Frost's eyes darted around the room, realizing he was losing control of the situation. "Don't be silly," he said, but his voice lacked conviction. "This woman is delusional, trying to turn you against me with wild accusations."

"Oh yeah?" Bao challenged. She gestured, and suddenly the air was filled with holographic displays, each showing snippets of Frost's secret files, test results, and plans for mass neural rewriting. "Still feeling delusional, Frost?"

The security team's weapons were now pointed squarely at Frost, their loyalty evaporating in the face of such damning evidence.

Bao turned her attention back to Jin's tank, trying to access the control panel. "Flynn, talk me through this. How do we get him out safely?"

"Working on it," Flynn replied. "These systems are complex, but... okay, got it. I'm sending you the sequence now. Be careful, Bao. The withdrawal process is delicate."

As Bao worked to free her brother, Frost made a desperate lunge towards a hidden panel on the wall. But before he could reach it, he was tackled to the ground by his own security chief.

"I don't think so, sir," the man growled. "You've got a lot of explaining to do."

The tank hissed open, and Jin's eyes fluttered. Bao caught him as he stumbled forward, weak, but alive. "Bao?" he mumbled, disoriented. "What... where am I?"

"It's okay, little brother," Bao said, tears of relief stinging her eyes. "You're safe now. It's over."

As if to punctuate her words, the sound of sirens filled the air. Police cruisers and news drones converged on the warehouse, their lights painting the night in red and blue.

"Cavalry's here," Flynn's voice chimed in Bao's ear. "I've sent them everything we've got. Frost is going down, and his whole operation with him."

Bao held her brother close, watching as Frost was led away in handcuffs, his empire crumbling around him. But even in this moment of victory, she knew their fight was far from over.

"Flynn," she said, "how much of Frost's research did we manage to save?"

"All of it," came the reply. "Why do you ask?"

Bao looked around at the rows of tanks, each holding a person whose mind had been tampered with. "Because we've got work to do. Frost might be stopped, but his technology is out there now. We need to find a way to use it for good, to help these people and make sure nothing like this ever happens again."

Jin, still leaning on her for support, managed a weak smile. "Always taking on the impossible, aren't you, sis?"

Bao grinned back. "Hey, someone's got to. Besides, with you and Flynn by my side, I'd say the odds are in our favor."

* * *

As dawn broke over Neo Atlanta, Bao Chen stood at the threshold of a new chapter. The battle against Frost was won, but the war for the future of augmented humanity was just beginning. She thought of all the minds that had been touched by Frost's experiments, of the massive power that technology held to both heal and harm. It was a daunting task that lay ahead, but as she looked at her brother and thought of Flynn waiting for them, Bao felt a surge of hope.

As they stepped out into the new day, leaving behind the details of Frost's twisted ambitions, Bao knew that whatever challenges lay ahead, they would face them together. In the end, it wasn't the technology in their heads or the augmentations in their bodies that would define humanity's path forward.

It was the choices they made, the bonds they forged, and the unwavering spirit that had driven them to fight against impossible odds. And in that spirit, Bao found a power greater than any neural implant or digital consciousness—the power of hope, of love, and the indomitable human will.

The sun climbed higher, its rays catching on the sleek surfaces of Neo Atlanta's high-rise buildings. The future was unwritten, full of both promise and peril. But with courage, compassion, and a little bit of high-tech ingenuity, Bao Chen and her team were ready to face whatever threat might come their way.

Chasing Storms

Loki Laats

T he poltergeist wouldn't shut up, so Jackie had given it the run of the house for now. It wasn't a problem—evening sunshine poured across the garden, and a cool wind rustled the leaves of nearby trees. She'd give the poor thing some time to cool off, and then go back in. Poltergeists were just confused, fractured spirits after all. Some, like today's guest, could be damn stubborn, but Jackie was too, so they were evenly matched. There had been more recently, but there were waves every year. Dead people were a lot like alive people— stubborn and messy as hell and refusing to file neatly.

She watched the leaves blowing for a few minutes in peace, then hauled herself to her feet. She heard the kitchen cabinets slamming. Too soon to go in yet. Instead, she clambered onto the roof. The valley stretched before her. She was settled right in the foothills of the Catskills, near the Susquehanna River. If she looked hard, she could see the remnants of asphalt and old houses.

Most of the established houses had simply been torn down and their materials repurposed as the community regrew. Solar panels dotted most of the roofs. She could see a team of skeletons on top of one of the roofs, repairing the panel. It'd been damaged in the storm yesterday. Summer sat at the bottom as expected, hands extended to either side of her as she focused on the movements of each skeleton. Tom, one of the engineers, stood next to her. She couldn't hear him, but Jackie knew he was instructing the skeletons through Summer. A few human engineers were up there too, double-checking the work. A little boy stood next to Tom, eagerly watching. Every so often he'd exclaim something, and the adults would laugh.

Jackie was way too young to have been alive during any of the Collapsing. She considered it a blessing, though she knew the Collapsing was not quite as calamitous as the name suggested. Wesley, the older hunter, had been young during the last years of it. According to her and the stories passed down, "the Collapsing" was a slow process, over decades, beginning in one century and ending in another. Many elders grumbled about such a dramatic name attached to such a protracted event, and Jackie wanted to honor that, but it was dramatic and commonplace, and she couldn't quite help herself.

The elders spoke of a time when nearly anything in the world could be attained quickly, so long as you could pay for it. Wes, too, had fuzzy but fond memories of "all I could ever want at my fingertips, the push of a button." No wonder people had difficulty letting it go. It sounded intoxicating. Things were slower now. Jackie couldn't watch TV shows from Korea or communicate instantaneously with anyone else no matter the distance. Traveling traders and messengers went around on solar powered trucks or cars, but they were much fewer and far between.

But at the same time, Jackie reasoned, nobody during the Collapsing or before it had what they had: genuine necromancy. The exact science behind controlling skeletons escaped Jackie, but Summer had summed it up like this: Skeletons could be powered by consuming something that gave them energy, just like living humans. Once people figured out how exactly to power a skeleton, they could control each skelly they powered. Each skelly only had a year, maybe two, of service

169

before it was laid to rest, and though there was no major overarching government, the objective truth of the matter was that anything that wasn't pure bone would spread diseases and thus shouldn't be used, on pain of everyone around you now refusing your business and company. Not every culture picked up necromancy, but many had.

Wesley emerged from her cabin and lingered slightly off from Summer. As one of the oldest and most important members of the community, Wes (often called "Auntie Wes" by the kids) had the unofficial authority to interrupt the proceedings. But Wesley was physically incapable of being rude and showed a particular disgust of interrupting others.

Luckily for Wes, the skellies and humans didn't work for too much longer. Summer called the skeletons, and the engineer called the humans, and they all congregated. It was then Summer turned in her chair. Jackie saw her wave to Wes and the older woman come forward to hand off a package. They briefly talked before Wes pointed over to *Jackie's house.* Jackie blinked, before realizing—Wes was going around handing out the dried meat people had ordered.

The two women were heading towards Jackie now. A skeleton fell neatly in line to push Summer's wheelchair. She hurried out to meet them, craving living (no disrespect to the skeleton) company. As she'd expected, Wes handed Jackie a package too with a smile.

"God, Wes, I don't know how we'd get on without you," Jackie said.

She now had a dilemma: she couldn't very well leave the meat outside to spoil in the sun but inside contained the damn poltergeist. Well, it was worth another shot trying to communicate with it.

"You'd figure it out, I'm sure," Wes said. "You're clever."

"Yeah, but then we'd have to *hunt* and *farm* and *prepare* by ourselves," Summer whined. "And I don't *wanna.*"

The two women both worked hard, but it was true that Wes's work was more physical than Summer's. She started to continue before stopping and frowning over Jackie's head. "It's a good thing when there are dark green clouds sweeping towards you against the wind, right? I think that's a good thing."

Wes frowned up at the sky like Summer. "I don't know what that is," she said with quiet horror. "Whatever it is, get inside. *Now.*"

Summer and Jackie locked eyes, then both hurried towards their homes. Behind her, Jackie heard Wes ringing the storm bell for just such an occasion. People had known even before the Collapse that climate change was going to accelerate before it calmed down. Now, people like Jackie had to deal with the severe storms and weather that seemed malevolent. But that was the price they paid for humanity leaving their scars on the planet, and the current humans were adapting as best they could to the natural chaos.

This, though. The sky being green was not necessarily unprecedented. It was known to do that sometimes during big storms, but these clouds were streaked with flickers of lime green through them. As Jackie started readying the house, the poltergeist barely shifted a chair. Jackie was silently grateful. Maybe the storm would scare it straight.

She was swiftly proven wrong. The poltergeist wasn't moving things anymore, but it was screaming like, well, the damned. "Would you be quiet?" she snapped.

The poltergeist rattled cabinet doors, then with apparent great difficulty picked up the pen she'd left for it and began to write in shaky letters.

NOTTME

"The hell you mean it's not you?" Jackie said. Maybe said. The screaming was so loud by now that she wouldn't have noticed if you popped a balloon in her ear. She slapped her hands over her ears, but that did nothing. Of course. The screaming was not just physical. It was psychic too. Which meant that there were a *lot* of angry ghosts in the area.

For a moment, Jackie was paralyzed. What could she do? The storm of ghosts—if that was indeed what was happening—was right above her. Wind smacked against her windows and roof. The screaming only got louder. And now the cabinets were shaking. The dishes inside danced madly along to the screeching of the ghosts. With needles in her ears, Jackie did the one thing she could think to do and took cover under her kitchen table. She'd intended to hold the legs as she'd seen people do for earthquakes, but ended up curled on the floor, useless hands over her stinging ears. Occasionally a mug or plate would break free from the cabinets and leap to crash on the floor, shattering into pieces.

After quite possibly years, the screaming died down. Jackie still lay there. This wasn't possible. It was every poltergeist she'd ever had to deal with coalesced into one entity. It didn't *happen*. Poltergeists were pieces of human consciousness fragmented by disease before death or death itself. They didn't get into groups. They most certainly didn't attach themselves to clouds.

Pounding on the door. Jackie yelped.

"It's Wes!" The call came from outside. "Jackie, can I come in? Are you alright?"

"It's unlocked," Jackie called back.

Wes let herself in and hurried upstairs. "Goodness. You, ah... stay there. Under the table or not, just stay away from the glass, alright? Where's your broom? I'll clean up."

By the time Wes was done, Jackie had collected herself enough to not only climb out from under the table but convince the equally confused innocent poltergeist to rest and move on.

She paced around the table (once it was shard-free), talking to Wes. "I mean, theoretically, spirits can band together just like the living do, but they aren't really *whole* enough to do that. Most are just perpetually confused. They don't do whatever the hell that was."

"Walk and talk." Wes headed out and Jackie followed her.

The damage seemed minimal, and people were now standing outside, holding their hands out as if testing for rain, asking each other what happened. Many turned a questioning eye to Jackie, but she always shook her head. They always looked disappointed. If the spirit ambassador didn't know what was going on, nobody did.

Talking to ghosts didn't require an innate talent or special equipment (mostly) like people apparently used to think. It was still an incredibly rare skill, and most people could never dream to be one, for the same reason there are very few nuclear physicists. Tapping into the spirit world was a fine-point art, one not helped by the layers upon layers of media and folklore giving people preconceived notions about what one does. If you asked Jackie, she would tell you that her mind was like a radio tuned to the spirit world. She would also launch into a diatribe of incredibly field-specific jargon, which was why most people did not ask Jackie. But the upshot most people understood was that Jackie was smart and knew what was happening.

As had been established, she did not! At all. With a mixture of disappointment and relief, Summer clearly didn't either.

"What in the absolute fuck was that?!" she said by way of greeting as she wheeled up to the two. "I've been asking around. Nobody's hurt bad. Couple'a scrapes or bruises. Lotta people are shaken up, but nothing we won't recover from. I think. Jackie—"

"No idea. Do you have anything? No. No. Okay." She carefully lowered herself onto a bench. "I hate this, actually." Controlling skeletons didn't go so far into the theoretical as talking to spirits did, but it was hard and specific work of its own, and Jackie was perturbed to see the other post-death expert as baffled as she was herself.

"I'm the only non-expert here," Wes began, "but Summer and Jackie, did you learn anything at all about storms or wind that target the dead when you were learning your trades?"

Both women shook their heads.

"But it's possible we're forgetting something," Jackie said.

"Speak for yourself," Summer replied with a soft laugh. Jackie couldn't help but grin. "Or maybe there's been research on it since we left. We should go to the college, see what they have. Worst-case scenario, we talk with the experts and get their help figuring out what the hell happened."

Though pre-Collapse colleges had largely been overly expensive and gatekeepers of knowledge, they did *have* knowledge, and they *were* distributing that knowledge to folks who could pay. Nowadays, they were places to continue preserving that knowledge and continue teaching—though the classes they taught and the knowledge they held were free to anyone who walked onto campus.

"It would be a two, three-day hike from here," Wes said. "We can take the road, though, so Summer can do it, and we can try to hitch a ride with a trader or something if we come across one."

Summer called up a skeleton, who took her chair handles. Preparations were made, and the next morning, the three embarked.

It was a long trip, but a good one. Autumn was just beginning to make an appearance. Fall came and went fast these days, so Jackie did her best to appreciate it while it was here. The road was littered with the occasional pre-Collapse wreck, but otherwise clear. People before and during the Collapse *had* tried to prevent everything from going to what they would have perceived as hell, so the highway was permeable, allowing rainwater to seep into the ground and not simply run off the road.

Cars and trucks powered by water and the sun were invented somewhere at the end of the Collapse or the beginning of the aftermath. Water-powered cars were easy—there had already been a design made for them that had been stolen. It wasn't all too hard to find it and tinker with it to create a functional vehicle; solar-powered vehicles had been invented not long after. They were rare, however, mostly because of the difficulties of manufacturing them. It was a lot harder to make an entire car, much less a line of cars, when you weren't extracting the Earth's resources at an unsustainable speed in an unsustainable way. But that just meant Jackie got to get out from her settlement, walk on the roads, observe the wildlife and the turning of the leaves. They passed other travelers. The others traveled on foot or bicycle, and most were amenable to walking together until their paths diverged. A few had stories of similar storms and approved of the mission to try and figure out how and why this was happening.

Finally, the college stretched out before them. It sat in what had been farmland and was now forest. Despite the world around it having fallen and rebuilt, it still looked academic. Red brick mixed with "modern" styles mixed with green roofs and walls. A few skellies tended a rooftop garden. It was good to be back.

"I want a shower," Summer declared as they moved through the campus. "Dorm showers have remained unappealing across the decades, but I smell like ass."

It didn't take too long to get set up with rooms in the dorms and take showers. While one showered, the two made casual conversation, and learned from other travelers more about the sweeping throngs of undead. All shared the same stories of confusion and fear. Though one spirit ambassador reported that he'd caught snatches of personality during his experience. Mostly confusion, frustration, and panic, this time amplified even further than normal poltergeists could do. Aside from the ominous storms and the pack movement, it wasn't *that* different from a normal poltergeist.

By the time everyone was ready to actually go speak to the professors, the trio had a group following them, all desperate for the answers they sought. Students and skeletons fanned out behind them, chattering and debating among themselves the best course of action, whether they were completely in the dark, the changes made to the dining hall (on

175

that front, at least, things seemed to be positive).

It did lend a weighty aura to the search for professors to speak with as they roved through academic halls. The buildings were by and large spacious and open. More windows had been put in where possible, and small plant boxes and pots had been built for use and enjoyment. Jackie could see and almost feel the past students here, pre- and post-Collapse, clustering in groups to discuss assignments or hurrying to the next class or gossiping about the latest inevitable drama.

There were, however, no professors to be found, even in offices where professors already had been. There was some concerned discussion about this before Wes just said, "Guys. They're in a meeting."

"Wes, how's it feel being the smartest one here?" Summer asked, before her skeleton pushed her faster down the hallway.

Yet Summer's haste did not grant her more luck. The meeting rooms and classrooms were empty. She didn't give up, and neither did the group. The trio and a few others all but flung themselves into an elevator, and the rest hustled down the stairs. They came out in a hallway that clearly was trying very hard to pretend it was not a basement. But the group was in luck. Voices could be heard floating from one of the subterranean lecture halls.

It took the professors a few moments to process that new people had entered the room. Jackie saw the mixture of confusion and eagerness on the professors' faces as they all eventually looked up.

Summer took the stage. "Professor Doherty, so good to see you again."

The professor stared at her for just a moment before smiling just as wide.

"Summer! And I recognize you too, Jackie. Come, take a seat. Tell me, why have you, ah, raised a small army to come see us?" The professor had the kind of face that inspired freshmen to call her *Mom* on accident, and she consistently wore shawls, no matter the weather.

"We were hoping y'all at the college could tell us what was up with the poltergeists howling through towns." Jackie took the proffered seat. "But, looking at what y'all have been doing here, you guys seem to be figuring that out already."

To Jackie's surprise, the professor laughed. "'Figuring that out already' implies that we have an idea of why this is happening. We have theories. Ideas. Nothing concrete."

"Most everything is a theory, in science," a different professor butted in.

"Yes, but there's a difference between evolution and throwing equations on a whiteboard," Professor Doherty said. "Which is, I confess, mostly what we've been doing here."

Summer and Jackie moved as one to peruse the equations. It was obvious now why the professors had moved down here—the lecture hall walls were lined with whiteboard material. The equations were made in all different hands. Someone had written down the Laws of Paranormal Activity, then amended a "known" in front of the title. Jackie surveyed the (known) Laws and came to the same conclusion the professors evidently had too—the ghostly storm violated these laws. They weren't possible, except clearly they were.

"These are unprecedented—" a professor started.

"If I have to hear 'unprecedented times' one more time, I'm going to lose it," Wes interrupted. "How long have y'all been working on this?"

Professor Doherty knitted her brow. "In between classes and meals and going home and all that, we've had this set up for about a week."

Jackie put her head in her hands and groaned. A week and the smartest people in the country had little to no idea why this was happening or how to stop it. She should probably be patient. Most scientific discoveries did not happen in a week. But who knew how long before the next storm? Before they got strong enough to do more damage? Before experiencing one became unbearable to sit through for spirit ambassadors?

She could hear Wes and Summer going around and reading the equations and little notes aloud, with Professor Doherty tagging along and explaining. The professor was clearly pleased to tell people about her work, but Jackie heard the same note of disappointment in her voice.

"'Folkloric precedent,'" Wes read aloud. She murmured over the notes and spoke to a professor.

Jackie looked up at her. "There have to be ways of placating restless spirits across cultures, right?" she asked.

"Well, yes, but, from reports, these storms are suggesting that the spirits are being swept along too fast and they're too disjointed to be able to be meaningfully calmed by these efforts," the professor said.

Jackie waved a hand and went over to the maps of reported storms. "Professors. In these other areas, did storms—real storms—happen before the poltergeists came?"

She saw nods dotted across the hall. Wes tilted her head, trying to connect the dots that Jackie was putting down.

"And we know that ghosts have been known to be able to interact with electricity. I propose..." She took a breath. "The poltergeists are being swept up by the lightning in those storms. We all know storms have been getting worse and will continue to until nature sorts itself out."

Some more scattered nods. The professors were murmuring. Jackie couldn't tell what by their expressions. What if she was wrong?

"There wasn't enough electricity contained in the storms before," Summer finished. Unlike the professors, she had a giddy note in her voice. "At least not to drag along that many ghosts. But we saw the clouds. The ghosts must've been fighting to escape the pull of the lightning and taken the clouds with them. But that just meant lightning in the clouds the spirits held."

Jackie pointed at her, grateful.

"I just... don't know what we can do about it." Jackie's pride at (sort of) understanding what had happened diminished.

Wes had wandered back over to Folkloric Precedents. "Hey. Jackie. It's okay. Besides," she cleared her throat awkwardly. "I don't go here, so maybe I'm wrong, but haven't humans been calming ghosts down for forever? Can't we just amp up our methods of calming them down like we amped up our storm protection? Half the reason they don't let go of the cloud is that they're angry, right?"

She looked at Jackie who nodded. Electricity attracted and could sometimes hold spirits, but spirits could just as often have a death grip on what they thought they needed or had to do. "Right. So if we can get the spirits to chill before they hit a settlement, we can get at least some of them to let go and not mess up our shit. Pardon my French."

Summer sighed. "That'd be difficult to do everywhere."

"But I believe it would work." The folklore professor beamed at Wes. "We'll need to start spreading the word."

"I know some traders who would be happy to," Wes offered instantly.

"And I can send some skellies with notes. We'll need to move fast. It's already hurricane season. I'd bet there's some spirit storms brewing after the hurricanes already," Summer added.

Jackie nodded. "I know a lot of spirit calming methods. I'll help you draft those notes. We're going to need to be pretty specific."

In a few minutes, the room was full of students and professors all helping each other. Humanity needed to adapt, and so adapt it would, once more.

Project Butterfly

N.H. Van Der Haar

Department: Organic Technologies & Administration
  Project: BUTTERFLY
  FGAN Number: 100274
Authorization Code: AC 11679
Current Status: Archived.
Project Abstract:

Shortly after the Second World War, our government passed the 1946 Covert Actions Bill. In a single pen-stroke, every single Government Department found itself equipped with unlimited authority and budgets to begin covert operations and projects free of all constraints. After decades of this kind of action, with the passing of the 1991 Acts of Retainment, I have been selected to survey the damage done and draw a line in the sand. Project Butterfly shall be that line. What had been originally meant to be an opportunity for national growth has ended in a network of secret waste and useless experimentation. Project Butterfly will unearth the disused and/or abandoned and find a use for them of some kind – From the Office of Administrator Dieter Winthrop.

Codename: MANTICORE
  Subjects: 5

Related Project/s: DECANTER

Synopsis:

The specimens codenamed MANTICORE are 5 Staffordshire Terri-
ers aged between 5 and 10. All specimens are hyperintelligent but
genetically asexual. They become more aggressive and animalistic, the
further away from each other they are. All the MANTICORE specimens
display a variety of personality quirks:

- Specimen 5-M enjoys writing jokes, riddles, and limericks.
- Specimen 4-M is fluent in Turkish, Greek, and Arabic, considers
  themselves an expert on the Ottoman Empire.
- Specimen 3-M cultivates Orchid varieties, including developing
  several new hybrids.
- Specimen 2-M has written several novels of varying genres and
  freely gives talks on their self-described masterpiece: '*Fable of the
  Flying Fang*'.
- Specimen 1-M plays the viola, piano and cello like a master and has
  composed 3 concertos.

Besides these quirks, MANTICORE behaves like any ordinary Staffordshire Bull Terrier. The dogs were created as part of Project DECANTER.
Files indicate that they were designed to be a *"non-human, universal
translator"*. The dogs became the obsession of Doctor Leonid Cove,
who allowed them a great deal of freedom as a Director in the Sub-
Department of Creature Sciences. Project DECANTER ended after the
death of Doctor Cove.

Resolution:

All MANTICORE Specimens will be allowed to express themselves but
must be kept in custody until further notice. Limited ethical testing of
Specimens will be allowed. The MANTICORE Specimens are charming

conversationalists. They have a significant morale benefit to the staff. Whoever takes over supervision should treat them with dignity and respect – From the Office of Administrator Dieter Winthrop.

Codename: SPHINX

Subjects: 19

Related Project/s: SPYGLASS

Synopsis:

19 paintings, each depicting a seated female figure. Each painting depicts a slightly different woman. Each range in size from 10 inches to a meter but is framed identically in gilded hardwood and an attached brass plaque naming each painting's as: 'The Other Woman'. Each work uses a different artistic style and medium. When the paintings are faced towards one another, they begin to argue with one another in French. The argument has no end until the paintings are pointed away from one another. Otherwise, the paintings speak rarely.

Related Data & Information:

There is little information regarding Subject SPHINX. Project SPY-GLASS was created by the Department of Cultural Regulation with a focus on "reducing anti-state tendencies in our nation's artists" but almost all the files were sadly lost. What we could learn was from the personal documents and interviews with Jervis Crane, the former Director who created Project SPYGLASS. He suffered a breakdown while trying to resolve the arguments with the paintings over a 48-hour period. This event and lack of obvious outcomes resulted in the closure of both Project SPYGLASS. While I do find these paintings disagreeable, I see no reason why they cannot be re-homed individually. Much of my staff have volunteered to take home a painting on the condition they treat the works with respect and engage in polite conversation when spoken to. I was able to arrange for ex-Director Crane (currently residing at the Tillykirk Sanatorium for Mental Affectations) to have a painting, who expressed much delight – From the Office of Administrator Dieter Winthrop.

Codename: BASILISK

   Subjects: 1 (deceased)

   Related Project/s: MAGIC METTLE

   Synopsis:

   Carcass of an Irrawaddy Dolphin (*Orcella Brevirostris*), measuring 3 meters in length and weighing 172 kilograms. Subject is in an advanced state of decomposition. Autopsy reveals nothing unusual, other than the cause of death being lethal injection.

Related Data & Information:

   Project MAGIC METTLE was a collaboration between business and government, aimed at creating *"genetically boneless fish as a cost-effective food source for corporate manufacture"*. This was, in fact, a cover for the keeping of a pet dolphin, created by Director Blount and his wife, Cynthia Widener, a Senior Executive for Widener Fisheries. Closure of the Project forced the mercy killing of their pet.

Resolution:

   Subject BASILISK remains burned. Ashes kept for archival purposes. I cannot imagine a more blatant waste of government resources. Director Blount and his wife are both deceased, regardless I recommend an investigation begin into any surviving staff who worked on Project MAGIC METTLE – From the Office of Administrator Dieter Winthrop.

Codename: WENDIGO

    Subjects: 9

    Related Project/s: LAKE, POND & PUDDLE.

    Synopsis:

Specimen WENDIGO consists of 9 human hearts. Each Specimen is individually sealed in (unlabeled) wine bottle and floating in an unidentified, orange liquid. Every hour, each WENDIGO Specimen beat once, in unison.

Related Data & Information:

All records related to Subject WENDIGO are incomplete or contradict each other. What little we have indicates, they were a simple by-product of experiments performed as part of Project LAKE, the goal of which is still not known. Doctor Blake Heathmont died suddenly after creating the WENDIGO Specimens. Both Project POND and PUDDLE were created by colleagues of Dr. Heathmont specifically to (according to what files remain) *"solve the riddle of the hearts"*.

Resolution:

Subject WENDIGO was a scientific riddle created by Dr Heathmont in competition with his rivals within the Sub-Department of Speculative Health. These vanity projects were why the Sub-Department was shuttered to begin with. All remaining files relating to Projects LAKE, PUDDLE and POND destroyed. Doctor Nigel Frand for my R&D department assured me that the vibrations created from the beating of the hearts can be used to generate electricity to supplement our existing energy grid – From the Office of Administrator Dieter Winthrop.

Codename: PEGASUS

    Subjects: 60

Related Project/s: SHAMAN

Synopsis:

Subject PEGASUS consists of 60 hermetically sealed containers of Saltwater Crocodile (*Crocodylus Porosus*) corpses, each weighing roughly 1,280kgs.

Related Data & Information:

According to the extensive files we have, Project SHAMAN aimed to: *"investigate the usefulness of aggressive reptilian species in non-conventional warfare".* According to interviews with former employees of the Sub-Department of Alternative Combat, the containers contain *"fallen soldiers of war"* awaiting military funeral.

Resolution:

Subject PEGASUS repackaged into coffins and given a formal military funeral at Mount Fuliginous National Cemetery. I can understand animal testing in extreme circumstances, but casual animal cruelty simply has no place in this government – From the Office of Administrator Dieter Winthrop.

Codename: DRAGON

Subjects: 1 (deceased)

Related Project/s: MISTY THRONE

Synopsis:

Subject DRAGON is the cryogenically frozen body of a deceased human female, aged in her late 40s.

Related Data & Information:

There are almost no files relating to Project MISTY THRONE, thankfully what we do have focuses primarily on Subject DRAGON. Autopsy and analysis reveal Subject DRAGON to be in-fact the remains of Empress Alexandra Feodorovna, Princess of Hesse and the Rhine and the last Tsarina of Russia (1872 - 1918).

Resolution:

Subject DRAGON's remains buried with dignity at the nearest Russian Orthodox Cemetery under name 'Irina Bolkonsky'. Tissue samples and blood tests will be kept for archival purposes. This kind of fantastical, overly ambitious super-science of freezing corpses for storage for more than fifty years is exactly why I have been brought on board to wipe the slate clean – From the Office of Administrator Dieter Winthrop.

Codename: GORGON

Subjects: 1

Related Project/s: STEEL BRIDGE, BUTTERFLY

Synopsis:

Subject GORGON is an overgrown *Monstera Deliciosa* covering almost all its enormous holding cell. Automated ceiling sprinklers and sunlamps in the roof ensure the continued growth of PEGASUS. Investigation of Subject reveals several spiders and gnats living within Subject GORGON holding cell.

Related Data & Information:

Project STEEL BRIDGE was created by the Sub-Department of Martial Wellbeing to create "*organic therapies for the use of mentally deranged veterans in combat scenarios*". Essentially, it was about convincing the shellshocked to fight using any means necessary. Some may have thrived in that kind of environment but 95% of staff did not and requested transfers almost immediately after starting on STEEL BRIDGE. According to files, this cell and Subject GORGON became the emotional safe space for staff forced to work on Project STEEL BRIDGE. The project was eventually closed owing to staff retention issues and the resignation of Director V.N. Chesterton.

Resolution:

Subject GORGON has been pruned, had its cell cleaned and will now be used as a safe space for Project BUTTERFLY. Chairs, tables, a complimentary library and a small koi pond will be installed. Despite its dark beginnings, I can see the benefit of such a cell for staff morale – From the Office of Administrator Dieter Winthrop.

Codename: CYCLOPS
   Subjects: estimated to be 100's
   Related Project/s: NAVIGATOR
   Synopsis:

Subject CYCLOPS is a community of hyper-intelligent Caribbean Hermit Crabs (*Coenobita Clypeatus)* that has developed a complex society. Food and fresh resources outlets still function and are worshipped as gods by the Subjects. Their very large enclosure has been fully explored and colonized by the crabs, who have erected several structures and begun to enter the human equivalent of the Medieval Period. Our remote analysts have already documented the crabs as having invented the wheel, organized religion, architecture, agriculture, money, art and culture.

Related Data & Information:

Subject CYCLOPS was created as part of Project NAVIGATOR, with the intention of creating tiny spies capable of being planted on enemy territory and collected later to relay key information. It appears this facility and the Subjects inside were forgotten about for decades owing to a government error.

Resolution:

I think disturbing this society would only cause harm to our government in the long term. At this stage in their society, the food and resource distribution network is essentially redundant and acts now simply as a safety net for those crabs born with nothing or in desperate need. The staff seem delighted to remotely study this society as it grows and develops, and I see this as a boon to morale overall. I can only hope that if this society exceeds our own one day, I hope they can do a better job than we have done so far – From the Office of Administrator Dieter Winthrop.

Of Potatoes and Stasis Pods...

Alex Grehy

Where shall we begin? Once upon a time? But time is meaningless in deep space, far from the spinning blue globe that references its passing.

MaxieP, Quantum Fairy Godmother, is sitting on a deckchair on the sunny side of Pluto. Though out here, the sun, like time, is more concept than reality. Still, it's a good place to observe the silver streak of a speeding spaceship hurtling past.

"That looks like a wish on the run. Show time!" she murmurs, clicking her fingers to activate her personal transporter. An instant later she arrives on the spaceship's bridge, invisible for the moment.

By the main console, two men are arguing.

"Hey, it's YOUR fault! You should have said not to touch the drive controls. You're the captain!"

The speaker has unkempt blonde hair which is growing out of the severe military crop that he'd started the journey with, the one that his commanding officer had mandated back on Earth. He has violet-blue eyes and a chiselled chin, but he's a little too dishevelled to be a hero. His vest and sweatpants would certainly not pass a parade ground inspection.

"Yes, I am the captain, but that doesn't matter to you, *Crewman* Axel

Moore. It's never mattered! You haven't lifted a finger since we got out of range of earth comms—until today."

The second man is slight with long, dark hair. His deep brown eyes are ablaze, his sharp features twisted with rage. His delicate fingers are plaited into tight fists, which he waves ineffectually. He knows from bitter experience that punching his beefy companion would be...unwise.

"I just wanted more speed. Space is a lot more boring than I expected. I thought we'd get home quicker. You should have told me it was dangerous!" Axel whines.

"Everything's dangerous in space! If you didn't know what you were doing, you shouldn't have done it! And you waited until I was asleep! And you didn't wake me until now! We're accelerating exponentially—our speed's doubling every hour. Even if we could decelerate, we'd be in the next galaxy by the time we stopped!" Cendrillo paces the bridge, but the tiny space doesn't allow him to vent the enormity of his anger.

"Bo-ring. I'm going into stasis until you fix it." Axel yawns.

"No! We both need to be awake to take turns on watch."

"Ain't nothing to watch now that we're outta the planets. You're the smart one—you fix, I sleep."

MaxieP, still invisible, watches Axel stomp down the corridor that runs from the bridge to the stasis pods.

"No! Axel!"

"How you gonna stop me, Cinderella?"

"For the love of dark matter, it's Cendrillo!"

"Whatever. Here's your big chance. You got the balls to get us to the ball, Cendrillo?" Axel's voice is thick with contempt.

"You can't fix this with balls or any other macho bullshit. Don't you understand? We...are...going...to...die...here!" Cendrillo runs after Axel and grasps the big man's arm in an attempt to stop him, to make him listen.

Axel slows and turns to face Cendrillo.

"That's up to you. G'dnight." Axel brushes Cendrillo's hand from his shoulder as if it were a speck of space lint.

Cendrillo slumps, helpless, as Axel steps into his stasis pod. The thump of the door and hiss of coolant stifles the sound of Cendrillo's sobbing as he returns to the bridge.

MaxieP follows him. *So this is the one,* she thinks, sensing his desperation. It's been her first call for a while. Since humans switched to automated space exploration, there hasn't been much for a Quantum Fairy Godmother to do.

She finds Cendrillo sitting in the captain's chair, aimlessly fiddling with the controls. In the viewer, dark space has brightened into the rainbow glare of a Doppler shift as the ship accelerates relentlessly.

"Maybe I should go into stasis too; sleep through this mess," Cendrillo mutters.

"Talking to yourself is not a good omen, you know!" says MaxieP, cancelling her invisibility field.

Startled, Cendrillo tries to move his chair back from the apparition that's just appeared in front of him, but the chair is fixed to the floor. Captains are not allowed to back away.

"Who...?"

"MaxieP, Quantum Fairy Godmother, at your service. Dreams delivered, wishes granted."

"What?"

"I hear you're in a pickle." MaxieP takes a clipboard from her coveralls. "Lessee. You're stuck with your childhood nemesis. You're being carried away from Simon faster than you could ever have imagined."

MaxieP looks up from her list.

"Simon's the love of your life, yeah? And you're fretting that your last words to him were: *I can't believe you wore that shirt for the launch party.* It's all looking bleak. Have I got that right?"

Cendrillo looks down at his feet, his cheeks reddening. Then he lifts his chin, looking directly into MaxieP's iridescent eyes.

"Yeah, that pretty much sums it up, except you missed the bit about sassy women turning up uninvited and telling me what I already know! I don't know which would be worse—that you're an alien or a hallucination!"

MaxieP plonks herself down in the crewman's seat and twirls around.

"Nice! I like a bit of spirit in my godchildren. Look, my job is to grant your heart's desire, even if you don't know what it is yet. So, what's it to be? True love forever?"

She waves her wand back and forth, grinning and muttering "tra-la-lah" under her breath.

"There's no-one to fall in love with out here—and don't even suggest Axel. If you're offering a deal on *aaw, maybe he wasn't so bad after all*, then I'm not buying. He's always been the same dumb ass all his life!"

Cendrillo reaches out and stops MaxieP's spinning seat.

"All his life? Is he your brother?"

"No! Our moms were friends, so they thought we should be friends too. Huh, some friend; he beat me up, threw my books down the toilet, pushed me off my bike. He made my life a misery on Earth!"

"Uh huh. So how come you're stuck with him in this tin can?"

"It's hard to say...just unlucky, I guess." Cendrillo spins his chair around to avoid her gaze.

"OK, if you can't tell me, show me." MaxieP walks around his chair and touches Cendrillo's forehead with her fingertips. "This Wi-Fi brain-to-monitor connection is THE latest thing in Fairy-Godmothering," she explains as she swivels Cendrillo's seat to face the display screen.

Cendrillo's memories tumble onto the screen. His mom drinking wine with Axel's mom. His mom saying *Cendrillo's such a sensitive boy*. Axel smirking as he overhears their conversation, like that's all the ammunition he's ever going to need. Axel raising his ham-hock fists.

Axel wrecking Cendrillo's science project. Axel taunting him in the school gym. Axel this, Axel that. Always Axel, Axel...

Then Cendrillo standing tall as he walks into MIT, free at last. No way would Axel's SATs get him into a top-flight university, or any university, for that matter. Cendrillo's smile as he meets Simon for the first time during new-student orientation.

"Axel always wins! It's like he's charmed or something," Cendrillo interjects miserably as his on-screen memory fixes on Simon's face. "I thought Axel was gone for good when he followed his daddy into the army. But guess who paid for this spaceship? The army! And guess whose daddy bought him a place on the space programme?"

Cendrillo's hands slap at the useless control console, then he lowers his hands to his lap.

"That sure sounds unlucky. Though in Godmother Academy we're taught that you make your own luck. Why didn't you stand up for yourself when he turned up?"

"Axel gave them some sob story about being proud to be partnered with his old school friend; of how he'd always been awed by my intelligence. The selection board thought he'd be good company for me. If I'd turned him down, they'd have thought I was a snob."

MaxieP gets up and stands by Cendrillo, who is staring at the monitor as if it were a window to infinity.

"Do you still care what they think? You're six billion miles from earth and counting."

"If we get back, Axel will find a way to come up smelling of roses and I'll get the blame again."

"That's rough." MaxieP puts a consoling hand on Cendrillo's shoulder.

"You can't fight bullies, even in deep space," Cendrillo says, shaking the woman's hand off his shoulder. "So, actually, I do care what *they* think. You may as well leave—I'll dream my life away in my stasis pod until we crash into a star in a thousand years' time."

MaxieP looks Cendrillo in the eye and winks.

"Would it help if I told you that Axel reprogrammed your stasis pod to stream slasher movies into your subconscious—forever?"

"Huh? What's streaming in his pod?"

"Disney movies. Deep down, he wants to be a princess; wants someone to sweep him off his feet, be his advocate and protector. It's a shame his daddy tried to beat it out of him."

"But he's so privileged...he can look after himself!" Cendrillo shakes his head.

"He's like a red giant star—huge, hot tempered, showy, but inside he's dying."

"So you're saying I should feel sorry for him? That I should just accept this?" Cendrillo gestures to the blurred velocity gauge measuring the spaceship's wild acceleration.

"No, I'm not saying that. There's no excuse for what he did to you. I may be Quantum, but at heart I'm a Fairy Godmother. I see to it that bullies get their just desserts, trust me. But for you? Just remember, forgiveness rewards the forgiver and kindness needs to set boundaries, because cruelty doesn't know how to."

MaxieP sits back on the crew chair and spins around, leaving a trail of sparkles in her wake.

"But let's get back to your happy ending—what'll it be?" she asks.

"Don't you know?" Cendrillo's lip curls into a sneer.

"I've got an inkling, but I'm quantum, right? It's the Schrödinger's Wish Uncertainty Principle. Your wish exists in potentia, but I won't know for certain until you say *I wish,* so..."

"I wish...no, this is stupid. Even if I wish it, by the time we decelerate and turn back to Earth, Simon will be an old man and I'll still be young, because of time dilation. It won't work."

"Just wish already—you worry about the what and I'll work out the how," MaxieP huffs.

"I wish I were back on earth with Simon, that we could find a way to be together even though he's an arboreal scientist and I study dark matter in deep space."

Cendrillo's shoulders sag, the weight of his longing is unbearable.

MaxieP nods. She's seen this a million times—there's nothing darker than the predawn gloom between the wish and the fulfillment. She twirls again.

"Got it, one true love with a side-order of togetherness coming up."

"How?"

"Magic!"

"I don't believe in magic!" Cendrillo states, crossing his arms across his chest.

"But you do believe that sufficiently advanced science can look like magic, don't you?"

"Yeah, can't argue with Arthur C. Clarke."

"Smart guy! Now, I need you to get me some things. First, I need two cockroaches."

"There are no cockroaches on a spaceship!" Cendrillo exclaims.

"Believe me, there's cockroaches everywhere. Check the hydroponics garden. And while you're there, get me something dense, preferably spherical."

Cendrillo gets up from the Captain's chair, shaking his head. MaxieP's list makes no sense, then he snorts, just what would make sense right now?

"Like the titanium balls from the drive shaft?" he asks.

"No, something living—for my magic to work, I need to persuade the object to transform. You can't negotiate with a lump of titanium!"

As Cendrillo scuttles off, MaxieP strolls down to Axel's stasis pod. His face is just visible through the pod's view screen—he's smiling beatifically.

"Cute," MaxieP mutters, before making a few adjustments to the controls. "Nothing teaches morals like a Disney movie—one hundred years should do it."

Satisfied, she returns to the bridge and checks the monitors. The ship is accelerating dangerously close to the speed of light, which might interfere with her calculations.

"Hurry!"

Cendrillo comes back to the bridge—he's carrying a flask with two cockroaches and a...

"Potato?"

"Yeah, it's the densest living thing on board, not counting Axel's skull."

MaxieP shakes her head. Spirit *and* a sense of humour—what a kid!

"Funny! Now let's get these roaches strapped onto the bulkhead by the main engine."

"But we're going too fast for a spacewalk!"

"Inside will do—I can maintain the hull's integrity as they transform."

Transform into what?" Cendrillo asks, his brow furrowed.

MaxieP stamps her foot impatiently. The downside of being a Quantum Godmother is that you're always dealing with scientists and their damn questions.

"Auxiliary booster engines—we need some directional thrust."

"Roaches can't be engines, they're just bugs!"

Cendrillo stands in the centre of the bridge, looking around in a state of bewilderment as MaxieP bustles around, her wand busy.

"Never underestimate the power of a roach, just look at Axel! Boom!" MaxieP offers a high-five, which Cendrillo ignores.

"But they're so small!"

"You provide the matter and magic will take care of the mass—first law of Quantum Magic Dynamics."

MaxieP waves a hand. The roaches expand, their black carapaces forming an oval thruster framed by chitinous legs. Looking out of the porthole, Cendrillo sees a perfectly streamlined roach engine extruding through the hull.

"Right, you got any weapons on this ship?"

Cendrillo looks shifty. They're not meant to have weapons, but there is one prototype space cannon on board. The military had paid for this scientific research trip as cover for their top-secret mission—to test the effectiveness of a new weapon. That was really why Axel was on board—a goon and his gun are rarely parted.

"We've got a cannon, but there's nothing to fire at, unless...have you seen something? Are we on a collision course?" Cendrillo clutches his chest, his breaths short and anxious.

"Relax. We just need to fire this potato into space."

Cendrillo laughs hysterically. He's convinced he's gone insane, but he's got nothing to lose by loading a potato into a space cannon. He fires, half expecting the barrel, or the potato, to explode. Instead, the tuber shoots off into space, a rapidly dwindling dot among the distant stars. Except it's not a dot, it's a shadow which expands rapidly, drawing the faint light of the stars into itself.

He looks around. MaxieP is clapping her hands, a triumphant grin on her face.

"A potato, excellent choice! Who knew that its heart's desire was to be a black hole? That'll be a legend back at Godmother HQ. Now, let's boost that thruster and catch ourselves a wormhole home."

* * *

A year later, Cendrillo stands in a clearing in the Amazon rain forest— it's the perfect place for their honeymoon. Simon looks up—a violet corona glows in the blue sky, surrounding the dark maw of the wormhole which now provides earth with perpetual free energy and a fast portal to the rest of the universe.

"It's a miracle," Simon sighs, leaning into Cendrillo's shoulder.

"It is. Of course, it's always been postulated that the singularity created by black holes might fold space and create wormholes but to actually find..."

Cendrillo falters. Simon is giving him that look, the one he gives him every time Cendrillo tries to put quantum physics into words.

"So there's a bigger miracle than a stable wormhole, huh?" Cendrillo says.

"Yes, stupid. It's a miracle that you came back at just the right time. Any sooner and I'd still have been mad at you for going; any later and I would have died of a broken heart!"

"Yeah, plus the wormhole means I can commute to work in deep space and be home for supper."

"It's also a miracle that you came back sound in body and mind. Is your crewman still stuck in his stasis pod?"

"Yeah, they've tried everything, but the pod won't unlock. He's alive and well, sleeping like a baby with the sweetest grin on his face. They're calling him *Sleeping Beauty*. I guess he finally got to be a princess, after all."

"And I got my Prince, so dreams do come true."

Far above in the forest canopy, MaxieP smiles as Cendrillo and Simon walk hand in hand back to their cabin.

She checks her clipboard:

Case File: Cendrillo

Heart's desire – Tick

Bully thwarted – Tick

Case File: Axel

Taught hard but valuable lesson – No

Evil intent redeemed by love - No

Hmm, still work to be done...

* * *

EPILOGUE

MaxieP activates her temporal transporter and emerges in a museum ninety-nine years after Cendrillo's return to Earth. No-one notices her arrival amidst the throng of journalists that surround the exhibit...

Axel Moore: Astronaut aka Sleeping Beauty, celebrating 100 years in stasis.

The crowd parts as the museum curator walks through them, opening an aisle for an old man in a wheelchair to follow him. The crowd applauds—Cendrillo is a celebrity. In the golden age of science that followed his miraculous return, human health and longevity have improved. But he and Simon have resisted anti-aging technology. Cendrillo knows this is likely to be his last annual visit to Axel's pod. A beautiful young woman pushes his wheelchair, his granddaughter, Bella, herself a respected social anthropologist.

The display on Axel's stasis pod shows him to be in perfect health; he is still smiling. The crowd counts down with the pod's digital clock...

"...three, two, ONE!"

100 YEARS 0 hours 0 minutes 0 seconds

Nothing happens.

100 YEARS 0 hours 0 minutes 10 seconds

"I'm sorry grandpa," Bella whispers in Cendrillo's ear. "I guess there's no quantum fairy godmother to save him with two roaches and a potato!"

"You remember that, huh?" Cendrillo says.

"It was my favourite bedtime story. I wish it had been true—science can do so much, but my research shows that humans still need a bit of

199

magic."

Cendrillo puts a hand on the stasis pod. "I forgive you Axel. I got to live my life, live my dreams, find my best self. I wish you'd had the chance to find yours too."

The journalists turn away—there's no story here.

"He needs true love's kiss!" MaxieP calls from the back of the crowd, giving a little twirl.

Impulsively, Bella touches her lips to the pod's observation window. A thin layer of glass separates her from Axel's face. She gasps as the pod cracks open with a glittering shower of sparkles. Axel blinks confusedly and steps out. Bella steps forward and kisses him on the lips.

There is an excited hubbub from the journalists, but Axel only has eyes for Bella.

"Hi, I'm Bella, welcome to the future..."

MaxieP moves through the crowd to stand by Cendrillo's wheelchair.

"True love eh, who'd have thought it?" she winks at Cendrillo.

"It certainly looks that way," says Cendrillo, remembering the electric attraction he'd felt for Simon all those years ago. "But can it work out? She's today's woman and he's a dinosaur!"

The glow from the open stasis pod bathes Bella and Axel in a silvery light.

"I'm sure they'll work it out, but a bit of magic never goes amiss."

MaxieP twirls again—she knows that time is just a function of perception. As Bella and Axel stare into each other's eyes, something flashes between them like a subliminal advertisement.

In the blink of any eye they experience a hundred catch-up conversations, a hundred dates, a hundred break-ups and make-ups—the components of a long and enduring relationship falling into place with engineered precision. They reach out to each other; as their fingertips touch, MaxieP twirls again and seals the love spell.

Hand in hand, Axel and Bella turn to face the crowd. Axel tears his gaze away from Bella for an instant and looks at Cendrillo.

"Cendrillo, I'm sorry...for everything." Axel's voice is sincere and full of regret.

"Take care of my girl," Cendrillo replies hoarsely.

"Forever..." says Axel, losing himself in Bella's gaze again.

Hovering in the ancient space shuttle exhibit, MaxieP checks her clipboard one last time:

And they all lived happily ever after – TICK.

Letter

Colleen Addison

Moving is super stressful, as you know, but I'm really starting to settle in here. I won't lie to you about how long that's taken.

At first, I wasn't certain; I missed you, and, somewhat surprisingly, the city, even the inbred cats that lurked around our favourite coffee shop, their misshapen mouths crying for handouts.

It's so different here, my new rural life. There's still the inbreeding; we never could help with that, could we? But it's not the same. The birds can fly. The seagulls can't get very far, admittedly, not anymore: too fat from the land's garbage. But they've still got wings. In the morning, on the days I go ashore, I can see their feathers spreading into the sunrise.

Initially, I was a bit lonely, as you are when you move to a new area. This place is a haven for water creatures, like we saw in the brochure. A waterman lives next door to me, and seahorses have all the lower floors.

I missed our old gang, though; I thought I'd never find a coven here, and it sure took some time. Finally, I met an octopus, and one of his eight legs pointed me in the right direction: *Sirens and Sea Stars*, a conservation program to get rid of the last of the plastic in the ocean.

Apparently, mermaids and the like are mistaking the few discarded makeup bags for moon jellies and choking to death, a horrible fate for the poor things. So I'm helping with that now, waving my wand a lot, though never as much as before.

Actually, it reminds me of the way the sparrows used to strangle themselves with telephone lines, except I always suspected that was on purpose.

You'll think it's a waste of my talents, I know. The incantations are far easier than our earth stuff. There's less despair here, and more, for lack of a better word, hope. The water is cleaner, or at least, better than the city.

Life is good. My new condo has walls made of soft corals and a floor tiled with sand dollars. I open my shutters, and schools of fish float by, their bodies shadowed sometimes by basking sharks.

The place doesn't get much sun, but when the light filters through the ocean, I do yoga, moving my body against the pressure. I'm getting fitter and fitter, the more because I swim everywhere now and have stopped using the dolphins.

In the evenings, there's sound too, not that rush-hour cacophony but the snapping bark of sea lions, the pulses of Pacific herring.

I miss you still, o fellow witch. I'm sorry I left. I couldn't stay, what with the sparrows and the strata fights and the fact that none of our spells had any effect anymore.

I hope you've forgiven me. And there's space here for two, just so you know. We can't fix the land, or at least, I'm too tired to try anymore. But there's still the sea.

Please come if you can. The water surrounds me as I write this, carving it into a rock on the ocean floor. There's the odd flash of plastic around still, as I said, but mostly, miraculously, and thanks to magic, it's all clear.

The Garden of the Sun

Cassandra Arnold

Aunt Sally's place was on the other side of town, down by the river, across the tracks, where the houses all perched on stilts, shaded by balsam poplars that dropped cotton-wrapped seeds into banks of summer snow and made me sneeze. I'd only been there once or twice during my childhood. She was not much spoken of in the family: my mother's baby sister, closer to me in age than my mother, in fact. The last time I'd seen her, I was twelve. Her hair had been dyed a vivid orange, purple-painted toenails peeped out of her silver sandals, and there had been some kind of row between her and my mother, conducted in furious whispers in the tiny kitchen that opened directly onto the backyard.

That yard was a magical oasis, the antithesis of our own barbered and butchered expanse of turf and woven plastic outdoor chairs and tables. It was brimful of plants, layer upon layer, reaching up into a sky that seemed bluer than I had ever seen it at home. There were tiny strawberries hidden at my feet, nasturtiums sprawling beside the path, raspberries at head height, and plums and apples hanging overhead. There were hammocks, a pond with fish and frogs, lamps suspended from the trees, and a stone sundial in the centre of a paved circle. I never got to examine the symbols carved into its rim.

My mother called, and I had to turn away with a strange ache in my heart that I couldn't explain. We drove home in a silence I knew not to break and we did not go back again.

So five years later, when I climbed the steps to go and sort out Aunt Sally's things when she died, I was surprised to find myself blinking back tears as I opened the front door and peered inside.

It should have been my parents, of course it should. But they were on a cruise to the Bahamas and the landlord wanted the place cleared out pronto, ready for a new tenant before the start of the new month. And I was on Spring Break, so...

I cleared my throat and stepped across the threshold. There was a skip coming in the morning and the Salvation Army would come and collect the good stuff at the end of the week. The parents had made it clear that nothing of Sally's was to enter their house. They had also sniffily declared that they doubted she had anything worth selling, so that was my two choices spelt out: trash or charity. Seemed kind of fitting in a way.

The house was small, two up and two down, with the kitchen added on as an afterthought at the rear. I walked through to the back, dumped the rolls of black garbage bags, newspapers and tape that I had come armed with on the counter top and leant on my elbows to peer out into the garden. It was as beautiful as I'd remembered it. With a sigh, I turned my back on the sight to head out to the car to fetch the boxes. Better get some work done first.

Clearing the kitchen was surprisingly easy. Good plates, bowls and mugs into a box for the Salvos, chipped ones into the trash. Bent forks, spoons and knives into the bin, good ones for charity. There were a few vases and ornaments, but nothing I liked the look of. All to charity. I was tempted to stop then and take a break. I'd opened the windows and I could smell the scent of the garden. Bird song drifted out of the thickets and once a bee buzzed in and out again, settling for just a second on a gaudy painted plate that I was lifting to wrap. Most of the pollen sacks on its legs were already swollen to bursting. I watched it zigzag its way out to the real flowers under the shade trees, then squared my shoulders and walked through to the living room, taking its industriousness as my own inspiration.

The room was spotless. The books on the shelves were neatly arranged by colour and size. The pictures on the walls hung straight with glass that sparkled as if freshly washed. A worn green leather couch was drawn up at right angles to the window, so that lying in one direction, there was a view of the garden, and in the other, of the neatly laid fireplace in the corner near the door. A crazy patterned quilt was slung over the back of it, ready for chilly nights.

Had she known she was going to die? Or had she always lived like this? Like a nun or a hermit. At any rate, the polar opposite of my mother, who spent her life battling an impossible tide of *stuff* that invaded our house and piled in drifts on every surface and in every corner.

On the wall above the fireplace hung a framed photo of a woman and a man. They stood in a garden a lot like Sally's, leaning one against the other. I walked closer, frowning. They seemed oddly familiar, although I would've sworn I'd never seen them before. They were dressed in the fashions of the turn of the twentieth century. She had the hem of her dress lifted in one hand. A hat dangled behind her shoulder, the tip of its feather decorations tangling in the branch of the holly tree behind them. It was an unusually casual pose for the time. But it was her eyes that gripped me. They were a pale hazel colour, and while his blue ones were locked on her in an attitude of devotion, hers stared out at me, her lips parted to speak, as if they had a secret that she longed to share.

I lifted the picture off its hook. There was nothing to show where it had been taken, or by whom. I was about to put it back when I flipped it over instead.

A slip of buff coloured paper was tucked into the back of the frame. I pulled it gently out, blowing off the dust of a crumbling spider web. It was a ticket. Or an invitation, really. Gold letters were embossed into the paper:

Admit One
To The Garden of the Sun
Afternoon Tea Included
Opening hours Noon to Sunset
(Excepting Saturday)

On the other side was an address I didn't know and three names: my grandmother's, my mother's, and mine. And through each of the names but the last one was a neat red line.

I don't know if anything else would have inspired me to keep working long into that Friday night and all the next day. I ignored texts from my parents asking how things were going, cancelled on my trivia team at the pub, skipped yoga at the gym, and kept going. I found nothing else exciting. As I slipped out of each empty room, my feet echoed on the bare boards. My voice came back to me distorted when I sang softly under my breath as I swept the front porch and turned the key in the lock. I had only the garden to go.

I wasn't expecting to have to do much there: pick up a few statues, untie the hammock, take down the fairy lights on the arbour around the pond, that kind of thing. I walked around to the back along a narrow brick path that ran along the shadowed north side of the house. Night had fallen while I worked and the way was lit only be the yellow haze of street lights. I moved slowly, kicking at clumps of moss that clung to the cracks between the bricks like green puffballs.

The ticket-invitation nagged at me. I was kind of glad now that M and D were away. If they had found it, I was sure it would never have made it to my hands.

I straightened my back as I reached out to open the gate into the garden. It felt like this would be the hardest part of the dismantling. A sound from beyond the gate stopped me in my tracks. A soft voice whispering, and a deeper one answering with a sharp command. The words were carried to me only faintly by the evening breeze. Whoever spoke must be in the far part of the garden. There was a crash and a muffled giggle, and what sounded like a slap. Then silence.

I pressed my face to the gate and peered through a gap in the planks. It was darker than I had realised out there. The canopy of the taller trees blocked out the light. I could see only as far as the bend where the path turned to wind through bushes toward the pond.

Could it be children stealing?

I thought about that for a long moment. I might not have been the only one to fall in love with everything that aunt Sally had done in her yard. There might be neighbours who loved the place, who had come to take a souvenir before it was all destroyed. I ran my hands over my face with a sigh.

Could anyone do any harm in there? Sally was already dead. I had nowhere to put statues or lights or hammocks or tiny decorated fairy doors.

And they might demand to know who I was just as easily.

I turned my back. Whoever was there could have whatever it was they had come for.

I was done.

* * *

When I woke, the sun was already high in the sky, just touching the top edge of the crystals that swung in my window and cast small rainbows onto the wall. I stretched languorously across the whole width of the bed, aware that I had not slept so deeply in months. Then I jerked upright, reaching for my phone.

What time was it? The Garden...

I rolled out of bed with a groan. It was nearly noon, and I didn't want to miss another moment of the day.

The GPS in my car wouldn't recognize the address on the paper. I ran back into the house to get a map.

Where the hell had I put it?

I threw piles of papers around the living room as I searched. They landed on other piles and the wobbly edifices fell in heaps around me, leaving scant patches of grey-blue carpet like pools of sky.

The whole bookshelf wobbled as I reached up to drag stuff off the top section.

No map.

The kitchen was no better. Magazines, junk mail, coupon... I sent them all scattering in my haste.

Nothing.

I ran my hands through my hair, knocking out the jewelled butterfly I had pinned there in honour of the occasion. It rolled under the fridge and vanished from view.

By all the gods, how had Sally been so neat and tidy? If only I was more like her...

I gave up in the end. I'd have to buy one at the gas station on the corner.

I ran back to the car and turned the key in the ignition. A low grinding sound was all that happened. I did it again and again. No motor leaping into life.

A terrible suspicion formed in my mind as I got out, kicked the door shut and looked desperately down the road for another option.

What if the other names had been struck out, not because they hadn't wanted to go, but because they couldn't?

I ran along the street, past the painted houses and clipped hedges and trimmed non-mess-making trees, my heart and my thoughts pounding in time to my feet.

I tried to summon an accurate memory of my grandmother as I ran. My mother's mother. Tall and lean and supple. She had scraped her grey hair back into a bun that kept her face taut. Only her lips had seemed young. Fuller and redder than any I had ever seen. And her eyes had been blue. A startling thing in a family of deep brown and hazel. It made her seem frivolous, out of place. Or was that her laugh? For what I remembered above all was her laughing.

She had died suddenly as well. One moment she was there, the next, she was gone. I didn't remember a funeral. If there had been one.

Stupid. Stupid. Stupid.

I cursed under my breath as I ran. There was something more than the ordinary to this, that was for sure.

I reached the bus stop to see the tail end of the Number 64 toiling into the distance. I leant over, my hands on my knees, gasping for breath. It was several years since my last high school track and field event and I was not getting any fitter bending over the bench and framing art for the would be trendy customers that came to our Michel's store.

Some of them had nice stuff, of course.

I shook my head, tempted to bang my head on the glass wall of the bus shelter, to get focus back on the problem before me.

Behind me, there was a discrete cough, and a deep voice said a hesitant hello, then continued.

"You alright, Ma'am? Did you need to catch that bus badly?"

I nodded without turning, my head suddenly dizzy, my breath catching.

"I did," I said, "very badly."

Brown leaves skittered around my feet, rustling like soft maracas as a knee-high wind twisted into eddies at the corner of the stop. Velvety guitar chords wound into their chorus. I turned then, all right.

Dark blue eyes laughed into mine, half hidden under a tangle of dreads and a green knitted cap. The rest of the guy was bent over the guitar, balancing it against his legs and fingering the strings with his eyes now closed and a smile touching his lips.

I frowned, trying to place him and his sound. He was playing louder now, the notes a lament that matched the clouds gathering in the west.

Suddenly, I had it.

I snapped my fingers and he straightened up, letting his fingers fall. The music dying under the squeal of a truck running the lights.

"You're Wiley Montana," I said, and it wasn't a question. "I saw you play last month at the Club."

He nodded and bowed. "At your service, Ma'am."

"I wish you were."

I bit my lip as the words leapt out. Flirting with strangers was not my normal scene. Even if the stranger was the lead player in the hottest band in town.

He slung the guitar over his shoulder and onto his back with a practised flip of the wrist. A lone drop of rain hit the pavement and rose again in a puff of dust and steam.

"Oh, but I am," he said, and there was a note of insistence in his voice that could have alarmed me. "See that pickup?" he turned and pointed two blocks down the road to a black Silverado. "Me and my beast there can take you anywhere you need to go."

I fingered the ticket in my pocket. I didn't need to look at it to tell him the address, but I was afraid he would laugh. I looked around as if the answer I sought would come from outside of me. Some sort of permission to be real.

Wiley was waiting, not fidgeting, not worried. He looked as if he had nothing else he would rather be doing than waiting for me to respond.

"I won't laugh," he said, "if that's what worrying you. What is it? A kitten shower? Tupperware party? Clown workshop? Fairy Princess training?"

I laughed, despite myself, and shook my head.

"I'm not quite sure myself," I said, "but can you take me to Ester-brook Road? Up on the Ridgeway." "Quickly?" I added. "I might be running out of time."

He raised one eyebrow, a skill I have never mastered.

"As I said, your wish is my command."

He broke into a brisk jog, steadying the guitar with one hand while the other fished in his pocket for keys.

"Come on," he called without looking back. "That storm is about to break."

I ran after him and hauled myself up into the passenger seat, with just time to notice the small silver dragon painted on the door. It was only as big as my hand, curled around the door handle like a sleepy guardian. I didn't see if there were similar ones, or other beasts, on the rest of the doors. Black clouds covered the sun and the rain began in earnest as Wiley swung the truck around in a tyre-wrecking skid and accelerated up the hill toward the north of the city.

"You know where it is, then?"

He shrugged. "I was raised here. Kids got to go exploring back then."

He leant forward and flipped the radio on. Sunday afternoon jazz filled the silence. I looked out of the window on my side. The water streaming past blurred the images.

"You haven't asked my name," I murmured dreamily, as the thought occurred to me. "The knight in shining armour rescues the princess and does not know who she is..."

"Ah, but does the princess herself know?"

He kept his eyes on the road, and his tone was light, but the question struck me as inexpressibly sad.

Did I?

Did I know anyone?

Why did Aunt Sally have that ticket in her house? What had she fought about so bitterly with my mother? Why had I never asked?

"Gemma Delaney," I whispered, and then corrected it, even more softly. "Gemma Phoenix Delaney."

I usually kept that secret. I wasn't named for a built-up bit of Arizona desert, but for the regenerating bird, but either way, I'd been teased too often. So generally, I just left it out.

Or lied.

Paula, Pamela, Patricia. There were plenty of boring P names to choose from when I needed one.

Wiley swerved to avoid water that was running along the side of the road. I gripped the edge of the seat and tried to see out of the windscreen between the swooshes of the wipers. We had left the built up area behind and were descending through dark woods to the river crossing. The black surface of the wet road shone in our lights. Leaves and twigs and pine cones fell around us and even the heavy truck shifted and bucked against the gusts of wind.

"I'll tell you my name if we get there. My real name. Wiley Montana is just for the stage. And for strangers."

A little shiver crept down my spine. If we get there...

"Don't you mean when?" I squeaked, unable to keep my voice to its normal range. "When we get there—"

The truck skidded across the centre line and back as Wiley hit the brakes and swerved to avoid a deer that had leapt from the verge right in front of us.

We rounded the corner, still fish-tailing, and then he slammed on the stop in earnest.

Water was surging up and over the bridge, its dark waves curling and roiling across our path. It was impossible to tell if it was deep from this distance. Debris rose and fell on its surface: branches, a chicken coop, the carcass of a drowned cow, bloated and grotesque even in the half light of the storm. As we watched, the trunk of a shattered tree reared up out of the water, the tip soaring above us like a giant's spear. It teetered in the air, murky water pouring off its twisted flanks, then crashed down onto the bridge with a sound that shook the vehicle under us. When the spray and flying wreckage had settled, it lay at an angle across the road, a massive roadblock that I knew we could not pass.

As Wiley and I began to breathe again, the rain eased and a band of clear sky began to push the clouds up from the western horizon, revealing the bulk of the Ridgeway ahead of us. I slipped out of the truck, not caring if I got soaked. As I let myself down, the painted silver dragon felt warm under my fingers.

Wiley slipped out on the other side and we walked forward to the edge of the swollen river. It was a short bridge, only wide enough for one vehicle at a time. Above my head, the Give Way sign creaked ominously. As the storm receded, I could see the bank on the other side. There was a gap between the level of the water and the underside of the fallen trunk.

"Wiley." Without realizing it, I gripped him by the arm as I pointed. "Look. We could go under. On foot. There's plenty to hold onto. We won't get swept away, I'm sure of it."

His face was pale and still. Drops of rain still lingered on his cheeks so that he looked as if he were crying. He reached down and took both of my hands in his. His skin was hot and dry, far hotter than mine, giving me a feeling of comfort, like wrapping my fingers round a mug of chocolate in winter.

"I can't," he said carefully.

I opened my mouth to protest, but he shook his head and squeezed my palms.

"Gem, we don't have time." He turned his wrist so I could see his watch.

Who wears a watch? But still. 4.30 pm. It would be dark by 6.

I looked again at the bridge and swallowed hard.

I had to cross that alone.

I pulled my hands free and began to run. If I stopped to think, I'd be too afraid to go on. Like gymnastics. Like sailing. Like the marathon.

Not this time, I begged myself. Don't quit this time.

I heard Wiley cheering behind me. I turned my head, nearly losing my footing under the flood.

"Your name," I shouted. "You didn't tell me your name!"

I could just hear him above the thump of other logs and flotsam hitting the rails beside me.

"Justin. Justin Phoenix Zephyr Masterton."

Two ridiculous names?

I stifled a giggle. I might have met my match in him.

I was half way across when I realized the water was still rising. It was chest deep already. The cold bit into me, so that I shuddered as I hauled myself forward, grabbing onto anything and everything to keep my feet under me. I knew my hands had to be torn and bleeding, so I didn't look.

A phrase ran through my mind, an echo from the past.

What you don't know can't hurt you.

Was it my grandmother's voice?

What you don't know can't hurt you.

"With all due respect," I yelled, pointing at the sky, not sure who or what I was addressing. "With all due respect, I do believe that it can!"

I punched my fist in the air, slipped on something vile that the water had left beneath me, and went down under the water, my arms flailing. For a moment, I couldn't tell which way was up, which down. Then I got my arm out of the water. I could feel the air against it.

Up. Definitely up.

I groped for something to hold, to haul me up. My fingers smashed into the edge of a branch. I yelped with pain. Water flooded into my mouth. I coughed and inhaled more, and oh, the burning. I was swallowing liquid fire. Drowning in flames.

I flailed again with my arms, both out now, both above me, and suddenly I was held in a grip stronger than mine, hauled out and up onto the trunk that spanned the broken bridge and let go so abruptly that I almost overbalanced again.

I opened my eyes.

Aunt Sally sat beside me, clad in a pale leather jacket over a white gown. She had a fishing pole in her hand, the line stretched out into the water on the far side of the road, a coloured float bobbing tranquilly up and down.

I would have squeaked some inane thing in surprise if I hadn't been so busy coughing. I spluttered for what seemed like hours, spitting out green tinged water, vomiting, holding my sides.

She reeled in the line and threw a small silver fish back into the flood with a kiss and a wave of her hand, then collapsed the rod and tucked it into a bag at her side.

When I was finished, she rose elegantly to her feet and reached out a hand. "Well, my dear, shall we go on?"

I looked up at her, balanced on that swaying trunk, a drowned rat tangled in a mass of twigs not far from her arm.

"It can do me harm," I croaked, the words hurting my throat and making me cough again. "What I don't know. Can't it, Aunt Sal?"

She sighed and shrugged, glancing once at the horizon, her eyes narrowed against the light.

"Why couldn't he come?" I said. "Why are we both called Phoenix? What the hell is going on?"

Her lips tightened and she reached into her bag and pulled out an oval instrument of brass and leather and iron. There was a circle of convex glass in the centre. She took a quick glance through it, turning a screw as if to focus on the water, then she tossed it to me with a quick grin.

"Look."

She was a woman of few words out in the open, it seemed.

I held the object to my eye. Through the glass, the water glinted a kind of steel blue. The lines of light ran in a mesh, like a net or a fence of molten wire. Where anything living touched the water, it gave off sparks and a vibrating hiss.

I'd seen that once before. When I was a child. In her pool. I was sure.

She held out a hand and I passed her the glass. She tucked it away, carefully, as one does something of great value.

"He's a Zephyr. He can't cross this."

There were too many questions to know where to begin. And the sun was visibly sinking toward the ridge.

But I needed one thing before I was prepared to go on. "Tell me your name. All of it this time."

"Let's get to the Garden. I'll tell you then." She turned to go, but I held my ground.

I could have counted my heartbeats as I waited for her reply. Even the water seemed to slow in its rush down river by my side. I did not look straight at her. I doubted that I could do that and not give in.

"Sally Gaia Masterton," she said at last, her voice a frustrated growl. "All right? Can we go now?"

I followed her, leaping as she did from trunk to branch to trunk, back into the water and onto the far bank.

I was filthy, soaked to the skin, shivering, and blue with cold. The woman I had known as my aunt looked as neat and ordered as she always did.

She looked at me with some concern, then back up the slope. The road curved away to the left, where it turned and zigzagged up the ridge along the contour lines at a grade that the first cars could have coped with. To our right, a rock-strewn dirt track headed up and into a tangle of undergrowth, some of which looked suspiciously thorny to me. Almost invisible on a mossy stone was a leaf-shaped wooden sign:

To the Garden

Sally tugged a green rip-proof jacket out of her bag and tossed it me without a word. Then she began to climb.

There are whole days and weeks of our lives that we will never remember later, and other moments that cannot be forgotten, no matter how hard we try. That path will be in the second category, I am sure.

When I got to the top, my jeans were in tatters, my face scratched and smarting where the salt of my sweat dripped into the wounds. Somewhere, I had lost the woven bracelet I had tied on my wrist in the morning. In its place was a darkening bruise that looked as if I had punched a wall.

Which a few seconds later I was tempted to do for real. The gate to the Garden of the Sun was closed and locked.

Sally looked at my expression and frowned. "You did bring the key?" she said. "The one I left by the pond?"

I closed my eyes and sank down on my heels, massaging my knees. They ached more than I could have imagined possible.

"I didn't get to the garden," I muttered. "I imagine the children took everything that was there."

"Children? What children?"

I told her about the gate.

She spat on the ground at my feet.

"Fifty years," she said bitterly. "Fifty years we plan this and you don't get the key because you're shy? I get you here, right to the door, and that's it? End of game? I don't believe it."

"You don't believe it?"

I was on my feet shouting at her before I had time to think.

"What about me? I have to clear out your whole house. I nearly drown to get here. You're dead, and now back again, and no explanations given, thank you very much. And you don't believe it?"

I waved my hands along the garden enclosure. "If this is as serious as you seem to think, then shut up and let me concentrate. Because there's another way in."

"How do you—"

I glared at her. "I feel it, okay? Now *be quiet.*"

Even as I spoke, the air was chilling as the evening fell. The shadow of the wall crept further out with each minute.

Sally sat down cross-legged and closed her eyes. Well, so much for that. I glanced at her once more, then tilted my head from side to side. Feeling... Seeking...

I blew out experimentally, gently, steadily, the way you do when you are coaxing fire from a lingering coal.

And there it was. Writing on the wall. Letters like tiny flames. I squinted at them hard to try to get them still, but they danced all the more. I blew again, even more softly than before. They brightened and flashed and vanished. I closed my eyes and they were there against my lids.

It was not English.

I read it anyway, in the kind of formal way people do in church or at graduation.

Singsong, singsong, blah di dah.

I read it twice and the second time I screamed as something cold and clammy fell onto my foot and croaked.

A frog. Well, probably a toad (as if I could tell). And in its mouth, a key.

I laughed and reached down and took it. It was a bit wet, but apart from that, it felt like any other bit of metal.

Sally opened her eyes and watched as I put it in the lock and turned. There was a click, and the door swung outward. Inside was another door, slightly smaller. In the centre, a serious of leather straps criss-crossed each other. Behind them, I could see another keyhole, out of reach. I fingered the straps, pulling one carefully to see what happened. It gave like elastic.

"Oh." I turned to Sally, genuinely surprised. "I know this. You gave me that computer game for Christmas once, remem—"

I swallowed the words back in disgust. *Fifty years in the planning.* What kind of manipulative...

I let my hands fall to my sides and leant against the wall. Not for long. Strands of ivy and creeper dug into my back. It was hard to be righteously angry like that.

"You know what? How about you tell me *why* I should get into this garden before I go on? I mean, what's in it for me?"

"Nothing," said Sally. "Nothing at all for you."

She turned her back. The toad hopped away with a sound like a miniature engine revving.

"Just a lot for the world."

She said it so quietly I didn't think she was even speaking to me. She reached into her bag and carefully lifted out a bigger instrument folded into a white cloth. She unwrapped it and held it out. Her eyes were dark and there were no longer any raindrops to hide the tears that balanced there.

It was a telescope, as beautiful as the water glass.

"Look," she said, her gesture taking in the whole city laid out across the river, and the land beyond.

I lifted the glass to my left eye, squinting the right one closed. Another network lay over the city, green this time, with pulsating nodes where there were parks and houses with particularly lovely gardens. Even the sculpture installations along the river path had nodes, small but present nonetheless.

In the distance, around the largest mall in Alberta, was a pool of black.

I lowered the glass and raised my shoulders. "And?"

"And we are losing," she said. She reached out and shifted a lever beside the lens.

"Look again."

My anger forgotten I looked. This time the network was like flame, a dancing web of light.

I drew in a sharp breath. I felt that fire touching me.

"Phoenix," I whispered. "Firebird within." And I knew something else, too, in that moment.

That web was mine.

I turned to Sally. "Who named me, then? Who named Wiley?"

She smiled for the first time that day, and laughed, the rich low chuckle that I had loved so much as a child.

"The Fairy godmothers, dear heart, with your parent's consent."

It was absurd. I didn't believe her for a second, but it was enough. There would be time to know more, but only if I entered the Garden.

Sally knew. She settled into silence as my fingers flew over the leather lacing, separating the strands so that nothing crossed and I could plunge the key into the next lock.

I knew the next puzzle as well. Shifting bars to open a path and expose the keyhole.

And the third puzzle. Matching colours and shapes to complete a pattern.

Did Sally *make* computer games?

I laughed at the thought. There were many people involved in the game. I had no doubt of that. Each with a talent of their own. Each bound to an element, not of their choosing. Theirs from birth. Before birth even.

"How does Wiley have two?" I asked, stretching out my hands and flexing my fingers as the next door slid open sideways to reveal a long dark tunnel. I peered into it. The floor sloped down and twisted out of sight. I wiped my fingers against each other, but the sweat returned. Like a water slide. The fear that had seen me laughed out of team sports at High School.

I clenched my bladder as a fierce urge to pee swept over me. That day at the top of the stairs to the water slide, that had been a defining humiliation all right.

Maybe this wasn't real? Maybe it was a test of my resolve, and when I walked forward, it would vanish and the gravel path I was standing on would continue flat and smooth, into a garden and that Afternoon tea I had been promised.

"It's real," said Sally. "And he has two because he entered the Garden, and studied and fought. Masterton is a title, not just a name, you know."

Her hand touched me lightly between the shoulder blades. "The sun..."

I suspected some part of the test was free will, since she didn't push me, and she might easily have done.

I jumped.

I screamed and flailed and emerged at the bottom in a tangled heap of limbs just as the sun's light fell off the edge of the giant sundial that lay in the entrance to the garden and night fell.

* * *

I had heard that happened in the Tropics, such a rapid change between light and dark, but this was not a tropical garden. I was already shivering, despite Sally's jacket. As I lay on the ground, still dazed from the fall, just glad that I was inside, snow began to drift down from a sky where stars still shone. Swift lights danced above my head. Fireflies, I decided. Dark shapes swooped silently after them. Bats perhaps. At any rate, the lights faded and scattered and I lay in starlight, fingering the snowflakes that settled as I watched. And truly, they were large enough to see that each one was different.

And beautiful.

I got to my feet, dusting myself off, wondering which things I had been taught were true, and which myth, or outright lie.

Not the ones I had thought before. That much was certain.

I looked around. It felt as if I was alone. To my right was a tea shop, the shutters drawn and a Closed sign in the window. To the left, a path ran off between Privet hedges. I'd got lost in a maze once, and I wasn't going to risk that tonight.

That left the middle road.

It was paved in white stone, cut into even squares. It ran ahead of me, glowing softly, under the arch of a Gatehouse and up to a mansion.

I couldn't think of any other word to use. The building was painted white, with wrap around verandas on all three floors. Red Virginia Creeper ran up the walls and onto the roof.

As I got closer, I could see a woman standing in the doorway, clad in a long red cloak and a crown of creeper.

I tried to hold my back straight as I walked forward. I needed shelter from the cold and I knew that this would be another test. The last one, I fervently hoped.

My stomach growled, reminding me how long it had been since I'd rushed from the house with only a spoon of dry instant coffee and a banana to set me up for the day.

Now, if I'd known *exactly* what kind of day it would be...

I let that thought trail away as the woman dropped me a perfect curtsy, better than *Downton Abbey* I would say.

I looked down at my ripped and filthy jeans and decided not to even try. I bowed instead and waited. I had already learnt something new from Sally about silence and timing and the power of a well-timed pause.

I was expecting her to ask me to light a candle, or set fire to the garland on the door behind her. Something Fire related. I had already figured out that the four elements were part of whatever this was. Earth, Fire, Air and Water.

Me, Fire.

Wiley (I couldn't yet think of him as Justin), Fire and Air.

Sally, Earth.

No one I knew of yet for Water.

Oh.

I stopped moving for a moment, letting a new thought flow into me. That was how it felt. Like Wisdom from some other place.

My mother and Grandmother were both called Nerida.

Mermaid.

I had never attached any significance to it before.

The woman in the doorway rang a small bell. I jumped back to the present. A man appeared from around the corner of the veranda. He wore black and silver. A flute was slung over his shoulder, just as Wiley had worn his guitar.

Another man appeared from the other direction, wearing green and brown. In his hands he held a horn of antler, polished till it shone.

I looked from one to the other.

The woman held out a woven sack to me. The neck was pulled shut with a red leather tie. I pulled the sack open and tipped out a rawhide drum. The surround was painted red, with black bulls running from warriors with flaming spears.

The woman nodded and flung open the door into the house. I followed the two men inside, the drum pressed against my heart.

The entrance way was of white marble, flecked with mica, or something else that sparkled in the light of glittering chandeliers. Before us, the floor was covered with a map. It took me a moment to realize that it was all of Canada. The States and Territories were laid out in detail, drawn with ink and ochre, I thought, onto stretched hide. I could see our town, crouched by the river, in the lee of the Ridgeway. To the West, the mountains rose and fell in waves to the sea. To the East, the prairies lay prone across the ancient land.

The map stopped before it reached the Maritimes.

We circled it slowly, our eyes locked.

I hadn't noticed the curtain to the far side of the room until it was pulled apart. A woman lay there on a blue futon, her skin as pale and dazzling as white coral sand. On the floor at her feet a conch shell rested on a cushion of seashell pink.

The woman who had let us in climbed a set of steps to a carved lectern and banged a gavel three times. Doors all around the hall swung open and beasts of all kinds stepped in. Elk, eagles, beavers, skunks, frogs, mice, Chickadees... I could not see them all, let alone name them all.

But I knew what they were. Our judges and jury.

I had never played a drum.

It was not the kind of instrument that my parents would have allowed in the house. Noisy. Uncouth. Not 'our kind of thing' at all.

Still, it fit nicely in my hand. I tapped it gently with two fingers to see what happened.

What happened was total silence and all eyes focused on me.

It seemed that whatever was happening, I had begun.

I closed my eyes and took a deep breath, thinking of Wiley on stage at the Club.

Justin Phoenix Zephyr Masterton.

Now, he knew how to project a persona to satisfy the crowd.

I let my fingertips fall like soft summer rain onto the stretched skin of the drum. My hands searched out the memories in the skin. Heat. Sun. Fire. Flame. Sweet Grass. Deep shadow. Heart-hammering lust in the time of the Rut. The tugging, intense suckling of young.

Fear of the End.

The fingers faltered and the beat slipped. I shared that fear. Lines of sweat were slid across my skin, making my face shine and my torn shirt cling to my back.

Still I drummed on, feeling the others in the room, their longing for sweetness, for sun and light and life and the going-on of things, generation after generation, life without end.

The pulse I created wove a net around the room. I let myself drop into it, feeding it with white-hot coals that I blew into leaping tongues of flame.

After a time, I saw, felt, sensed, breathed, a knowledge of the others playing beside me, weaving the net with me. Fire, Earth, Air and Water. We made a new thing that was Many and One.

And somewhere in that drumming, I said *Yes. This I what I will become.*

* * *

I don't remember how it ended.

I woke by the sundial as the sun crested its edge. I was covered in melting snow. A drum lay by my head. Sally and Wiley, *Justin,* had a picnic spread on the grass. Soft white cheese, rosemary and olive bread, fruit, and chilled sparkling wine.

I'd never been so hungry in my life.

My fingers and palms were raw and blistered. I blew on them to soothe the burn. Justin popped food into my mouth and Sally lay back, smiling like a cat who has just given birth.

As I suppose she had in a manner of speaking.

"So how come the red lines?" I asked lazily with my mouth half-full. "What happened?"

"Your Grandmother couldn't do the puzzles," said Sally. "And your mother, well, she was already deeply in love with your father and she

226

couldn't let that go."

I chewed in silence, thinking on that.

If Sally had asked me outright, back at my house, to give up all the dreams I had for my life and become what, a warrior for balance, would I have done it?

If I had never felt the drumming, never seen the nets that ran through and under and across everything, binding us all into a creation of such beauty that I knew I could never know it enough, never study it enough, never protect it enough?

I bit my lip, knowing that I would have refused, and hating myself for that answer.

Justin shifted on the grass and raised his glass.

"A toast," he said. "To all those out there," and he nodded to indicate over the wall, in the world we had left behind for the moment, "who weave the net without knowing that they are magic. Without ever making a conscious choice. Without the risk of knowing that they are special and becoming prima donnas..."

I threw a bunch of grapes at his head and followed it up with a jug of water.

He leapt to his feet and pelted me with dried figs.

The laughter was what I needed clearly. I rolled around on my back, gasping for breath, tears pouring from my eyes.

Sally watched us, a smile lighting her sapphire eyes.

She took the empty water jug, filled it from the fountain against the outer wall and tipped it on both our heads.

"May your babies be Earth and Water," she said. "We need a new generation to carry the Flame."

First published in 'Elemental Foundations', Zimbell House Publications, 2017.

Fates & Flora

Natasia Rose Langfelder

I t was a little after 3 am when Lila woke up alone. Alone. As usual. She pulled the cool white sheets up to her chin. No matter how hot it got, the sheets were always cool. Alexi insisted on buying designer CoolBoiTech sheets. Even though she had moved in almost a year ago, his apartment was still his apartment, and it looked like the quintessential bachelor pad. She groaned and shut her eyes hard to try to block out the purple neon lights that always snuck in through the cracks in the blinds. She heard the bathroom tap dripping against the porcelain. She hated when Alexi left it leaking. He was rich enough to not be affected by the water rations - yet. Yet. She warned him it was coming; she had seen the reports herself. Artax was running out of water. The aquifers beneath the city were at all-time lows and even water-rich Bree was considering halting water exports.

She kept trying to warn him. "Having money won't protect you forever," she said, brandishing her cereal spoon at him like a weapon. "It's coming for all of us."

He laughed at her. "You worry too much, little doll. We will be fine. Everything will be fine."

His smile was wide and full of gleaming white teeth. He left her to bear the worry alone. She got up and twisted the faucet closed, then dove back into the safety of the soft feather bed. Alexi thought of money as a shield against the woes of the world. But when an entire city falls, no one is safe. They will eat the rich in the streets.

They will feast on your bones, she thought. I will join them.

Lila had seen it before. He knew she had, but he had not asked. As usual.

When the alarm went off at 7 am, he was back in bed. His back was to her. She turned off the alarm and slipped out of bed. She didn't ask him where he had gone, and he pretended to sleep through the alarm. She was beginning to think of it as a game they played. She indulged in a short shower, relishing in the warm trickles of water as they poured over her flesh. If she was a better person, she would shave her head. But she kept her white hair short in back and collarbone length in front to appease her vanity. She changed into her work uniform—sensible black flats, black slacks and an eggshell blouse, and launched herself into the world. The city of Artax was not and would never be home, but it was a better option than the barren wastelands that surrounded it.

Artax was shaped like a 5-pointed star, bordered by walls that stood over 100 feet tall and edged with barbed wire. She and Alexi lived in the center of the city, in a high rise that stood in a cluster with other skyscrapers. Residential and corporate buildings spangled with blinking neon advertisements reflecting off each other's hard metal and glass facades. She was trying to get used to it. This is home, she told herself, as she ran to catch the train to the lab.

The routine of going to work soothed her, helped her not think of the final days in Leda. The buildings got shorter and further apart as the glass tube raced out of the heart of the city. The botany lab was located at the northern point of the star, alongside the rest of research and development for Artax. Everything from botany to agriculture and weapons development was clustered together in a heavily guarded compound that spanned miles.

Lila passed five different checkpoints to get to the wet labs. She was working on forced transpiration, seeing if there was a way to engineer a plant that could efficiently soak up contaminated water and spit it back out as clean water. Her plan was to engineer a plant that would have a high concentration of stomata on its leaves, which opened to release water frequently, or even always, like a dripping faucet. The latter would be ideal and a huge scientific breakthrough.

The problem really was that the contaminated water was killing the plants before they could get to the water-producing part. In her weaker moments, Lila daydreamed about being the celebrated scientist who single-handedly saved the planet. She flushed just imagining being the one who could master the process. To be the person who changed the world. She tried to squash the thought. It was ridiculous to think she could be the one... and yet. It was what got her out of bed each morning. Hubris kills, she warned herself. But without her work, what did she have?

If you looked at Lila through the harshest lens of reality, the only reality she could abide, she was wasting time and resources killing tiny plants. If Alexi told her the definition of insanity was doing the same thing over and over and expecting different results one more time...

Lila entered the pristine white locker room, stashed her bag, and walked through the sterilization chamber to her station. On it she had five plants in glass cases, their roots reaching deep into water that had been collected from the Lepya Wastelands to the north of Artax. They were all dead. As usual.

"Hey," CJ, the closest thing Lila had to a friend in Artax, appeared in the doorway of her lab. "A bunch of us are going out tonight, if you want to come with."

"I don't know."

"C'mon, Li, it's Friday. You never do anything. You never go out. You're becoming an old lady right in front of my eyes." CJ lifted her hand to her brow for dramatic effect.

"Yes, it's Friday. Maybe Alexi will want to do something."

CJ's face tightened a bit at the edges. Lila had said the wrong thing. "Don't feel bad for me. I don't care that he cheats."

"There's that Leda straight-forwardness. Hard to get used to people who say exactly what they mean." CJ leaned against the door frame and wrapped her orange ponytail around a finger. "Just come out, have a few drinks. We'll be at Mermaid Junkyard on the second south point. My girlfriend works there. I want you to meet her. I think you'll like her."

"I never like anyone. Just you and maybe Alexi."

"Okay, maybe I don't think you'll like her. But you need to get out. We're gonna head out early but just come when you're done. Promise?"

"Promise."

Lila arrived at the bar at 8, which she considered late enough to spare herself hours of insipid chit-chat but early enough to not be rude.

"Li, over here," CJ waved.

She was standing at a wooden high top, and a dark, muscled woman had an arm around her. The rest of their colleagues had shed their white lab coats and looked, well, like normal people having fun. Lila sidled in on the side of CJ that was not occupied.

"Take your coat off. Stay a while."

"I'm Feather," said the woman, holding out her hand. Lila shook it. She appreciated the firm handshake, even if the hand itself was callused and rough. "Ceej talks about you all the time."

CJ blushed and pushed her glasses up. "I do not!"

Feather laughed. It was a genuine laugh that came from deep in her belly and made you feel warm all over. Lila decided she did, in fact, like CJ's girlfriend.

Five beers later and Lila was telling Feather her tiny dead plant woes. Feather furrowed her brow. "I have an idea. I want you to meet my sister."

"Why?"

"She can talk to dead people."

* * *

The next day Lila found herself on the train to the south point to meet Feather and her sister.

"Do you want me to go?" Alexei had asked, as he lounged in bed.

"No, it's fine."

She tried not to be offended when he smiled, happy to be off the hook. She didn't want him there anyway.

Fortune's Flora was a small storefront on the southern point. It took up the bottom floor of a small cement apartment building. The awning was faded but clean and potted trees spread their leaves outside a plate-glass window that showcased fridges filled with freshly cut flowers. Lila opened the door, and a bright brass bell announced her arrival. A small, pale girl with white hair was standing at the cash register.

"Can I help you?" the girl asked. Her fringe brushed the top of her eyelashes. In place of eyeballs, the girl had two metal orbs that glowed a faint green. Lila froze.

"Li!" Feather came out from behind one of the fridges. "Misty, this is Li, the friend I was telling you about."

"Charmed," said the girl.

Feather swung the sign behind the door to "Closed" and turned a key in the lock. "Let's go in back."

Misty untied her apron, which was white rimmed with a lime green that matched her eye mods. Underneath, she was wearing an A-line white dress that made her look like a child's doll. Misty stepped through the door behind the fridge and Lila followed. They were in a small cement room, with a round table in the center flanked by two wooden chairs.

"Please sit." Misty gestured and sat in one of the chairs.

Lila sat facing the strange child. Feather closed the door behind them. Her large figure looming over them made the room seem impossibly small.

"Feather has told you about my gift." It wasn't a question.

"Yes, but I'm not..."

"You doubt I can help you." Misty finished the thought. "And my eyes scare you."

"Yes."

"I traded my eyesight on this physical plane in order to enhance my gifts in the spirit world. I have eye mods, so I can still see when I have the inclination."

"She plucked her own eyes out of her head when she was six," Feather interjected. "Scared the shit out of me and mom. Blood everywhere. Worst day of my life."

"Everything has a price." Misty arched an eyebrow at Lila, prompting her to wonder what the price of this visit would be.

"Aw, Misty. We were going to go anyway. Don't be like that."

"Are you sure you two are related?"

"I wonder that all the time," said Misty. "Feather told me about your conundrum. Luckily for you, I've already been working on something that might help." Misty whipped out a battered touch pad and set it on the table between them. "Before The Great Rive, the government hid stashes of heritage seeds all over the continent. The idea was that in case of a catastrophic event, we could use these seeds to feed the population, purify the air and the water. Allen said it's like Noah's Ark for plants. It holds everything we could dream of and everything we couldn't possibly hope to imagine. He's very poetic, really."

Purify the water. Lila felt light-headed with hope.

"Unfortunately, after The Great Rive, no one left alive remembered or cared about the caches. Leaving them ripe for opportunists, such as my sister and myself."

"So, you can sell flowers no one else sells?"

"One would think that would be a priority, wouldn't one?" Misty asked. "But some of us are drug dealers."

Now it was time for Lila's eyebrows to rise. "Does CJ know that?"

Feather put her hand behind her head, looking a little sheepish. "Nothing crazy, just fire moss. But Misty said there's seeds for something called marijuana. One of the spirits was telling her about it. I could have my own thing out there; one that's not habit forming and will just make people feel good."

"What a noble and entrepreneurial spirit," Lila deadpanned.

"For a drug dealer," Misty added.

Meeting two people she liked in as many days? *Maybe my luck is changing,* Lila thought. "So what exactly is the plan?"

"Allen, the scientist, helped me draw a map to a cache in the Lepya Wastelands." Misty pushed the touch pad over to Lila. "My proposal is this. We take Feather's bike to the facility, unless you have a mode of transportation?"

Lila shook her head.

Misty sighed. "I guess that means I'm riding in the sidecar. Anyway, he gave me the last code he had. He's been dead for a while, so it might have changed. I don't foresee it being a huge hindrance. He said he believes some of his colleagues are there and to mention his name."

"Alive colleagues or dead colleagues?" Feather asked. "I need to know how much ammo to bring."

Feather removed her leather jacket. Underneath, she had an exoskeleton mod to reinforce her ribs and spine and arm mechs on her right bicep. Lila stared.

"I work as a barback. I carry a lot of kegs," Feather explained as she opened the large cabinets on the back wall. She strapped on dual holsters and two ammo slings. Lila doubted that barbacks needed that many bullets but decided not to say anything.

"Dead."

"Perfect."

"Allen says the cache is basically just a glorified bunker, cut into the mountainside, with different rooms for different types of plants. The rooms and seeds should be clearly labeled and filed."

"This sounds too easy."

"It does, doesn't it? From what I can account for, our major challenge is going to be getting into the bunker. If there are no coherent spirits around for me to commune with, we won't be able to get in if the code is expired. Sometimes the older spirits lose their," Misty paused, "humanity. And if they have, they won't be useful to us."

"What if someone already broke in and took the seeds?" Lila asked.

"We aren't the biggest flower shop, but I assume if someone had rare or valuable seeds, they would have eventually tried to sell them to us. Or the government would have started putting those seeds to work to drive down food costs."

Feather snorted and started pulling backpacks and helmets out of the bottom cabinet.

"My sister thinks the government would toss the seeds to keep us poor and starving. I think they would make themselves water rich, at the very least. Either way, I think we would have heard rumblings." Misty smiled. "Overall, I'm very happy with this plan."

"And it helps to have an extra pair of hands to help us carry out our haul." Feather winked.

"So, when are we leaving?"

"Now."

"Impossible, I'm not prepared."

"You can have CJ's sandsuit. You two are the same size. She left it last time she was here." Feather threw it onto Lila's lap.

235

"I'm not prepared mentally, either. This is a huge thing."

"We have to go now." Misty stood. "Once you know you can have something that could change the world, wouldn't you want to get it as fast as possible?"

Lila unzipped the sandsuit. "Turn around," she said to Feather.

Feather grinned and faced the wall while Lila changed. A sandsuit should be skintight, but it was a little loose on her. She ran her hands up and down the suit to try to smooth out some of the wrinkles and felt a lighter in the inside pocket. Strange, she wouldn't have thought CJ was a smoker. But then again, she wouldn't have thought her sensible friend would date a gun-toting, mod-enhanced drug dealer.

A half hour later, Lila was holding tightly onto Feather as they careened toward the edge of Artax. The borders of the domed city were easy to pass through, but few wanted to leave the comforts of civilization for the blaze and uncertainty of the desert.

Misty, clad in a white leather sandsuit, rode in the sidecar. She held the touch pad in her lap and screamed directions at Feather. Lila could hardly hear anything over the sound of the motorcycle and the helmet didn't help. It occurred to her that she was completely at the mercy of two virtual strangers. Even if she did feel closer to them than anyone she had met since she fled Leda.

By the time they found the right hill, they were all covered in the fine red sand of the wastelands. Feather brought the bike to a slow stop. "I'm going to have to leave the bike here and we can walk up. I'm afraid of it sinking in the sand."

Their sandsuits protected them from the worst of the grit, but Lila could still feel the crunch of sand in her mouth. They decamped and marched up to the steel door. Lila sank almost to her knees in the sand with every step. She held the empty saddlebags over her head so they could fill them with seeds. Her arms and legs burned with strain, but the thought of bringing those seeds back to Artax, fat with heritage flora from days long past, produced a rush of adrenaline she could feel pulsing through her veins. Misty held onto the backpacks while Feather piggybacked her to the entrance. They collapsed in front of the door.

"Is Allen around?"

"No, he doesn't like leaving the city," Misty said, distracted. She turned off her eye mods with a tap to the temple and turned around a few times, looking into the distance.

"Tap in the code while I'm looking," Misty ordered.

Feather punched in a few numbers and the panel flashed red. "It's a no go. Did you get anyone?"

"Not yet. Hold please." Misty turned in a few circles.

"Is this," Lila gestured to Misty, "going to take very long?"

"It depends," Feather answered, idly drawing the pistol at her hip. "Spirits tend to stick to places that were important to them. They don't go very far. The question is whether or not this place was important enough to anyone for them to want to hang around it for eternity."

"If what Allen said was true, there would be hundreds of souls here," Lila huffed.

Feather laughed. "I think you, CJ, and my sister both hold seeds near and dear to your hearts. But I can't think of anyone else who does. Oh, I guess your dorky coworkers,"

Lila huffed again.

"Oh, don't get offended for them. You don't even like them."

Lila considered. "No. I don't. But imagine their faces..." She trailed off. They waited for Misty, lost in their own dreams.

Misty ran over. "I got someone! Her name is Dr. Erica Svengald. She was in charge of the lab for a while. She says back when it was very rare for women to hold such positions." Misty paused, listening. "She wants to help us. She says she wants the seeds to flourish instead of rot. She says they have finite lifespans." Misty frowned. "Some of them might already be useless."

Lila's heart slipped into her stomach. She hadn't had much faith they would find the bunker, but being this close raised her hopes perilously high.

Misty entered the code from Dr. Svengald. Lila realized she was holding her breath. The panel flashed green, and the door clicked.

"Hurry." Feather braced the door with her shoulder and pushed it open, drawing her gun with her other hand. "Stay behind me."

Feather led the way into the bunker. It was larger than Lila thought it would be. Gray metal arched over their heads; fluorescent lights beamed down from recessed light fixtures. They descended a short staircase. The main tunnel had three branches that shot off each side. Down the middle there was a row of small trees, maybe as tall as Lila, encased in glass domes. They were still alive. She gasped and ran a finger over the nameplate on the dome of the first tree. "Red Pine Bonsai - *Pinus densiflora*," she read aloud. "It's beautiful."

"It is. Now let's ransack this joint."

Misty sniffed. "Must you be so crude?" She turned to Lila. "If you want the water purification, it's the middle room on the right, air purification is next to it."

"I'm going to go first and secure the rooms," Feather said. "You both stay here until I'm done."

Feather disappeared into the first room. Misty and Lila waited. Lila could tell Misty was talking to the ghost. Her mouth twitched sometimes, and she was nodding frequently.

Feather popped back into the hallway, "Roll out, ladies. Li, I'm going to stick with Misty, while you get whatever it is you want. Be alert, be careful and let's get out of here as quickly as possible. This place feels like a tomb. Let's make sure it doesn't become one."

Feather and Misty headed to the furthest room on the left, and Lila rushed to the middle on the right. She knew she should go slower, be more careful, but now that she was so close... The room was empty in the middle. The wall was covered from ceiling to floor with neatly labeled metal drawers. The far wall was labeled "Water Filtration." To her right, the label read "Water Oxygenation," and to her left, "Algae & Moss." Each drawer was also labeled. Lila's head spun. Did she need semi-aquatic or aquatic? Submerged or floating?

Feather had given her a huge backpack, so she decided to start with two from each wall and just go around and around until the bag was full. Maybe she would leave room to grab some air purifying seeds if she could. She opened the drawer closest to her and a burst of cold air hit her in the face, colder than any cold she had ever felt. The seeds were each stored in airtight silver packets. She gently pulsed the packet between her hands. She could feel individual vials inside. "Water Hyacinth - *Eichhornia crassipes*," she read. She shoved it in the backpack. She filled the pack until it was almost too heavy for her to lift. Then she ran into the air purification room and shoved a few packets into the legs of her sandsuit and secured her boots over them.

Feather peeked her head in. "You get everything you need?"

Lila nodded.

"Let's blow this place." Feather motioned for Lila to pick up one of the saddlebags. Feather picked up the other and waved Lila ahead of her. She still had her gun drawn. Misty was almost at the entrance, but as she reached out for the handle, there was a loud click. "Hey, did that just lock?"

"I'm sure it's fine." Misty typed the code into the panel. They waited. Misty spun around just as the panel started coding red. "I've made a grave miscalculation." Her already pale face was completely drained of blood. "Dr. Svengald is malevolent."

"What?"

"She's insane. She's too far gone. She says she doesn't want us to leave with the seeds. She wants us to stay here and grow them. She wants to watch them germinate and fruit. She's not going to let us leave." For the first time, Misty seemed like a child instead of a robot. One by one, the overhead lights flicked off.

Lila could see red emergency lights start flashing from each room. "What are we going to do?"

"Stand back, get into the other room. I'm going to shoot it."

Lila grabbed Misty and backed them up into the first room off the corridor. "Lila?"

"Yes?"

"I didn't say anything because I didn't think it would have been received well. But shooting the control panel is more likely to make things worse than better."

Lila clapped her hands over Misty's ears as the shots rang out. A second later, sirens began to wail.

"Fuck, fuck, fuck," Feather yelled from the hallway. She popped her head into the room. "Stay here and DO NOT MOVE. I'm going to check the rooms for emergency exits." She moved down the hallway, gun first.

"I have an idea," Lila screamed over the alarms. "Is the doctor still here?"

Misty switched off her eye mods. "Yes, she's standing right here with us. She's very satisfied with herself."

"Tell her there's new technology. Tell her I have a way to bring these seeds back from the dead, but I need to get to my lab. Which means she needs to let us out," Lila screamed over the sound of the alarms.

"She says you're full of shit."

"Tell her I can't guarantee it, but I can try. And—" Lila paused as Misty delivered the first half of the message. "If she doesn't let us out, I am going to burn every seed in here. Even if it kills the three of us."

"Feather wouldn't let you risk killing me."

"Tell her."

Misty flinched. "She's just screaming."

"Can she see me?"

"Yes."

Lila ripped off the backpack and unzipped the sandsuit to get to the lighter in the inside pocket. She flipped open the lighter. If they died locked away in here, humanity would never get the seeds anyway. So, what did it matter if she was the one who had to make the choice between the lives of three nobodies from a dying species on a dying planet or possibly finding a long-term solution that could sustain human life? She wanted to live. She wanted this strange little girl to live. She wanted her friend's shady partner to live. Still, her entire body screamed as she made her decision. She held the lighter up to the backpack and let the flame start to lick at the bottom. "Tell her I'm serious."

Misty fell to the floor with her hands over her ears, shrieking in pain. Feather ran back into the room and her eyes widened as she looked back and forth between Lila and her sister.

"What the actual fuck is going on?" She pointed the gun at Lila. "Explain now."

"We're threatening the good doctor. She gives us the code to get out or the seeds go bye-bye."

Feather holstered the gun, picked her sister up off the ground, and cradled her. The backpack caught fire. Lila's face was wet with tears she didn't realize she was shedding. Misty whispered into Feather's ear and Feather sprinted towards the panel. Lila followed, holding the blazing backpack by its top loop.

"She said to put out the fire and she'll give us the code."

"No. Code first." The flames were close to the top loop. Lila felt her hand burning, but she held tight, brandishing the backpack in front of her like a weapon, even though she couldn't see where her enemy was.

Still cradled in her sister's arms, Misty held out a drooping arm and keyed in a code. They waited. The sirens stopped wailing, and the red lights faded and blinked out. Slowly, the white lights turned back on. The panel blinked green. *Go.* Feather slammed her back into the door, and she and Misty tumbled out. Lila ran after them. She threw the backpack into the sand and smothered the flames. She allowed herself to collapse onto the sand, weeping.

"The seeds are dead. They couldn't have survived that." She held the charred backpack to her chest and rocked back and forth.

"Feather, put the poor woman out of her misery," Misty said weakly. She stood up and brushed herself off.

Lila felt Feather's large hand clap her back. "That's the backpack I use for my fire moss. It's lined with CoolBoiTech fabric. It's basically like being in a refrigerator."

Lila looked up, incredulously.

"Don't look at me like that. I don't want to spontaneously combust when I'm offloading my shit, you know?"

"So, what now?" Lila asked.

"Now we go home. Misty and I are going to get rich as hell. And you, you can save the world."

About the Authors

Colleen Addison completed a Master's degree in Creative Writing, followed by a PhD in health information; she then promptly got sick herself. She now lives, writes, and heals on a small island off the coast of Vancouver, Canada. Her recent work has been published in Halfway Down the Stairs, Flash Fiction Friday, and A Story in 100 Words. She has been nominated for a Best of the Net award.

Cassandra Arnold is a retired Australian doctor, who worked for Doctors Without Borders (MSF) from 2009 to 2014. Her memoir *Beyond Borders* is a poetic photo-journal of her posts in Niger in 2009 and 2012. After 12 years in Calgary, Canada, she returned to Australia with her partner, David, in the fall of 2023.

Her art, poetry, and stories are inspired by her love of nature, and her heartbreak at the loss of species and increasing effects of climate change. Website: cassandraarnold.com Instagram: @cassandra_art_and_stories

Emecheta Christian is a brilliant writer whose work explores themes of self-actualization, belonging, and the complexities of the human experience. His works have appeared in esteemed literary journals and anthologies such as The Potter's Poetry, Indiana Review, Oxford American, Four Way Review, the Academy of American Poets Poem-A-Day Series, and elsewhere. He has been recognized with several awards, including the Iroko Award and The Dorothy Hewett Award.

Emecheta's unique voice and evocative imagery have garnered him a growing reputation as a voice of change in the global literary scene.

Social media: https://web.facebook.com/emechetac/

Sarah Das Gupta is an 82-year-old, retired English teacher from Cambridge, England, who has taught in UK, India and Tanzania. She lived in Kolkata for some years. Her interests include equestrian sports, the countryside, Medieval History and early music.

She has had work published in journals and magazines online and in print, in 20 countries, from New Zealand to Kazakhstan. She has recently been nominated for Best of the Net and a Dwarf Star Award.

Alex Grehy (she/her) writes relatable works that engage the reader's emotions and helps them to make sense of the world around them. Her words have been published in a range of anthologies and ezines worldwide and are also available via a global network of prose & poetry dispensers run by French publisher, Short Edition.

Alex is known for her vivid prose and thought-provoking verse. Her first poetry collections, Last Species Standing and A Listener Speaks (Alien Buddha Press) are now available on Amazon.

Alex is inspired by a reflective life filled with narrow boating, rescue greyhounds, singing and chocolate.

Facebook: alex.grehy.7. Blog: http://idealreaderblog.wordpress.com/

Dorothy Johnson-Laird is a poet and social worker who lives in New York City, and has a passion for African music. She has published reviews and essays about it on www.afropop.org and www.worldmusiccentral.org.

Her recent poems are in: Aji, Cantos, Pomona Valley Review, Pedestal Magazine, among others. Her poems are also in the anthology, Alchemy and Miracles: Nature Woven into Words.

She is at work on her first book of poetry. More of her writing can also be found on:

https://www.facebook.com/profile.php?id=100083698660157

Robin Kathaas is a poet who was born and raised in Belgium, but now lives, laughs, and loves in Brighton, UK. Their cat is more interesting than they are. They can be found on Instagram at @robin.kathaas (unless they get sick of Instagram, in which case they can be contacted via postal dove, maybe, if you ask the dove nicely.)

Loki Laats is an author who rediscovered their passion for writing at the tail end of college. They are seeking to create fantasy worlds that intrigue and inspire.

Jen Lailey (she/her) has come to writing a little later in life. She works as a GP-psychotherapist in Thunder Bay, Ontario and lives on a boreal forested property just outside the city where she gardens and walks the trails. She and her husband have 3 daughters and are new to an empty nest. Jen appreciates writing as a way of understanding her own experience and saying what can be difficult to express in the usual day to day conversations.

Natasia Rose Langfelder is a born and bred Brooklynite. By day, she's a mild-mannered content marketer and by night...she's a mild-mannered writer. Natasia's work has been published in ThreePenny Review, Cloaked Press, Wicked Shadow Press, Sirens Call Publications, and more.

When she's not working or writing, you can find her hanging out with her wife and their teacup Yorkie. You can read more of her work at https://www.natasiarose.com/

Carys Owen is a poet, artist, community builder and nature-lover who respectfully lives on the unceded territory of the K'omoks First Nation on Vancouver Island, Canada. Her office is on the beach, by the river, in the forest, near a mountain.

She once published a collection of poetry along the Community Centre Trails of Quadrant Island—posting a poem at every fork in the path. It was called 'Lost in the Woods'. Some people reported being unable to locate all of the poems...

See more at https://carysowenpoetry.ca/. Instagram: @carysowen-poetry

Daniel A. Rabuzzi (he/his) (danielarabuzzi.com), a Pushcart nominee, has been published in, among others, Crab Creek Review, Asimov's, Harvard Review, New Letters, Hopscotch Translation, Chicago Review of Books, and Lady Churchill's Rosebud Wristlet.

He earned degrees in the study of folklore & mythology and European history. A lifetime birdwatcher and amateur botanist, he lives in New York City with his artistic partner & spouse, the woodcarver Deborah A. Mills (https://www.deborahmillswoodcarving.com/).

Rod Raglin is a journalist, photographer, editor of an online community newspaper and author of thirteen self-published novels, a collection of short stories and two plays. He lives in Vancouver, Canada.

To read excerpts of his work visit his Amazon author page at https://www.amazon.com/-/e/B003DS6LEU. For links to short stories and poems accepted and published individually, or in an anthology, visit https://revuecommunitynews.com/rod-raglin-author

Bobby Rollins is (gratefully) prone to daydreams, some of which he puts into words. He writes in the hopes his stories make people laugh and think, both of which he'd like more of in the world.

Ali Rowland is an older, neurodivergent writer from Northumberland. Her short fiction has been published in The Amphibian Literary Journal, The Letters Page, Wensum and Flash Fiction North. Ali has just completed her second novel. Her first poetry collection 'Rooted' was published by Maplestreet Press in 2024.

You can follow her work at Musings of a Mad Woman on Substack.

William Scarborough is currently a graduate student at The University of Akron, focusing his research on the works of Kim Stanley Robinson. His short story, The Obituarist, represents his first venture into writing climate fiction. He currently resides in Columbus, Ohio.

Ginger Strivelli is an artist and writer from North Carolina. She writes both fiction and non-fiction. She has written for Marion Zimmer Bradley's Fantasy Magazine, Circle Magazine, Third Flatiron, Autism Parenting Magazine, Jokes Review, Cabinet of Heed Literary Journal, The New Accelerator, and various other publications for thirty years.

She loves to travel the world and make arts and crafts along with her storytelling and educating through her writing.

John A. Tures, originally from El Paso, Texas, is LaGrange College professor and a regular newspaper columnist and magazine writer who has published in a number of news magazines and newspapers across the USA (https://muckrack.com/john-tures) and scholarly journals (https://scholar.google.com/scholar?hl=en&as_sdt=0%2C11&q=%22J ohn+A.+Tures%22&btnG=).

He published "Deep Plots" in Ariel Chart, International Literary Journal (https://www.arielchart.com/2023/11/deep-plots.html) about a green cemetery with a different kind of environmental justice.

He has two pieces in the DeKalb Voices Review and the nonfiction piece "Bridge Builders" (https://www.storyhouse.org/johnt.html)

published by The Preservation Society.

He also has "LaGuerrera," published by the Anti-Misogyny Club (https://www.theantimisogynyclub.com/gallery/laguerrera).

His Twitter or "X" handle is @johnntures2.

The author would like to thank his family and Sharon Marchisello for their help.

N.H. Van Der Haar is a quietly queer and autistic writer. Previous work can be read at The Victorian Reader, Antithesis Magazine and Farrago Magazine. He enjoys brisk walks and riding trains. He can be found online on Instagram: @nic_noc_nac.

Regina Rae Weiss earned an MFA in Creative Writing and Literature from Stony Brook University. Her recent fiction appears in *The Saturday Evening Post, Still Point Arts Quarterly, Idle Ink* and elsewhere. Her nonfiction has appeared in *The Philadelphia Inquirer, The Huffington Post* and is forthcoming from *White Wall Review.* She also has a graduate degree in Social Policy.

Elizabeth Whitton is an award-winning speculative fiction author. Her debut contemporary fantasy Young Adult (YA) novel, *Houses of the Old Blood*, was winner of the 2018 Aurora Award for Best YA Fiction, while her YA novel,*The Gold Flame of Senica,* along with five of her short stories, were Aurora Award finalists. My great thanks go to her for offering her story, The Green Witch, for this collection.

Elizabeth is an active member of IFWA, ARWA and the Alberta Writers Guild. She is happiest when pounding on her laptop late at night while ignoring pleas from her family to go to bed. She lives in Calgary, Alberta, just an hour away from the spectacular Rocky Mountains.

Website elizabethwhitton.com

X @EAGWhitton.

Instagram elizabeth_whitton.

Facebook EAGWhitton.

If you enjoyed this book, do please leave a review on Amazon
or other places of your choice.

It really does make a difference.

Acknowledgments

First and foremost, my heartfelt thanks to all the authors who contributed their work to create this volume. Without the range of their voices and experience, this book would not be the treasure that it is.

Then, as always, thanks to my partner David Wood for enriching my life; my writing groups in Ballarat and Calgary who inspire, critique and encourage me; my sister Diana, who cheers me on, and my late father, Laurence Hardy, who shared his love of books with me when I was young.

Also by Gilbert and Hall Press

Alchemy and Miracles

83 poets weave the miracles of nature into words.

In this carefully chosen collection, you will find beauty, humour, grief, longing and joy.

Wonderfully readable, these poems will inspire you to explore nature with a poet's eye, and discover a myriad of places and viewpoints to delight in.

"Beautiful poetry from authors all over the world celebrating nature and our need to protect it. This book is a must have for everyone."
Amazon Review

The Winter Fae

Fairies, elves, demons... Secrets and desire... Dark humour, magic, wonder...

Twelve stories that will transport you into other worlds, or twisted versions of our own.

If you had magic, what would you do with it? If you loved someone, how far would you go?

"A magical compilation of thought provoking and inspiring stories. A mix of eco-fiction, urban fantasy and romance all tied together – a little something for everyone."
Amazon Review

The Light Inside
Nature. Spirit. Healing. Joy.

In this new collection, Instagram poet Cassandra Arnold takes you on a whirlwind tour across Canada, England and Australia, through winter, summer, autumn and spring.

She dives wholeheartedly into the challenges of life in our consumerist world, finding your home in nature, and reclaiming your authentic self.

You can listen to the author read her poems on Instagram, where she is @cassandra_art_and_stories.

The Greenleaf project
Meaning, purpose and someone to love. Is it really too much to ask for?

1997 Australia.

Bridget Fletcher has a 16-year-old son, friends, a cat, a dog, the beach, and a community she adores. It seems idyllic.

But secretly, she fears life is passing her by. And she still has nightmares about her ex-husband claiming his son.

When she stumbles on The Greenleaf Project, she discovers an online world of connection and purpose she never believed possible and dives into a contest to transform the town.

Sickened by the corporate world, Arthur Ross turned his back on his successful career and vowed to reconnect to nature. Bridget and The Greenleaf Project might be just what he is searching for.

Can Bridget win the contest and Arthur's heart, or will she lose everything she fought so hard to gain?

"This lovely story will charm you, make you think about how your choices affect the environment and most importantly, help you consider what you really want in your life! The characters are interesting and full of personality.
I enjoyed every minute of this book."
Amazon Review.